# THE BROKEN LANCE

They're not fighting for their Emperor.
They're not fighting for their country.
They're definitely not fighting fair…

IF YOU'VE GOT a job so dangerous, so suicidal that
even the bravest men balk in terror, then it's time
to call in Reiner Hetsau and the Blackhearts.

Convicted men, fated to die in the hangman's
noose, the Blackhearts have one chance of salvation. The Old World has plenty of dark deeds
that need doing for the good of mankind, and
the Blackhearts are just the scum for the job.

Their latest assignment takes them to a remote
border fort. All communications with this bas-
tion have ceased and the Imperial authorities are
starting to get nervous. If it's been overrun, it
could be the herald of an invasion. Or has the
fort's commander himself gone rogue? The
Blackhearts can only be sure of this: the odds are
going to be stacked against them, and they may
not come back alive!

A WARHAMMER NOVEL

# THE BROKEN LANCE

## NATHAN LONG

## A BLACK LIBRARY PUBLICATION

First published in Great Britain in 2005 by
BL Publishing,
Games Workshop Ltd.,
Willow Road, Nottingham,
NG7 2WS, UK

10 9 8 7 6 5 4 3 2 1

Cover illustration by Christer Sveen.

A CIP record for this book is available from the British Library

ISBN13: 978 1 84416 243 7
ISBN 10: 1 84416 243 5

Distributed in the US by Simon & Schuster
1230 Avenue of the Americas, New York, NY 10020, US.

Printed and bound in Great Britain by
Bookmarque, Surrey, UK.

See the Black Library on the Internet at
**www.blacklibrary.com**

Find out more about Games Workshop
and the world of Warhammer at
**www.games-workshop.com**

THIS IS A DARK age, a bloody age, an age of daemons and of sorcery. It is an age of battle and death, and of the world's ending. Amidst all of the fire, flame and fury it is a time, too, of mighty heroes, of bold deeds and great courage.

AT THE HEART of the Old World sprawls the Empire, the largest and most powerful of the human realms. Known for its engineers, sorcerers, traders and soldiers, it is a land of great mountains, mighty rivers, dark forests and vast cities. And from his throne in Altdorf reigns the Emperor Karl-Franz, sacred descendant of the founder of these lands, Sigmar, and wielder of his magical warhammer.

BUT THESE ARE far from civilised times. Across the length and breadth of the Old World, from the knightly palaces of Bretonnia to ice-bound Kislev in the far north, come rumblings of war. In the towering World's Edge Mountains, the orc tribes are gathering for another assault. Bandits and renegades harry the wild southern lands of the Border Princes. There are rumours of rat-things, the skaven, emerging from the sewers and swamps across the land. And from the northern wildernesses there is the ever-present threat of Chaos, of daemons and beastmen corrupted by the foul powers of the Dark Gods. As the time of battle draws ever near, the Empire needs heroes like never before.

# ONE
## An Untested Tool

THE HAMMER BRANDS were gone. The shameful scars that had been burnt into their flesh had been removed at last by a sorcery so painful it made the original branding a pleasant memory by comparison. The skin of their hands was clean, unblemished, as if the red iron had never touched it. But the blood beneath that skin, that was another story.

Reiner Hetsau and his convict companions; the pikemen Hals Kiir and Pavel Voss, the Tilean crossbowman Giano Ostini, and Franka Shoentag, the dark-haired archer who only Reiner knew was not the boy she pretended to be, had been given the deserter's brand by Baron Albrecht Valdenheim as a way to force them to help him betray his brother, Count Manfred Valdenheim. He had promised them that when their service to him was done, he would remove the brands. But after they learned that he intended to betray them as well as his brother, they had helped Manfred instead, in hopes that he would make good on Albrecht's promise.

And he had. Manfred had been so impressed by the unorthodox ways in which Reiner and his companions had escaped their predicaments, by their ability to adapt and survive in any situation, and by their utter disregard for what respectable men might call right and wrong, that he had decided to make them agents of the Empire whether they wished it or not. The country, he said, had need of blackhearts who would not flinch at dishonourable duty. So he had ordered his personal sorcerer to remove the brands – which marked them deserters who could be shot on sight, and therefore useless as spies – and instead bound them to him with a much more subtle leash.

He had poisoned their blood.

It was a latent poison, which would lie dormant within them unless they attempted to leave Manfred's service or betray him. Then a spell could be read that would wake the poison and kill them wherever they might run, within the Empire or beyond.

There might be some, Reiner thought, as he folded his compact frame into the bay of a mullioned dormer window and looked out over the moonlit rooftops of Altdorf, who would be happy with the arrangement. Manfred had installed them in his townhouse and given them the run of the place, allowing them to read in the library and practise at swords in the garden, and had provided them with warm beds, fine food and obsequious servants – a soft life in these days of hardship and war, when many in the Empire were maimed and starving and hadn't a roof over their heads to call their own – but Reiner hated it.

The townhouse might be the epitome of comfort, but it was still a prison. Manfred wanted their existence kept a secret, so they were not allowed beyond its walls. It tortured Reiner that Altdorf was just outside and he couldn't reach it. The brothels and gambling halls, the dog-pits and theatres he called home, were within walking distance – on some nights he could hear singing and laughing and perhaps even the rattle of dice. But he couldn't get to them. They might as well have been in Lustria. It was agony.

Not that the others didn't suffer as well. When Manfred had recruited them, he had promised the Blackhearts action – secret missions, assassinations, kidnappings – but for the last two months they had done nothing but sit, waiting for orders that never came, and it was driving them stir crazy. It wasn't that Reiner relished the thought of risking life and limb for the Empire that had falsely branded him sorcerer and traitor, but endlessly waiting to be sent to one's death was a misery all its own – an edgy, endless boredom which set him and his companions at each other's throats. Casual conversations suddenly erupted into shouting matches, or broke off into sullen silences. Though he liked them all, Reiner's companions' tics and mannerisms, which he had once found amusing, now grated like brick on flesh: Hals's incessant barbs and jokes, Pavel's little clearing of the throat before he asked a question, Giano's moaning about how everything was better in Tilea, Franka's...

Well, it was Franka that was the real problem, wasn't it? Reiner had made a terrible mistake falling for the girl. He hadn't thought it would happen. After he had gotten over the shock of learning her true sex he hadn't given her a second thought. She wasn't really his sort – a wiry hoyden with hair shorter than his own – nothing like the laughing, lusty harlots he usually favoured, with painted lips and voluptuous hips. But that day on the crag above Nordbergbusche, when together they had killed Albrecht, they had exchanged a look that had awakened a flame of desire in him he knew could only be quenched in her arms. The trouble was, though she had admitted to him that she shared his passion, had in fact kissed him once with a fervour that had nearly carried them both away, she refused to consummate their lust. She...

The latch in the door behind him clicked. Reiner turned from the window as Franka entered the room, candle in hand. He held his breath. She closed the door, set the candle on a dresser, and began unlacing her jerkin.

'Slowly, beloved,' said Reiner, twirling his moustaches like a stage villain. "Tis too nice a job to rush.'

Franka gasped, covering herself, then let out an annoyed breath when she realized who was sitting in the window seat. 'Reiner. How did you get in here?'

'Klaus was asleep again, as usual.'

'And so should you be.'

Reiner grinned. 'An excellent idea. Turn down the covers and let's to bed.'

Franka sighed and sat on a divan. 'Must you continue to persist?'

'Must you continue to resist?'

'The year of my vow is not yet up. I still mourn for Yarl.'

Reiner groaned. 'Is it still two months?'

'Three.'

'Three!'

'Only two days have passed since you last asked.'

'It feels like two years.' He stood and began to pace. 'Beloved, we could be dead in three months! Sigmar knows what madness Manfred has in store for us. He could send us to Ulthuan for all we know.'

'A man of honour would not press me on this,' said Franka, tight-lipped.

'Have I ever said I was a man of honour?' He sat on the divan beside her. 'Franka. There is a reason for a soldier's loose morals. He knows every day that he might die tomorrow, and therefore lives each night as if it were his last. You are a soldier now. You know this. You must seize what stands before you before Morr snatches it from your grasp forever.'

Franka rolled her eyes as he opened his arms in invitation. 'You make a compelling argument, captain, but unfortunately I have honour – or at least stubborn pride – enough for the both of us, and so…'

Reiner dropped his arms. 'Very well, very well. I will retire. But could you not at least grant me a kiss to dream on?'

Franka chuckled. 'And have you take advantage as always?'

'On my honour, beloved...'

'Did you not just say you had no honour?'

'I... er, yes, I suppose I did.' Reiner sighed and stood. 'Once again you defeat me, lady. But one day...' He shrugged and stepped to the door.

'Reiner.'

Reiner turned. Franka was beside him. She stretched up on her tiptoes and kissed him lightly on the lips. 'Now go to bed.'

'Torturer,' he said, then turned the latch and left.

UNSURPRISINGLY, REINER FOUND it difficult to sleep, which was unfortunate, for he was woken much too early the next morning. He had been dreaming of Franka unlacing her jerkin and pulling off her shirt, and it was a rude shock to open his eyes to the ugly face of dear old Klaus, the guard in charge of watching over him and his companions, glaring down at him.

'Get yer boots on, y'lazy slug,' Klaus barked, kicking Reiner's four-poster.

'Piss off.' Reiner pulled the covers over his head. 'I was with a lady.'

'None of your sauce!' Klaus kicked the bed again. 'His lordship requests yer presence in the yard, on the double.'

Reiner poked an eye above the blanket. 'Manfred's back?' He yawned and sat up, rubbing the sleep from his eyes. 'Thought he'd forgotten about us.'

'Manfred never forgets nothing,' said Klaus. 'You'd do well to remember it.'

'WHAT HAPPENINGS?' ASKED Giano as the Blackhearts shuffled sleepily down the curving mahogany staircase behind Reiner and Klaus to the townhouse's marble-floored entryway. The curly haired Tilean was still doing up his breeches.

'No idea,' said Reiner. Klaus motioned them through a service door and they entered the kitchen.

'It's something different, though,' said Pavel. He stole a pastry from a tray and stuffed it in his mouth. 'Makes a change,' he said, spitting crumbs.

Reiner chuckled at the sight. The pikeman was as ugly as a wet rat, and utterly unconcerned about it: long necked and scrawny, with a patch over his lost left eye and a scarred mouth that was missing three front teeth.

'Probably just sword drills again,' said Hals, Pavel's bald, burly, red bearded brother-in-arms. 'Or worse, horsemanship.'

Klaus opened the kitchen door and they stepped into the gravelled stable yard. 'Maybe not,' said Franka. 'Look at that.'

Reiner and the others looked ahead. A coach with louvred windows sat just inside the back gate. Two guards stood before it. The Blackhearts groaned.

'Not the coach again,' said Hals.

'We'd all kill each other before we got where we were going,' agreed Pavel.

Klaus stopped in the centre of the yard and called them to attention. They straightened, but only half-heartedly. Months of enforced familiarity with him had bred contempt for his authority. They waited. The morning fog hid the world beyond the stone walls in a pearly embrace, and though it was summer, the sun was not yet high enough in the sky to chase the night's chill away. Reiner shivered and wished he had thought to don his cloak. His stomach growled. He had become used to a regular breakfast.

After a quarter of an hour, the gate to the garden opened and Count Manfred stepped into the yard. Tall and broad, with silver in his hair and beard, the count looked the part of a kind, wise king out of legend, but Reiner knew better. Manfred might be wise, but he was hard as flint. A bright-eyed young corporal in the uniform of a lancer followed in his wake.

Manfred nodded curtly to the Blackhearts. 'Klaus, open the coach, then retire to the gate with Moegen and Valch.'

'M'lord?' said Klaus. 'I wouldn't trust these villains near yer lordship…'

'Obey my orders, Klaus. I am perfectly safe.'

Klaus saluted reluctantly and crossed to the coach. He took a key from one of the guards and unlocked it. Reiner expected Manfred to order them into it, but when Klaus opened the door, four men ducked out and stepped down to the gravel. The Blackhearts exchanged uneasy glances. The men were filthy, unshaved, and half starved, and wore the remains of military uniforms.

'Fall in,' said Manfred.

The four men shambled over and lined up next to the Blackhearts, squaring their shoulders reflexively.

Manfred faced the Blackhearts. 'We have work for you at last,' he said, then sighed. 'There have actually been many jobs on which we would have liked to have used you. There is much turmoil in Altdorf at the moment. Much finger pointing over our losses in the recent conflict, and much clamouring for changes at the top – particularly among the younger barons. It would have been nice to have used you to "calm" some of the more strident voices, but we were hesitant to try an untested tool so close to home where it might fly back into our faces.' He clasped his hands behind his back. 'Now a perfect test has presented itself. Of utmost importance to the well-being of the Empire, but far enough away that you will not embarrass us if you fail.'

'Your confidence in us is inspiring, m'lord,' said Reiner wryly.

'Be thankful I have any at all after your insubordination at Groffholt.'

'Did you not recruit us particularly for our penchant for insubordination, m'lord?' asked Reiner.

'Enough,' said Manfred, and though he didn't raise his voice, Reiner did not feel inclined to push his insolence any further.

'Listen well,' said Manfred. 'For I will not repeat these orders and they will not be written down.' He cleared his throat and looked them all in the eye, then began. 'Deep in the Black Mountains is an Empire fort which guards an isolated pass and protects a nearby gold mine. The mine helps the Empire pay for reconstruction and defence in these troubled times, but in the last few months the mine's output has slowed to a trickle, and we have not received from the fort satisfactory answers to our queries. I sent a courier two months ago. He has not returned. I do not know what has befallen him.' Manfred frowned. 'All that is certain is that the fort is still in Imperial hands, for an agent of mine saw recruitment notices for the fort's regiment going up in Averheim not a week ago.' He looked at Reiner. 'This recruitment is your opportunity. You are to sign on, install yourselves in the fort, discover what is occurring, and if it is treasonous, stop it.'

'You have reason to suspect treason?'

'It is possible,' said Manfred. 'The fort's commander, General Broder Gutzmann, is rumoured to be angry that he was kept in the south when the fate of the Empire was being decided in the north. He may have become angry enough to do something rash.'

'And if he has?'

Manfred hesitated, then spoke. 'If there is a traitor in the fort, he must be "removed", no matter who he is. But know that Gutzmann is an excellent general and loved by his men. They are fiercely loyal. If it is he you must remove, it should look like an accident. If his men discovered that he was the victim of foul play, they would revolt, and the Empire is stretched too thin now to lose an entire garrison.'

'Pardon, m'lord,' said Reiner, 'but I don't understand. If Gutzmann is such an excellent general, why not bring him north and let him hunt Kurgan like he wants? Would that not stop his grumbling?'

Manfred sighed. 'I cannot. There are some in Altdorf who feel that Gutzmann is too good a general, that if he won great victories in the north, he might begin to have ambitions – that, er, he might seek to be more than a leader of soldiers.'

'Ah,' said Reiner. 'So he was kept in the south on purpose. He has reason to be angry.'

Manfred scowled. 'No "reason" can excuse stealing from the Emperor. If he is guilty, he must be stopped. Do you all understand your orders?'

The Blackhearts nodded, as did the newcomers.

Manfred glanced at the new men, then back to the Blackhearts. 'This will be a difficult mission, and it was felt you should be returned to full strength. Therefore we have found you some new recruits. These four men will be under your command, Hetsau. Corporal Karelinus Eberhart,' he indicated the young junior officer who stood to his left, 'will also obey your orders, but is answerable only to me. He is my eyes and ears, and will report to me at the end of this venture on...' He paused, then smirked. 'On how true and useful a tool you and your Blackhearts are. His report will determine whether we will be able to employ you in the future, and consequently, whether we will suffer you to live henceforth. Do you understand me?'

Reiner nodded. 'Yes my lord. Perfectly.' He shot a look at Corporal Eberhart, who was gaping at Manfred with wide blue eyes. Reiner chuckled. The poor lad didn't expect Manfred to be so open about his role in the enterprise. He was unused to the count's bluntness. Reiner was not. Manfred was not accustomed to hiding his cannon behind roses.

'Are these men subject to the same constraints as we, m'lord?' asked Reiner, indicating the four new recruits. 'Have they been...'

'Yes, captain,' said Manfred. 'They have agreed to the same conditions. Their blood bears the same taint as your own.' He laughed. 'They are now your brothers. Blackhearts one and all!'

# TWO
## We Are All Villains Here

NOT TWO HOURS after Manfred gave them their orders, the Blackhearts left Altdorf for Averheim, largest city of the south-eastern province of Averland, and the closest to the Black Mountains and the pass General Gutzmann's fort guarded. The count, with his customary thoroughness, had arranged everything: fresh clothes and weapons for the new men, horses for those who rode well, a cart for the others. The cart also carried the company's equipment: weapons, armour, cooking kit, tents, blankets and so on. It looked to be a much more comfortable journey than when last they had been recruited into skulduggery, thought Reiner. Then they had crept into enemy territory during a freezing Ostland spring, and packed only what they could carry on their backs. Now they travelled openly through the heart of the Empire, with inns and towns at every stage. Perhaps this was a good omen. Perhaps this foretold an easy duty. This job certainly didn't seem as difficult as the last.

Reiner breathed deep as they took the south road out of Altdorf and began riding though the farms and free-holds that surrounded the city. What a treat to be out of doors again. Just the passing of the scenery was thrilling to him. The simple act of moving was such a wonderful feeling that for a moment he almost felt free.

So enthralled was he by these novel sensations that it wasn't until Altdorf's walls were fading into the morning haze behind them and the dark line of the Drakwald was rising ahead that he noticed that no one had yet spoken. An awkward silence hung about the party, the old Black-hearts and new eyeing each other uneasily. Reiner sighed. This wouldn't do.

'Now, sir,' he said, turning to the new man who rode behind him to his right, a slight fellow with a mushroom cap of mousey brown hair above a sad, sharp face. 'How did you come to be in this sorry fix?'

'Hey?' said the man, startled. 'Why pick on me? What do y'need to know for?'

Reiner chuckled with as much good humour as he could muster. 'Well sir, If I'm to lead you, it would seem advisable to know something of you. And don't worry that you will shock us. We are all villains here, aren't we, lads?' He turned to each of his old companions in turn. 'Pavel and Hals killed their captain when he proved incompetent.'

'We didn't, though,' said Pavel.

'Kurgan killed him,' said Hals.

They both laughed darkly.

'Franz murdered his tent mate for making unwanted advances.'

Franka blushed.

'Giano sold guns to the Kossars.'

'Who know is crime?' asked Giano, turning up his palms.

'And I,' said Reiner, putting his hand to his chest, 'am charged with sorcery and the murder of a clergywoman.'

He grinned at the man, who stared around at them all, blinking. 'So you see, you're in good company.'

The man shrugged, suddenly shy. 'I... My name is Abel Halstieg. I am, er, I was, quartermaster for Lord Belhem's Cannon. They claim I bought poor quality powder and pocketed the savings, thereby causing the destruction of the unit.'

'How so?' asked Reiner.

'Er, the guns misfired and our position was overrun. But it rained that day. The powder may have become damp.'

'And since it was cheap powder in the first place...' drawled Pavel from the cart.

'It wasn't cheap powder!' insisted the quartermaster.

'Of course it wasn't,' said Reiner, soothing. 'So, can you aim and fire a field piece then?'

Abel hesitated. 'With help. If pressed. But my talents fall more on the supply side.'

'So it appears,' said Reiner, and turned away before Abel could contest the inference. 'And you, sir?' he asked the other mounted newcomer, a sturdy, stone-faced veteran with long, dark hair pulled back into a braided queue.

The man looked briefly at Reiner, then returned his gaze to his horse's neck, where it had been since the journey's beginning. His brows were so heavy that his eyes remained in shadow despite the brightness of the day. 'I took money to kill a man.'

The man's brevity took Reiner off guard. He laughed. 'What? No protestation of innocence? No extenuating circumstances?'

'I am guilty.'

Reiner blinked. 'Ah. Er. Well. Will you tell me your name, then? And in what capacity you served the Empire?'

There was a long pause, but at last the man spoke. 'Jergen Rohmner. Master-at-arms.'

'An instructor of the sword?' asked Reiner. 'You must be quite the blade.'

Rohmner did not reply.

Reiner shrugged. 'Well, welcome to our company, captain.' He turned to the cart, where the other two new recruits sat amongst the gear. 'And you, laddie,' he said, addressing a smiling, gangly archer with a thatch of red hair and jug ears that stuck from his head like flags. 'How come you here?'

The boy laughed. 'Heh. I killed a man too. Nobody had to pay me for it, though.' He shied a pebble at a passing fence post, startling a pair of crows. 'Me and my mates was posted in some muddy Kiss-leff berg, drinkin' their cow piss liquor, when this fool of an Ostland pike bumps me elbow and spills me drink. So I...'

Reiner rolled his eyes. It was a very old story. 'So you and your mates hit him a little too hard and he had the bad manners to die.'

'Naw, naw,' said the boy, grinning. 'Better'n that. I followed him back to his billet, trussed him up in his bedroll, and set his tent afire.' He laughed, delighted. 'Squealed like a skinned hog afore he died.'

There was silence as the rest of the company stared at the youth, who carried on skimming pebbles into the wheat field on their left, oblivious.

At last Reiner cleared his throat. 'Er, what's your name, lad?'

'Dag,' said the boy. 'Dag Mueller.'

'Well, Dag. Thank you for that illuminating story.'

'Aye, captain. My pleasure.'

Reiner shivered, then turned to the last of the new recruits, a round bellied old veteran with apple cheeks and extravagant moustaches, gone a little grey. 'How about you, sir. What's your tale of woe?'

'Not a patch on the last, I assure you, captain,' said the man with a sidelong glance at Dag. 'My name is Helgertkrug Steingesser, but ye may call me Gert. The brass named me deserter and instigator, and the charge fits well enough, I suppose.' He sighed, but his eyes twinkled. 'Y'see, there was a girl, a big, fine girl. Lived on a farm near where I was billeted in Kislev with the Talabheim City crossbowmen. Her man had died in the war. In fact, all the men of her village had died. It was a village of women. Lonely women. Big, fine women. And it came to me, y'see. The land was fertile, the country beautiful. A man could do worse, I said to myself, than settle down here and raise big, fine children.' He leaned back against their baggage, chuckling. 'And maybe I said it to more than myself, for when I decided to go, a score of my lads came with me, to fill in, so to speak, for the women's dead husbands. Unfortunately, the Empire didn't feel it were done with us. There were a battle the next day and we was missed. When the brass caught us up they accused us of running 'cause we was afraid. I take exception to that. We wasn't afraid. We was... er, eager for companionship.'

The Blackhearts laughed, partly because it was a funny story, but mostly out of relief that it wasn't another horrible one.

Reiner grinned. 'Welcome, Gert. And if y'find another village of lonely women on our way, don't keep it to yourself, hey?'

Franka shot Reiner a sharp look, but the rest laughed. Reiner turned at last to the fresh-faced blond corporal, Karelinus, who rode at his side. 'And you, corporal, how did you come to be minder for such a pack of reprobates? In Manfred's black book, are you?'

'Eh?' said Karel. He had been staring at Dag, and seemed to find it hard to turn away. 'Er. Actually, no. I, er, I volunteered.'

Reiner almost choked. 'You...?'

'Oh yes,' he said, turning on his horse to face the others. 'You see, I am betrothed, or at least I would be betrothed if it were possible, to Count Manfred's daughter, Rowena. But a count's daughter can't very well marry a lowly lance corporal. I must be a knight at least, mustn't I? Unfortunately, my father has had some reverses lately, and wasn't able to pay the tithe to win me a place in one of the knightly orders.' He grimaced. 'I'm afraid I made a bit of an ass of myself when I found I couldn't get in, cursing my fate and vowing to Rowena that I would win my colours on the battlefield or die trying.' He brightened. 'But then m'lord Manfred very helpfully suggested that I take this assignment. He promised me there would be plenty of opportunities to achieve my vow before we returned. That it was just the thing. A real gentleman, Count Manfred. Not every father would do as much for their daughter's betrothed.'

Reiner coughed convulsively, and he could hear Pavel and Hals mumphing with suppressed laughter. Even Franka, who knew well how to hide her thoughts, was having difficulty suppressing a smile.

'I beg your pardon, corporal,' said Reiner when he had recovered. 'A touch of congestion. Very decent indeed of the count to give you such a plum assignment. He must think very highly of you. Very highly indeed.'

They rode on through the rolling farmland, and the ice having been broken, the conversation began to flow at last. Hals, Pavel and Giano traded war stories with the crossbowman Gert, while Reiner and Franka listened with bemused wonder as young Karel prattled on about his close relationship with Count Manfred and how nice everyone was in Altdorf. Abel, the artillery quartermaster, hung at the edge of their conversation, trying to turn it to questions about their arrangement with Manfred and what was expected of them. The swordsman Jergen rode on in silence, his eyes never lifting from his saddle bow, while on the cart, Dag, the lanky archer, out of pebbles, lay on his back and watched the clouds sail by as if he hadn't a care in the world.

THEY CAMPED IN the woods that night, for though there were inns aplenty along the way, Manfred had forbidden them to sleep under a roof on their journey. He wanted them to appear hungry dogs of war when they arrived in Averheim, desperate to sign on to service as far from the centre of the Empire as possible, and hungry dogs hadn't the gelt to buy a cot by the fire.

The next day passed much as the first, riding at a quick but not punishing pace through league after league of thick oak forest, the gloom of which pressed in on them and stifled their conversation. They passed fewer travellers here; a heavily guarded train of merchants travelling together for protection, a company of knights trotting by double file, pennons flying from their lance tips, a group of Sigmarite fanatics on pilgrimage from Nuln to Altdorf and travelling every inch of the journey on their bare knees. It seemed to Reiner proof of Sigmar's grace that the mad holy men hadn't yet been set upon by the horrors that lurked in the trees.

On the third day, just as the sun was beginning to burn away the morning haze, they at last came out of the Drakwald and into the Reikland, the heartland of the Empire, an endless plain cross-hatched with fields and orchards. After so long in the forest, it was a beautiful verdant sight. But the initial impression of fertile plenty was proved an illusion when they got closer. The fields were green, yes, but as often green with weeds as with crops. The Empire had had a great army to feed these last few years, and fields that in happier times had been allowed to lie fallow to replenish the soil had been exhausted as the farmers tried to meet the demand for fodder. The crops that did grow were meagre and stunted, and the pigsties and cow pastures the Blackhearts passed were nearly unpopulated.

It was all so fragile, thought Reiner. And so precious. For if this died, if the fields withered and the cattle became skin and bones, then the Empire died. The knightly orders might prate about blood and steel and the Drakwald being the hard oaken soul of the Empire, but the knights ate beef and bread and cabbage, not acorns and squirrels, and no one ever fought to defend a forest as fiercely as a farmer defended his farm.

LATE THAT AFTERNOON they travelled along a stretch of road with pear orchards on both sides. The pears weren't quite ripe, it being only the middle of summer, but in the rays of the westering sun their rosy blush was enticing. Reiner felt his stomach growling.

On the cart, Dag sat up, sniffing. 'Pears,' he said. And without another word, he hopped down and started trotting towards the trees.

Reiner grunted, annoyed. 'We've plenty of fodder,' he said. 'No need to forage.'

'I only want one or two,' Dag said, and ducked through the first rank of trees.

Reiner sighed.

'Not much on obeyin' orders,' said Hals.

'Well, he's mad, ain't he?' said Pavel.

Gert harrumphed. 'T'ain't no excuse.'

A few moments later barking erupted from the orchard. The company looked up and saw Dag laughing and running through the trees, arms full of pears, with a big farm dog at his heels. He stumbled over a root and the dog caught him, sinking its teeth into his calf.

Dag fell, crying out and dropping the pears. He rolled onto his back, and before Reiner knew what he meant to do, drew his dagger and jabbed the dog in the belly. It squealed and recoiled, but Dag tackled it and held it down, stabbing it repeatedly in the eyes and neck.

'Sigmar!' choked Karel. 'What's he doing?'

'Mueller!' bellowed Reiner. 'Stop!'

The others cried out too, but before they could dismount, their cries were echoed.

'Hie, ye brigand!' came a voice. 'What do ye to my dog?'

Six farm hands ran out of the trees, armed with pitchforks and clubs, and surrounded the archer. There was a boy with them, who stared blankly at the dead dog. A farmhand clubbed Dag across the back.

Reiner cursed. 'Come on, then.' He dismounted and jogged into the orchard with the others following. 'Hoy!' he shouted.

The combatants didn't heed him. Dag was up, a mad grin splitting his face as he squared up to the farmhand who had struck him. 'And what was that for, yokel?' He held his bloody dagger in a loose grip.

'For? Why, ye killed my dog, ye madman!'

'Then yer in need of killin' as well, for letting him bite.' And before the farmhand could answer, Dag flicked blood at his eyes. The man flinched, and Dag lunged, slashing.

'Stand down, Mueller!' screamed Reiner. 'Stand down!'

The farmhand reeled back, clutching a bleeding shoulder, but as Dag followed, the other farmhands rushed in, swinging their bludgeons. Reiner sprinted forward. Damn the boy! There would be murder done, and Manfred's job botched before it began.

There was a scrape of steel beside him and Jergen blurred past. He hauled Dag out of the ring of farmhands with one hand and swung his sword in a circle with the other. Pitchfork tines and the tips of staves dropped to the grass around him, lopped off like dandelion heads. He ended on guard, Dag hurled behind him, and the point of his longsword touched the wounded farmhand's neck. The man froze, as did his companions, staring at their truncated weapons.

Reiner and the others stared as well, stunned by Jergen's speed, strength and terrifying precision.

'Well… well done, Rohmner,' said Reiner, swallowing. 'Now stand down, all. We'll have no more dramatics if you please. I…'

'Who put his hands on me?' cried Dag, bouncing up. 'No man puts his hands on me and lives!'

'Enough, Mueller!' shouted Reiner, turning on him. 'Shut your fool mouth.'

Dag glared at Reiner, eyes blazing, but Reiner, more by instinct than intent, glared right back, forcing himself not to blink or look away. Dag's anger seemed to surge. He growled in his throat and raised his dagger, but after a long moment, he shrugged and laughed.

'Sorry, captain,' he said. 'Ain't mad at you.' He sneered at the farmhands over his shoulder. ''Tis these gape-gobbed yokels who can't keep their curs to heel that…'

'Ye were stealin' our pears, ye thievin' murderer!' cried the farmhand Dag had wounded – though he didn't move, for Jergen's blade was still at his throat. 'T'ain't bad enough we've to send all our crops north to feed Karl-Franz's army – for starvation prices, too – now ye uniformed bandits come south to snatch the food from our mouths?'

'And kill our dogs,' said another.

'Snatch the food from yer mouth?' retorted Hals. 'Look at all the plenty around ye. Livin' in luxury while we been freezing our fundaments off in a Kislev snow bank, protecting yer worthless hide. There's gratitude for you.'

Reiner's men, who had up to this point sided with the farmhands against Dag, were beginning to range behind Hals.

'And why didn't you pick up a pike?' asked Pavel.

'Aye,' said Abel from behind him. 'Cowards.'

'Because someone had to stay behind and feed ye, y'ass!'

The two sides began to edge forward, drawing daggers and hefting clubs.

'Hold, curse it! Hold! All of you!' cried Reiner. 'Let us not all go mad. There's been enough blood shed already. Adding to it won't solve anything.'

'But he killed my dog,' said the farmhand. 'He cut me!'

'Aye,' growled Hals. 'So take it up with him. It weren't nothing to do with Captain Reiner and…'

'It is to do with me,' said Reiner. 'For, much as I could wish otherwise, I am your captain, and if I cannot control you then I am to blame.'

'Like him and his dog,' said Dag, triumphant. 'If he'd have kept him to heel…'

Reiner spun on him. 'His dog was doing its job. You, you stone skull, were disobeying orders. You were in the wrong, do you understand me?'

Dag frowned for a moment, looking from Reiner to the farmhands and back, then seemingly light dawned. He grinned and gave Reiner a broad wink. 'Oh aye, captain. I understand ye perfectly. I've been bad. Very bad. And I won't do it again.'

Reiner groaned. It was like talking to a post. 'I shall make certain of it.' He turned back to the farmhands. 'So, since I am to blame, I will be the one to make amends. Now, I know no one can put a price on the loyalty of a dog or the pain of a wound, but gold is all I have and not much of that, I'm afraid. So what will you ask in recompense?'

REINER WAS WORRIED that there would be difficulties over who would tent with whom that night, since he was sure no one would want to sleep next to Dag, but surprisingly, Jergen volunteered – with a monosyllabic grunt – and the rest of the company breathed a sigh of relief.

Reiner and Franka tented together; a boon for Franka, who would therefore not have to guard the secret of her sex both night and day, but torture to Reiner, who would have to endure her nearness without being able to touch or kiss her.

As they curled up in their separate bedrolls Franka rose up on her elbow. 'Reiner.'

He looked up when she didn't continue. 'Aye?'

She sighed. 'You know I'm not one to advocate murder in cold blood, but… but this boy is dangerous.'

'Aye,' said Reiner. 'But I cannot.'

'But why not? He's mad. He'll kill someone.'

'Is he mad?' asked Reiner.

Franka raised an eyebrow. 'What do you mean?'

Reiner leaned in and lowered his voice. 'Do you think Manfred is a fool?'

'What has that got to do with it?'

'Manfred admitted as we left that this job was a test, aye?'

'Aye.'

'So, if you were Manfred, and you wanted to know what we did, how I led, if we betrayed you or the Empire, is Karelinus Eberhart the man you would ask to bring you your report?'

Franka frowned for a moment, then a look of comprehension spread over her face. 'You think there is a spy.'

'There must be. Karel can't be anything but a decoy. He's a babe in the woods. One of the others must be working for Manfred as well.'

'And you think it is Dag? You think he only pretends to be mad?'

'No. But I can't be certain. It could be any of them. And if it is him and word gets back to Manfred that I killed him...'

'He'll think you discovered his spy and killed him,' said Franka, then sucked in a sharp breath. 'Any of them? We'll have to watch our tongues.'

'Aye,' said Reiner. 'No talk of running away, or killing Manfred, or flushing the poison from our veins.'

Franka groaned. 'We must find out who it is, and quickly.'

Reiner nodded. 'Aye.'

They stared into the dark corners of the tent for a moment, thinking, then Reiner noticed that their shoulders were touching. He turned and his lips brushed Franka's hair. He nuzzled her neck. 'Let's have a kiss.'

Franka jerked away from him and punched his shoulder. 'Don't be daft. Do you want to be caught?' She rolled over and pulled her blanket up over her shoulders. 'Go to sleep.'

Reiner sighed and lay back. She was right, of course, but that didn't make it any easier to control himself. It was going to be a very long journey.

# THREE
## The Finest Army in the Empire

THEY REACHED AVERHEIM without further incident. Whether Dag had been cowed by Reiner's scolding, or it was just that there was nothing to tempt him to violence, the boy remained calm and cheerful, watching the clouds and whistling tavern songs.

At twilight on the fourth day they passed close enough to Nuln to see the orange glow of the great furnaces illuminating the undersides of the black smoke that belched from its many hundred forges. There had been a time, thought Reiner, that the city known as Karl-Franz's anvil, the city that made the guns and swords and devastating cannon that protected the Empire, and that housed the College of Engineers and their wondrous weapons of war, had filled him with a sense of pride. Its superior warcraft was what set the Empire above all other lands. Now, however, the place only inspired in him a chill of dread. All the smoke and flame reminded him too much of the last time he had seen such furnaces and such forges. He could almost feel their heat, and the walls of that terrible red cave closing in on him again.

Two further days of dusty roads and sunburned necks, and they saw at last the grey stone walls of Averheim rising behind bare-branched arbours and patchy wheat fields. The spires of the temples of Sigmar and Shallya, and the towers of the elector count's castle, jutted over the walls and glinted in the noon sun.

Reiner stopped the Blackhearts before they came within view of the main gate. 'Right, lads,' he said. 'Here's where we part company. I don't want the recruiters to know we know one another. Too suspicious if we come in as a group. Sign up where you fit. Pavel and Hals as pikemen, Karel as lancer, and so on. Franz will play at being my valet. When we get to the fort, talk to your comrades, listen, and if you hear interesting things – murmurs of mutiny, treason, what have you – you will "befriend" Franz in the mess and tell him what you have heard, and he will relay it to me. Are we clear?'

A chorus of 'Ayes' answered him.

'Then luck be with you. And remember,' he added, 'no matter how tempting it might be to escape with my eye not upon you, Manfred's poison is still in our veins. His leash is still around our necks. It would bring you up short if you ran. It would choke the life out of you.'

The Blackhearts nodded, grim.

Reiner smiled, trying his best to look the brave commander. 'Now be off with you. When next I see you, we will all be honest soldiers again.'

AN HOUR LATER, Reiner and Franka rode through Averheim's broad city gate and began winding their way through the cobblestone streets to the Dalkenplatz, the great market in the city's centre. There in the shadow of the city jail was spread a sea of bright stalls and tents where one could buy fruits, vegetables, freshly butchered meat, and meat on the hoof. There were knife sharpeners, candle makers, tanners and cloth sellers, farmers, fishmongers, potters and tinsmiths. Bread and pastries were for sale, as well as sweetmeats, cider and beer. Rotund halflings from the Moot rolled wheels of cheese almost as tall as themselves through the crowd. It made Reiner hungry.

'Franz,' he said with a wave of his hand. 'Go and buy us some meat pies and a jug of cider.'

'What's this?' said Franka, looking up sharply. 'Putting on airs?'

Reiner smirked. 'If we are to be master and servant, we should practise a bit, hey?'

Franka rolled her eyes. 'Trust you to take advantage.' She dismounted and bowed flamboyantly. 'As your lordship desires.' Then she stuck out her tongue and disappeared into the confusion of tents.

After they had finished their snack, the two sought out Gutzmann's recruiters. They were not hard to find. They had taken over a tavern on the side of the square, a sway-roofed two storey building with mullioned windows. Tall banners had been raised on either side of the door – the griffin of the Empire and the white bear on deep blue that was Gutzmann's standard – and a cheerful, bearded fellow in a shining breastplate and blue breeks and doublet stood outside, looking every young man who passed in the eye saying, 'Yer a strapping lad. How'd you like to string yer bow for good old Karl-Franz?' and 'Three squares a day in General Gutzmann's army. And a bonus just for making yer mark.'

There were precious few young men left in the local population, which seemed almost entirely made up of women in widow's grey, children and old men. Still, there was a slow, steady stream of volunteers shuffling through the tavern's doors. Some indeed were young men – some too young by far – but many more were hardened professional soldiers, wearing the colours of every city in the Empire, men with missing eyes and ears and fingers, men with hard-used faces and well-used swords, who wore their leather jacks and their dented helmets and vambraces as if they had been born in them. And there were some of an even rougher sort: gaunt, thick bearded villains in buckskins and rags, with no weapons but bows and daggers, men with the clipped ears and noses of felons and clumsy burns meant to cover the fact that they had been branded murderer, deserter or worse.

As Reiner and Franka rode up to the tavern the friendly sergeant saluted, grinning. 'Welcome, m'lord. Come to lend a hand?'

'Aye, sergeant. That I have.'

'Yer an officer, m'lord?'

'Junior officer,' said Reiner as he and Franka dismounted. 'Corporal Reiner Meyerling. Late of Boecher's pistoliers. Seeking active duty.'

'Very good, m'lord. Right this way.'

Reiner handed the reins of his horse to Franka. 'Wait here, boy.'

'Wait…?' Franka's fists curled, then relaxed as she remembered her role. 'Yes, my lord.'

The sergeant ushered Reiner through the tavern door, elbowing aside the lesser recruits. Reiner saw Pavel and Hals in the line and gave them a wink. They hid their smiles.

The pikemen's line led to a table where more smiling soldiers in polished armour talked to each recruit in turn, asking them where they had fought before and why they had left their previous service. The recruiters didn't seem too picky. A majority of the men were asked to raise their right hands and pledge to serve the Empire 'unto death,' then sign their names in a big, leather-bound book, or at least make an X if they couldn't write. Once pledged and signed, they were given a few coins and a blue and white cockade to pin to their caps. Only a few men were turned away. A few others were taken away in irons, cursing.

The sergeant led Reiner around this scene to a table at the back of the tavern where a lance corporal sat with his spurred boots up, tapping his teeth with a quill pen. At Reiner's approach he abruptly sat up and affixed a big smile to his face.

'Corporal Bohm,' said the sergeant, 'may I present Corporal Reiner Meyerling. A pistolier.'

'Welcome, corporal!' said Bohm, sticking out his hand. 'Matthais Bohm, bugle with General Gutzmann's third lance.' He was a handsome youth with a swoop of brown hair over bright, eager eyes. He had the height and brawn of a knight, but not yet the hardness or gravity that came with experience.

'Well met, sir,' said Reiner, shaking his hand.

Bohm motioned Reiner to a chair, and they sat on opposite sides of the table.

'So,' said the youth, opening a small leather book. 'You wish to sign on with us?'

'I do,' said Reiner. 'Can't have my barking irons rusting, can I?'

Bohm laughed agreeably. 'Well, we can help you there, I think. But if you wouldn't mind telling me of your previous service. And, er, your reasons for coming here.'

'Certainly,' said Reiner, relaxing back into his chair. Manfred had ordered him to assume a false identity for the mission, and Reiner had spent much of the journey thinking of the tale that would be most pleasing to Gutzmann's ears. 'Before Archaon's invasion, I was stationed with Boecher's Pistols at Fort Denkh, and when that monster Haargroth came racing through the Drakwald on his way to Middenheim, we joined with Leudenhof's army to stop them. Quite a set-to as you can imagine.'

'We've heard stories,' said Bohm, enviously.

Reiner sighed. 'But though I did my part,' he coughed, 'and I think I can modestly say that I pulled more than my weight – I continued to be passed over for promotion.'

'Why so?'

Reiner shrugged. 'I hate to make a charge of nepotism against so august a name as that of Lord Boecher, but it seemed that his sons, and his sons' circle, won the lion's share of honours and commands. And when I was foolish enough to bring a complaint, it only got worse.' He spread his hands. 'The Meyerlings are a small country family. No influence at court. Not enough money to buy what can't be honourably won, and so when I at last realized that there would be no advancement for me under Boecher, I took my leave.'

Bohm shook his head. 'You'd not credit how often I hear that tale. Good men ignored in favour of bad. Well, you've come to the right place. General Gutzmann knows too well the perils of politics and preference, and has made a vow that merit only will be the way of advancement in his army. We welcome all who have felt slighted in other regiments and companies. We are the home of the dispossessed.'

'That is why I sought you out,' said Reiner. 'Lord Gutzmann's fairness is spoken of across the Empire.'

Bohm beamed. 'It is gratifying to hear.'

He turned the little book toward Reiner. 'If you would put your name and rank on this line, and pledge to serve General Gutzmann, Sigmar, and the Empire to the best of your abilities unto death, you will be instated in Gutzmann's army at your full rank, privileges and pay.'

'Excellent.' Reiner raised his right hand and made the pledge, smiling inwardly as he noted that General Gutzmann came before Sigmar and the Empire.

After he had signed Bohm's book, the young corporal shook his hand, smiling broadly. 'Welcome to the finest army in the Empire, Corporal Meyerling. It is a pleasure to have you with us. We leave tomorrow morning from the south gate. Be there at daybreak.'

Reiner saluted. 'A pleasure to find a home, corporal. I will be there without fail.'

As he was leaving, Reiner bumped into Karel coming in. The fool boy grinned at him and almost spoke, but Reiner kicked him in the shin and he yelped instead. A born spy, that one, Reiner thought.

THE NEXT MORNING, Reiner rode, slumped miserably in his saddle, through winding cobbled streets to Averheim's southern gate with Franka at his side. A moist, pre-dawn mist made looming half seen monsters of the brick and timber tenements that leaned their upper storeys over the narrow lanes. The fog without was mirrored by a fog within. Reiner had hoped, since he and Franka were separated from the others, that they would at last be able to get a room together alone, but maddeningly, there had been no private quarters available. With all the recruits in town, and it being market day, the city had been full to bursting. Even with all Manfred's reikmarks, Reiner and Franka had had to settle for sharing a cramped room with four longswords from Talabheim who spent the night singing marching songs. Reiner had drowned his frustrations in too many jars of wine, and now had a throbbing head as thick as army porridge.

He was not alone. Gutzmann's recruitment bonus had been nicely calculated to be just enough to get drunk on but not enough to tempt one to leave town, so the men who formed up before the tall, white stone gate under Gutzmann's banners and amidst supply wagons loaded with sacks of wheat, barrels of cured meat, apples, and cooking oil, as well as bags of oats and bales of hay, were a sad, quiet bunch, clutching heads and puking behind rain barrels. The sergeants, so friendly and cheerful the previous afternoon, were showing new faces now; pulling barely conscious recruits out of doss houses and taverns and bullying and kicking them into line. Other soldiers herded reluctant groups of fellows who, having thought better of joining up, had tried to sneak out through other gates, but hadn't been wise enough to remove the blue and white cockades from their caps.

As they made their way through the crowded square, Reiner saw a few of the other Blackhearts. Giano gave him a wink, and Abel a slight tip of the head. Pavel and Hals were hanging on their pikes like they were all that held them up. Hals had a black eye.

At the head of the line, Reiner joined Matthais and Karel and the other junior officers.

'Good morning, Meyerling!' said Matthais cheerily.

'The only thing good about it,' said Reiner, rubbing his temples, 'is that it will eventually be over.'

'Are you unwell, sir?' asked Karel, concerned.

Reiner gave him a withering look.

'Reiner Meyerling,' said Matthais. 'May I present Captain Karel Ziegler of Altdorf.'

'A pleasure to make your acquaintance for the very first time, sir,' chirped Karel.

Reiner closed his eyes.

After a quarter of an hour in which Reiner stared blankly into space, the sergeants at last chivvied the supply wagons and the new recruits into a rough marching order, Matthais bellowed 'For'ard!' in Reiner's ear, and the column staggered out the gate and into the fog. Reiner wished he were dead.

REINER RECOVERED CONSIDERABLY after the first meal stop. Whether Matthais's claim that Gutzmann's was the finest army in the Empire was true or no, the general certainly did well by his men as far as rations went. Reiner didn't know what the foot soldiers were being fed, but Franka served him cold ham and cheese and black bread with butter, as well as beer to wash it down with; all of better quality than he'd had in other regiments. The beauty of the day was a restorative as well. They rode through rolling farmland with the buzz of insects all around them and the young wheat rippling in the breeze. A broad blue sky soared above, piled high with fluffy white clouds.

When he at last felt human enough to talk in complete sentences, Reiner urged his horse up to the head of the line, where Matthais was singing the praises of Gutzmann to the new junior officers with the fervour of a fanatic.

'The Empire has yet to use him to his full potential,' said Matthais, 'but rest assured, General Gutzmann is the greatest commander in the field. His victories over the orcs in Ostermark and over Count Durthwald of Sylvania are held up as models of strategy among the knightly orders, and his reduction of the Fortress of Maasenberg in the Grey Mountains when the traitor Brighalter made his rebellion has never been equalled for speed and brilliance.'

'Indeed,' said Karel. 'I have studied it myself. The way he drew Brighalter out from cover was masterful.'

Matthais smiled. 'Consequently, he has won the undying loyalty of his men, for his brilliance keeps losses at a minimum. No one dies unnecessarily in General Gutzmann's battles, and the men love him for it. Also, he shares out the spoils with magnanimity. His men are better paid and better cared for than any others in the Empire.'

'Is there anything this paragon doesn't excel at?' asked Reiner dryly as he swatted at a mosquito on his wrist.

Matthais failed to hear the irony. 'Well, the general is nothing with the bow or the gun, but with sword and lance he is nigh unbeatable. His feats of martial valour on and off the battlefield are legendary. He defeated the orc chieftain Gorslag in single combat and led the charge that broke Stossen's line at Zhufbar.'

Reiner groaned to himself. And this was the man he must kill if it proved that he meant to betray the Empire? To stem the tide of praise, he decided to change subject. 'And what will our duties be when we arrive? What is the situation in the pass?'

Matthais took a sip from his water skin. 'I'm afraid there is presently little chance for glory, though that could change. Our little pass is not of the same strategic importance as the Black Fire. It is much smaller and closed for much of the year by snow and ice. And it is buffered from the dead lands beyond by the small principality of Aulschweig, which has been a good neighbour to the Empire for five hundred years, and is enclosed entirely within one valley. We also protect the gold mine situated at the north end of the pass.'

'There's a gold mine?' asked Reiner, feigning surprise.

Matthais pursed his lips. 'Er, yes. The mine is a primary source for the Empire's treasury.'

Reiner laughed. 'And the officers' retirement fund, no doubt!'

'Sir,' said Matthais stiffening. 'We do not joke about such things. The gold belongs to Karl-Franz.'

Reiner straightened his face. Was the boy pretending, or did he mean it? 'No. No, of course not. My apologies. A poor jest. But if that's all there is to our duties, it sounds a bit sleepy. You promised when I signed on that I'd get some use of my pistols.'

'And you will,' said Matthais, brightening. 'You'll not lose your saddle calluses under General Gutzmann's command, never fear. There are bandits in the hills to be chased down, trading caravans to be escorted across the border, and squabbling among the rulers of Aulschweig to keep an eye on. 'And,' he grinned, 'when there's nothing else to do, we have games.'

Reiner raised an eyebrow. 'Games?'

# FOUR
## 'Tis Always the General

REINER LEARNED WHAT Matthais meant by games four days later, when at last they reached the fort in the pass.

The journey there was uneventful, a dull slog due south from Averheim through farm and dairy land with the Black Mountains rising like a row of rotting teeth beyond them the entire way. Just after noon on the third day they reached the foothills and felt the first chill breezes nosing down from the heights above. By nightfall, when they stopped to make camp in a thick pine forest, summer had fallen away completely and Reiner was pulling his cloak from his pack and wrapping it around his shoulders.

'Why couldn't Manfred send us somewhere warm?' he muttered to Franka as they lay shivering in their tent that night. 'First the Middle Mountains, now the Black. Isn't trouble to be found on the plain?'

It only got colder the next day, as the long column of recruits wound along a torturous path deeper and deeper into the jagged range. At least the sky remained blue and the sun hot, when they weren't in the shadow of some crag.

That afternoon the path tipped down into a small cleared valley and widened into a well-maintained road. Meagre freeholds appeared on the left and right, where stunted cattle grazed on scrubby grass. At the end of the valley the column passed through the mining town of Brunn, which, though small, was still able to support a large, garishly painted brothel. Reiner smiled to himself. That alone proved that there was a garrison nearby.

On the road beyond the village they began to come across parties of men with picks over their shoulders. Those heading south whistled and chatted as they marched. Those coming north were covered in dirt and trudged along in weary silence. Reiner was thus not surprised when, a short time later, Matthais pointed out a branching path, well worn with cart tracks, that he said was the way to the gold mine.

Not a mile beyond that, the steep, thickly wooded hillsides of the ravine opened up, slowly revealing the column's destination. Coming upon it from the north, it was an odd looking fort, for it was one-sided. There were almost no defences on the Empire side, only a low wall and a wide open gate. Beyond that rose various barracks, stables and storehouses, and an imposing inner keep on the right where Matthais said the senior officers had their quarters. Beyond that were the massive southern battlements, a thick, grey stone wall almost as tall as the keep and stretching the whole width of the pass. The top was notched and crenellated with slots for archers and sluices for boiling oil. Squat catapults sat atop four square towers, all pointing south. In the centre was a great gate – a wide tunnel through the thickness of the wall – with massive, iron-bound wooden doors and an iron portcullis at both ends.

As they got closer, the new recruits were startled to hear a great cheer echo through the pass. Reiner's eyes were drawn to the broad, weedy expanse on the Empire side of the fort that stretched between the two walls of the pass. On the right were neat rows of infantry tents – many

more than were needed to house the fort's original com-
pliment of troops. To the left, the ground was devoted to
horses. There was a fenced off area for them to roam free,
a training ring, and a proper tilting yard, with lanes for
jousting and straw dummies for practising lance charges.
It was from here that the cheer had rung.

Reiner and the other new officers shot questioning
looks at Matthias.

He smiled. 'The games. Would you care to see?'

'Certainly,' said Karel.

So, while the veterans began herding the foot soldiers
to their new quarters and assuring them that they would
be fed and given their new kit in short order, Matthais led
the new sergeants and junior officers toward a big crowd
of soldiers of every stripe who ringed the tilting field,
whistling and shouting.

There was a canopied viewing stand on one side, to
which they made their way, turning their horses over to
squires and stepping up onto the wooden platform. A
handful of men sat on the long benches – infantry captains by their uniforms – but unlike the enlisted men
who watched so avidly in the sun, the officers hardly
looked at the field, talking instead amongst themselves in
low voices.

'Greetings, sirs,' said Matthais, bowing to them. 'I return
with the new blood.'

The officers looked around and nodded, but there were
no glad cries of welcome.

'Any for us?' asked one.

'Yes, captain.' Matthais indicated three of the new men.
'Two sergeants of pike and a gunnery sergeant.'

'And ten lance corporals,' said another captain dryly.

The captains returned to their conversation.

Matthais grinned sheepishly at the new men and indicated that they should sit along the first bench.

Once seated, Reiner turned to the field and discovered
that Matthais's game was 'tent-pegging,' an old parade
ground drill where riders took turns trying to pluck

brightly painted wooden tent-pegs out of the ground on the tips of their lances while at full gallop. It was a difficult trick, for the pegs were short, and broom stick thin, and it was more dangerous than it first appeared, for if one lowered one's lance just the slightest bit too much, one could catch it in the ground and be catapulted from the saddle.

This happened just as Reiner thought it. A knight flew through the air and landed in a cloud of dust on the hard-packed earth. The crowd of soldiers erupted in cheers and jeers as the knight pulled himself stiffly to his feet. He saluted the soldiers, then walked his horse off the field.

Reiner frowned, puzzled, for the fellow was no youthful lancer, but a hardened knight, in his middle years, long past his training days. He looked around at the other men on the field. There were many young men among them, but just as many looked to be senior officers.

Reiner turned to Matthais. 'Who are the players in this game?'

'Why, all officers corporal and above. The general insists every man be fighting fit.' He sat down next to Reiner. 'We run in sets of five, with all who share the lowest score dropping out before the next heat. Any man unhorsed is out as well. We play until there is only one.' He laughed. 'And 'tis always the general.'

Reiner nearly choked. 'The general plays as well?' He squinted out at the field, the lowering sun harsh in his eyes.

Matthais pointed. 'In the dark blue sleeves. You see him? With the cropped hair and the dented breastplate?'

Reiner stared. The man Matthais had indicated couldn't possibly be a general. He looked hardly older than Reiner himself, a laughing, handsome knight in simple armour, who slapped the backs of those who had made their pegs and joked with those who lost. A captain or obercaptain? Certainly. But a general? He lacked the gravitas.

New pegs were set and a bugle blared. Gutzmann and another knight took their places in their lanes. A soldier dropped a flag and they spurred their mounts into a gallop, lowering their lances as one. As they reached the end of their lanes there was an audible 'tock' and Gutzmann raised his lance high, a bright red peg squarely pinned on his shining lance point, while the other man came up empty. The crowd of soldiers cheered uproariously. It was obvious who their favourite was. Reiner decided that the fellow was a general after all, and one to be reckoned with. These lads would follow him into the maw of Chaos without a qualm. Woe to the fool who brought him low and let his troops discover it. Reiner shivered, hoping fervently that it wasn't Gutzmann who was stealing the gold.

As Gutzmann circled back to the top of the lane, he saw the new men in the stands and trotted over. The infantry officers fell silent as he approached, watching him.

'Well met, Corporal Bohm,' he said, reining up. 'So these are our new companions?'

Matthais bowed. 'Aye, m'lord. And a likely lot they are. Ready for anything.'

'Excellent,' said Gutzmann. He bowed from the saddle to the new recruits, his eyes merry. 'Welcome, gentlemen. We are glad to have you.'

Up close, Reiner could better see the general's age. Though he was as fit as a man half his years, skin drum tight over corded muscles, there were deep lines around his pale grey eyes and silver in his neatly trimmed beard and at his temples.

A knight called from the field and he turned his horse, but then looked back. 'If any of your lads would care to try his luck, he would be more than welcome. We've only recently begun.'

Matthais laughed and held up his hands. 'My lord, we have been riding since before dawn. I think the gentlemen are more interested in rest and a hot meal than tilting at pegs.'

'Of course,' said Gutzmann. 'Foolish of me even to ask.'

'No, no,' said Karel, standing. 'I for one would love to play.'

Reiner and the other new cavalrymen glared murder at the boy. If he had said nothing, there would have been no shame in allowing Matthais's excuse to speak for them, but now that one had volunteered the rest would look weak if they demurred.

'And I,' said Reiner through gritted teeth.

The others followed suit as well, and were quickly brought fresh horses and lances. As Reiner trotted out to the lanes he realized that this had become a test. Whether Gutzmann and Matthais had staged it on purpose or not, they and the other officers would now be watching the new men – to judge their martial skills, of course – but more importantly, Reiner thought, to see how game they were, how much enthusiasm and energy they could muster in the face of an unexpected and unwanted challenge. To see how well they 'played the game.'

It was a game Reiner needed to win. If he wished to learn the fort's intrigues, he would have to become part of the inner circle, and with so horse mad a garrison this seemed the best way to do it. Fortunately, though Reiner was only an adequate sword, riding had always come naturally to him, and he had been even more skilled with the lance than the pistol. Only his slight frame had stopped him from becoming a lancer instead of a pistolier. He hoped at least to best Karel. The boy needed a lesson.

Gutzmann's officers watched as the general assigned the new men lanes. They were impressive specimens, tall and broad shouldered to a man, with proud faces and regal bearing. Even though Reiner was of an age with many of them, he felt a boy beside them. And though they called friendly welcomes to the recruits, their expressions remained noncommittal.

Reiner missed his first peg – unsurprising, since neither the horse nor the lance was his own and the ground was unfamiliar, but he made his second, the impact with the peg sending a pleasing shock through his arm and shoulder. Then, after missing on his third and fourth runs, he caught the fifth square in the centre. It was gratifying how quickly the old skills came back. He hadn't couched a lance since before the war, but what his mind had forgotten his body remembered, and soon he was riding just as old master Hoffstetter had instructed him to – rising in the saddle before impact, letting the lance glide along the ground at the correct height, so that instead of stabbing desperately at the peg at the last second, you guided your lance easily into line.

Many of the new officers took only one peg. Some took none at all. So Reiner and Karel, with two apiece, made it into the next round with several of the others. But they would have to improve if they wanted to stay in the game long. Gutzmann's knights all took three or four pegs. Gutzmann took all five.

After three more runs Reiner and Karel were all that were left of the new men. And after another two, Karel was gone as well, having knocked the peg out of the ground that would have tied him with Reiner, but failing to keep it on his lance tip.

Gutzmann gave Reiner an approving nod at the start of the next round, and the other officers began sizing him up. A bearish knight with a bristling black beard pulled up beside him. Reiner had noted him before. A loud, hearty fellow with an ear-splitting laugh and a steady stream of jokes – the sort of man Reiner would have left a tavern to avoid.

'You do well, sir,' said the knight, sticking out a thick-fingered hand. 'Lance Captain Halmer, third company.'

Reiner recognized the name. 'A pleasure, sir. You are the captain of Matthais's company. He spoke highly of you.' Reiner shook the man's hand, then winced in his crushing grip. 'Meyer…ling. Pistolier.'

'Welcome, corporal. It's not often a new man gets this far. Luck to you.'

'And to you.'

Have to watch that one, thought Reiner, wringing the pain from his hand.

Reiner stayed in the running for two more rounds, getting three each time while others got two or less. But the round after that he took only one peg on his first four runs. As he watched the other knights make their fourth runs and bring their tallies to three or four, he knew this would be his last run. Halmer only had two, but he had yet to take less than three and always seemed to come through in the clinch.

Only this time, he didn't. On his fifth run, Halmer's horse stumbled a bit and his point went wide. He had only taken two pegs. Reiner's heart thudded in his chest. His turn was next. If he took his last peg, he would tie Halmer for last, and they would both drop out – petty vengeance for Halmer's crushing handshake – but Reiner had never claimed to be above petty vengeance. He could feel the lance captain's eyes upon him as he circled back to the top of the lanes. He knew the situation as well as Reiner did, and his anger was palpable.

Reiner could barely keep himself from grinning. Suddenly he knew he could take the peg. He had never felt more alive and in command of his abilities. Then he checked himself. He had been commanded to worm his way into the fort and learn its secrets. Making enemies of the officers wouldn't further that aim. He would have to miss the peg and let Halmer win. The temptation to ride his last run with his lance at parade rest had to be fought off too. Halmer would not love him for letting him win, and neither would Gutzmann. The general wasn't the sort of man who would tolerate a man not trying his best. So Reiner must make it look good.

As the soldier dropped the flag, Reiner spurred his horse forward and lowered his lance. It whispered through the sparse weeds of the field like a shark through a shallow sea, homing in on the peg. He knew his aim would be true. He knew he could pink the peg right in its centre. It took every ounce of self control to twitch his lance just a hair to the inside, and he almost played it too close. The peg spun from the ground as he hit its edge.

Reiner reined up, laughing and cursing, then rode back, rueful, to the top of the lanes. 'I had it, my lords,' he said. 'Truly I did. It was the wind from my horse's nostrils blew it aside.'

Gutzmann and the knights laughed, and Halmer joined in, but Reiner felt the captain staring after him, cold eyed and suspicious, as he turned in his lance and rode back to the sidelines.

Franka glared out at the field as she took his reins and helped him from the saddle. 'I wish you'd beaten him. Boasting bully.'

'I wish I could have allowed myself the pleasure.'

Franka turned big eyes on him. 'You let him win?'

'I let Manfred win,' said Reiner, sourly. 'Even from Altdorf he makes me dance.'

# FIVE
## Paragons of Martial Virtue

AFTER GUTZMANN HAD won the game to the cheers of the soldiers, the officers retired to the fort's keep for dinner in the great dining hall. The new sergeants and corporals were invited to eat with their new comrades, and as the one who had stayed in the game the longest, Reiner was singled out by Gutzmann to join him with his senior staff at the table on the raised dais at the head of the room. The table was long, but even so, it barely had space enough to hold all the officers in attendance. It looked as if Gutzmann had almost doubled the fort's original complement of men – many more than was needed to guard the pass. Both cavalry and infantry captains sat at the table, but Reiner noticed that the cavalrymen sat in the centre seats, nearest Gutzmann, while the infantry were relegated to the wings.

The general made a place for Reiner beside him on his left, forcing a grey-haired, square-bearded knight to shift down. 'Corporal Reiner,' he said as Reiner scooted his chair in and tried to keep his elbows close to his sides, 'May I present Commander Volk Shaeder, my right hand.'

The venerable knight inclined his head. 'Welcome, corporal. You stayed nine rounds I hear. Quite an accomplishment.' He had the soft, grave voice of a scholar, and wore ascetic grey robes over his uniform, but he was as tall and broad as the rest. A silver hammer of Sigmar hung from his neck by a chain. It looked to Reiner as if it weighed as much as an anchor.

'I would be lost without Volk,' said Gutzmann. 'He sees to the day to day business of the camp and lets me gallivant about playing at soldiers.' He grinned. 'He is also our spiritual navigator, keeping us always pointed toward Sigmar.'

Shaeder inclined his head again. 'I do my humble best, general.'

'To Volk's left,' continued Gutzmann, 'is Cavalry Obercaptain Halkrug Oppenhauer, Knight Templar of the Order of the Black Rose, or Hallie, as we call him.'

A bald, red-faced giant gave Reiner a friendly salute, beaming through a flowing golden beard, his blue eyes twinkling. Reiner recalled that he had been one of the last to drop out of the game. An amazingly nimble rider for a man his size. 'A fine display today, pistolier,' he said. 'Too bad you haven't the weight to make a lance.'

Reiner returned the salute. 'I curse my luck every day, obercaptain.'

'And on my right,' said Gutzmann, motioning with his hand, 'is Infantry Obercaptain Ernst Nuemark, Champion of the Carrolburg Greatswords, and hero of the siege of Venner.'

A tanned, clean-shaven man with close-cropped hair so blond as to seem white leaned forward, and nodded solemnly at Reiner. 'A pleasure to make your acquaintance, pistolier,' he said. He didn't seem terribly pleased.

'The pleasure is mine, obercaptain,' said Reiner formally. This was the first time Reiner had seen Obercaptain Nuemark. He hadn't attended the games.

'And where is Vortmunder?' asked Gutzmann, looking around.

'Here, general,' said a captain, standing. He was a wiry, bright-eyed fellow with dark hair and moustaches that had been waxed into jutting points.

'This is your captain, Meyerling,' said Gutzmann. 'Pistolier Captain Daegert Vortmunder. He is a good man. Heed his words.'

'I will, general. Thank you.' Reiner bowed in his seat to Vortmunder. 'Captain.'

'Welcome aboard, corporal. If you can shoot as well as you can ride, we will get along fine.'

'I will endeavour to impress you, captain,' said Reiner.

The first course was served and the officers fell to. The food was excellent.

Gutzmann poured Reiner wine. 'Matthais tells me you fought in the north. With Boecher, was it? Tell me how the end went.'

Something in Gutzmann's voice made Reiner hesitate. Though the general's expression was as friendly and open as ever, there was a hunger in his eyes that made Reiner shiver.

'I'm afraid I was far from the final battle, my lord,' said Reiner. 'I was wounded trying to stop Haargroth's advance, and sat out the end.'

'But you must know more of it than we, stuck as we are on the Empire's hindquarters. Tell me.' It was a command.

Reiner coughed. 'Well, you know the start, I'm sure, my lord: old Huss making dire predictions of invasion from the north, proclaiming his farm boy the reincarnation of Sigmar. Nobody paid any attention until we heard the first news of Erengrad and Praag. Thank Sigmar – or Ulric, I suppose – that Todbringer was quick on the uptake. And von Raukov of Wolfenburg as well. They put enough men in front of Archaon's hordes to slow 'em down for a time and organise a defence.' He sighed. 'That was the hardest part, I think. Getting so many disparate groups to fight alongside one another. Elves from Loren. Dwarfs from the Middle Mountains. Makarev's Kossars. Todbringer practically had to drink from the chalice and swear to the lady to get the Bretonnians in. And still it almost wasn't enough.'

'They had cannon, this time, the northmen,' said Gutzmann.

'Aye, terrible things that seemed almost alive. Their missiles were balls of flame.' Reiner took a sip of wine and went on. 'We had some successes, but there were too many of the devils. It was like trying to stop a river with a gate. And other fiends crept out of the shadows to take advantage of our weakness. Filthy, goat-headed beastmen from the Drakwald, greenskins. They fought amongst themselves as much as they fought us, but it didn't stop the tide.'

'And all the while Karl-Franz and the counts and barons of the south are dithering about who should go and who should stay, and not getting under way,' snapped Gutzmann.

Reiner hemmed noncommittally. 'It may be as you say, my lord. I was at Denkh at the time, preparing for the coming onslaught. The hordes soon took Ostland and then the west of Middenland. That was when I had my moment of glory, such as it was. Took a sword in the leg on my second charge and that was me done, and Haargrath pushed on to Middenheim with the rest of Archaon's horde.' He shrugged. 'I don't mind telling you I'm not sorry to have missed the siege.'

'A bloody business, then?' asked Shaeder.

Reiner nodded. 'Tens of thousands dead by all accounts, commander. Archaon and his henchmen pounded the Ulricsberg for more than a fortnight. Fortunately the Ostland boys had held them off long enough for Todbringer and von Raukov to get their lads in and shore up the defences. Still, it was close for a while, and the northmen were over the walls in places, but then we had a bit of luck with the greenskins. Their chief got it up his snout that he had to be first in, and so went after Archaon. And with the elves and Bretonnians and Kossars harrying the northmen from the forest, they began to lose heart and fell back to Sokh to regroup.' He sat forward. 'Karl-Franz arrived that day and attacked at once, but Archaon held him off, and the battle raged for three days, with Valten and Huss coming in on the second, and engaging Archaon himself in combat on the third.'

'It was there that Valten received his mortal wound, yes?' asked Shaeder.

'Aye,' said Reiner. 'Huss carried him off while Archaon was engaged with the orc chieftain, who had attacked as well.'

Gutzmann snorted at that.

'On the fourth day,' Reiner continued, 'the armies set to again, and it looked grim, for the beastmen attacked Karl-Franz's cannon from the rear, but before either side could win any real advantage, a third force appeared.'

'Von Carstein,' said Gutzmann.

'So my lord has heard,' said Reiner.

'Only rumours. Go on.'

'He raised the dead, my lord. Men of the Empire and of the north alike awoke where they had died and attacked both sides indiscriminately. Archaon's forces fled north while Karl-Franz withdrew his army to Middenheim. The Sylvanians followed, and von Carstein called for the Emperor's surrender and the surrender of the city, but Volkmar stepped out and told him to be on his way, and though I can scarcely credit it, he did. He turned about and buggered off to Sylvania again without another word.'

'And that was it,' said Gutzmann dryly.

'Yes, my lord. Middenheim held, and Archaon's army was dispersed.'

Gutzmann snorted again. 'And Altdorf calls it a great victory.'

'Your pardon, my lord?'

'The Empire was saved not by the reincarnation of Sigmar or the might of Karl-Franz's knights, or the much vaunted Company of Light, but by an orc warboss and an undead sorcerer.'

Reiner coughed. 'Er, they may have been in at the end, my lord, but the brave defensive actions of the men of Ostland and Middenland that kept the hordes at bay cannot be discounted. Middenheim would surely have fallen without them.'

'And if they were well led,' cried Gutzmann, 'the hordes would never have reached Middenheim at all! How many men died unnecessarily because our hide-bound counts continue to think that the only way to defeat an enemy is to fight him head to head, no matter the circumstance. If they hadn't insisted on swinging Sigmar's hammer at targets better slain with a stiletto, it might have been over in weeks, not months.'

'My lord,' said Reiner, annoyed in spite of himself. Gutzmann might well be the tactician he thought himself, but he hadn't faced the hordes. He hadn't stood toe-to-toe with a Kurgan warrior. Reiner had. 'My lord, they were a hundred thousand strong. And the smallest of them as big as two normal men.'

'Exactly!' said Gutzmann. 'A hundred thousand titanic men who must eat pounds of food every single day to keep up their strength.' The general leaned in, eyes gleaming. 'Tell me. You fought them. Did you notice their supply lines? Were they victualled from some northern stockpile?'

Reiner laughed. 'No, my lord. They were barbarians. They had no supply lines. They barely had an order of march. They raped the lands they moved through for their dinner.'

Gutzmann jabbed a finger at Reiner. 'Exactly! So, if one of our noble knights, our paragons of martial virtue, had had the forethought to harvest all the crops and slaughter all the game in Archaon's path, then burned the farms and forests before he reached them?' He banged the table with his palm. 'The northmen would have starved on their feet before they were halfway from Kislev, or more likely fallen to eating each other, the savages. Either way, they would have reduced their numbers considerably with almost no losses on our side. Instead Todbringer and von Raukov sent hastily equipped, unprepared forces against them, which, though they may have slowed them down, also fed their cooking pots and kept them strong.' He laughed bitterly. 'The knights of the Empire so love their tests of arms that they sometimes think that it is better to fight without winning than it is to win without fighting.'

Reiner was no student of military science. He had no idea if Gutzmann's theories would pass muster with other generals, but they sounded sensible.

Gutzmann shook his head. 'It is madness that I should have been sent here while Boecher and Leudenhof and fools of that calibre were sent to defend the Empire in its darkest hour.'

Commander Shaeder leaned forward, eyes anxious. 'But of course we must do as the Emperor bids us, my lord. Certainly he knows better than we how best to defend our homeland.'

'It wasn't Karl-Franz who banished me!' snapped Gutzmann. 'It was that hen-house of Altdorf cowards who were so afraid of my victories in Ostermark that they imagined I would break it from the Empire and crown myself its king. As if I would ever do anything to harm the land I love.'

'Then why,' said a captain of pike from down the table, 'do you turn your back on that land?'

'None of that!' barked Shaeder, glaring at the captain. 'You forget yourself, sir.' A few of the cavalry officers slid nervous glances toward Reiner. Reiner's heart pounded. What was this? This sounded exactly the sort of thing Manfred had asked him to look out for.

'I do not turn my back on the Empire,' said Gutzmann quietly. 'It turns its back on me.' His mouth twisted into a sneer of disgust. 'I wonder sometimes if it would notice if I were gone.'

The table fell silent. Gutzmann looked around, as if only now remembering where he was.

He laughed suddenly, and waved a hand. 'But enough of hypotheticals. This should be a merry occasion.' He turned to Reiner. 'Come, sir. What are the new songs in Altdorf and Talabheim? What do they play on the stage? We are starved for culture here in the hinterlands. Will you sing for us?'

Reiner nearly choked on his wine. 'I'm afraid I am no singer, sir. You would be hungrier for culture when I finished than when I started.'

Gutzmann shrugged. 'Very well.' He turned to the hall. 'Anyone else? Will any of the new men give us a song?'

There was a long pause as the recruits squirmed uncomfortably. But at last Karel stood, knees shaking.

'Er.' He swallowed, then began again. 'Er, if my lords would care to hear a ballad, there is one that the ladies ask for at the moment.'

'By all means, lad,' said Gutzmann. 'We are all ears.'

Karel coughed. 'Very good, my lord. Er, it is called, "When will my Yan come home?"'

Reiner braced himself for the worst, but after a few more hesitations Karel stood straight and began singing in the voice of a Shallyan choir boy; high and pure. The room sat silent and rapt as he sang the story of the farm girl waiting for her lover to come back from the war in the north, only to have him return on the shoulders of six of his friends, dead from a poisoned arrow. It was a heartbreaking song, sung with a heartbreaking sweetness, and when at last the farm girl decided to wed her lover in death by scratching herself with the arrow that killed him, Reiner saw many a knight dabbing his eye.

It only seemed to make Gutzmann angry, though he masked it well. 'A beautiful song, lad. But how about something jolly now. Something to lift our hearts.'

After a moment's thought Karel broke into a song about a rogue brought to ruin by a false nun, which had the whole hall singing along by the second chorus, and after that the atmosphere became relaxed and the conversation turned to light topics and filthy jests.

Towards the end of the meal, when pudding laced with brandy had been served and Gutzmann was involved in a loud conversation with some knights to his right about tent-pegging contests of yore and who had fallen and who had broken an arm or leg, Captain Shaeder leaned toward Reiner.

'You must forgive General Gutzmann,' he murmured. 'He is a passionate man, and the inaction of this posting frustrates him. But we are all loyal men here.' He laughed stiffly. 'If the general had a few more years, he would understand that no post is less important than another. And there are many who would be happy with any post at all.'

'Very true, commander,' said Reiner. 'And I took no offence, fear not.'

Shaeder inclined his head, nearly dipping his beard in his pudding. 'You ease my mind, sir.'

AFTER THE MEAL was done, Matthais volunteered to lead Reiner to his quarters, apologizing that he must bunk in a tent outside the north wall, rather than the pistoliers' barracks within the fort.

'We are too full at the moment,' he said.

'Aye,' said Reiner. 'I noticed. Don't quite understand why. The way you described our situation there doesn't seem the need for so many men.'

'Er, yes, well…' Matthais coughed, suddenly awkward. 'I believe I mentioned before some trouble in Aulschweig?'

'Aye. Infighting amongst the rulers or some such.'

Matthais nodded. 'Exactly. Younger brother wants older brother's throne. The usual Border Princes' nonsense. But there's a danger of it coming to a boil presently. The younger brother is Baron Caspar Tzetchka-Koloman, a blow-by who has a castle just the other side of the border. The older is Prince Leopold Aulslander. Altdorf wants Leopold to remain in power, as he is the more stable and level-headed of the two, so we may have to intervene if Caspar makes his play. Thus, extra troops.'

'Ah,' said Reiner. 'All becomes clear.' Or did it, he wondered. Matthais's explanation made sense, but the angry pike captain's outburst at the dinner table still rang in Reiner's ears.

'At least you'll have a tent to yourself,' said Matthais, 'if that's any consolation.'

Reiner's heart leapt, all thoughts of intrigue gone. Alone with Franka? 'Oh, I think I will manage.'

Matthais had been laughing and merry as they left the hall, but now, as they walked through the fort in the cold night air, the young knight lowered his voice. 'Er, I hope you read no treason in General Gutzmann's words tonight, corporal.'

'Not at all, Matthais,' said Reiner. 'His seems a reasonable enough complaint, considering the circumstances.'

Matthais nodded earnestly. 'Then you understand his frustration?'

'Of course,' Reiner replied, pretending the sort of bluff courage he knew lancers of Matthais's kidney valued. 'Any man would be disappointed to be kept so far from the front.'

'But you see the unfairness of it,' the youth pressed as they exited through the north gate. 'The deliberate slight. The danger into which the Empire was placed because of fear and favouritism.'

Reiner hesitated. Matthais's eyes were shining with almost religious fervour. 'Oh, aye,' he said at last. 'A damned shame. Absolutely.'

The young captain grinned. 'I knew you'd see it. You're a bright fellow, Reiner. Not a stubborn old fool.' He looked up. 'Ah. Here we are, your canvas castle.'

He reached for the tent flap, but it opened from within.

Franka bowed in the opening. 'I have laid out your things, my lord.'

Matthais nodded approvingly. 'You're wise to bring a valet from home. I've had to make do with a local boy. Horrible fellow. Steals my handkerchiefs.' He executed a clipped bow. 'Goodnight, corporal. Good luck with your new duties tomorrow. You'll like Vortmunder. He's a bit of a Kossar, but it's all bluster.'

'Thank you, captain. Goodnight,' said Reiner, returning the bow, then letting the flap drop.

He waited for Matthais's footsteps to fade, then turned to Franka, grinning. 'Ha! Alone at last. I have been waiting the last four months for this moment.'

'And you will wait yet another three, my lord,' she replied tartly. 'For my vow is as strong here as it was in Altdorf.'

Reiner sighed. 'But we have the opportunity now! In three months we might be on the march, or trapped in Manfred's townhouse again, with no chance for privacy.'

'It will only make it the sweeter when the time comes.'

'Bah!' Reiner started unlacing his jerkin. Then he stopped and looked back at Franka. He smirked. 'Unlace me.'

'What?'

'You are my valet, are you not? Unlace me.'

Franka rolled her eyes. 'You wish to continue the charade out of the public eye?'

'And why not. It will keep us from slipping when we are in company.'

Franka scowled. 'My lord, you seek to cozen me.'

'Not at all. I don't ask to unlace you, do I?'

Franka snorted. 'Very well, my lord. As my lord wishes.' She stepped forward and began tugging roughly at his laces.

'Easy, lass,' Reiner laughed, as he fought to stand still. 'You'll scuttle me.'

'"Lass", my lord?' said Franka, ripping open his last stays. 'You call your valet "lass"? My lord's eyes are failing, perhaps.' She grabbed his collar and began yanking it down from his shoulders.

'Franka... Franz... you...' With his arms trapped in his sleeves Reiner couldn't keep his balance. He staggered and fell. Franka tried to catch him, but instead went down with him, tipping the cot over. They ended in a muddle of blankets, the light wood frame on top of them.

Franka flailed a slap at him, laughing. 'You did that a'purpose!'

'I didn't!' Reiner cried. 'You were too rough, sir!'

He caught her wrist to stop another slap and suddenly they were in one another's arms, clinging desperately and kissing deeply. They moaned their desire, their hands moving feverishly. Reiner rolled to pull her on top of him, but Franka broke away with a sob.

Reiner sat up. 'What's this?'

'I am sorry, captain,' she said, hiding her face. 'I do not mean to tease, but I am not as strong as I pretend. This is why I beg you so not to press me. For it would take so little to make me give in, and then I could never forgive myself.'

Reiner sighed and pulled her head to his chest. 'Ah Franka, I...'

There were feet approaching the tent. 'Corporal Meyerling!' came a voice. 'Are you within?' It was Karel.

Reiner and Franka leapt up like guilty schoolboys. Reiner tore off his jerkin and tossed it to Franka. 'Here, take this and put it away. And dry your eyes. Hurry.'

Franka turned to Reiner's travel chest as Reiner righted the cot and piled the blankets on top of it. 'Come in,' he called. Karel ducked through the flap, his saddle-bags and armour over his shoulders.

'Corporal Ziegler?' said Reiner.

'They are overbooked, corporal,' Karel said, smiling. 'Thought they had more tents, but they didn't. I said you wouldn't mind if I bunked with you.'

Behind him Franka made a barking noise that might have been a sneeze, but probably wasn't.

Reiner ground his teeth. 'Not at all, sir. Not at all. Come in. Take the other cot.' He glared at Franka. 'Franz will sleep on the floor.'

FOR OBVIOUS REASONS, Reiner found it difficult to fall asleep that night, and so while Karel snored happily on his cot, and Franka slept curled in her bedroll, Reiner sat outside the tent, wrapped in his blankets, staring at the stars.

Part of him cursed Karel's inopportune interruption. Part of him thanked him. Reiner had no wish to hurt Franka, but whenever he was in her presence, the urge to crush her to him was overwhelming, and he forgot all promises and honour. Three months! Blood of Sigmar, he might explode by then!

A movement to his left caught his eye. He craned his neck. Three figures were slipping through the tents toward the north road. They all wore long cloaks with hoods pulled far forward to hide their faces.

Reiner frowned. The men might of course have a perfectly innocent reason for being abroad at this hour. A patrol, perhaps. And it was cold. They might wear cloaks to keep warm, but something in the furtiveness of their movements spoke of some dark purpose.

So much cheer on the surface of this place, Reiner thought, sitting back. The games, the songs, the love the soldiers had for their commander. But things stirred in the depths. Both Matthais and Shaeder had tried subtly to discover how Reiner felt about Gutzmann. Was he sympathetic to the general's frustrations, or did he believe the Empire right in all things? Strange – or perhaps not so strange – that Reiner found himself drawn more to Gutzmann's side. The general wanted to escape the suffocating embrace of authority, and so did he.

# SIX
## Where Does He Lead Us?

THE NEXT MORNING, after entirely too little sleep, Reiner was awakened by Karel, who sprang out of his cot and began donning his new uniform, whistling all the while.

Reiner opened one eye. 'Would you mind very much jumping off a cliff?'

'Did you not hear the bugle?' asked Karel. 'The day has begun.' He took a deep breath. 'I can smell our breakfast cooking in the great hall from here.'

Reiner waved a hand. 'Go on without me, lad. I will follow momentarily.'

Karel grinned as he stepped to the door. 'Don't tarry too long, slug-a-bed, or you shan't get any bacon.'

Reiner groaned, nauseous. Who could think of bacon at this hour?

'I begin to see why Manfred wanted that boy out of his hair,' said Franka, rising from her bedroll.

'Aye.' Reiner sat up, rubbing his face. He sighed. 'Well, Franz, lay out my uniform. Time to go learn my new duties.'

Franka saluted sleepily. 'Aye, sir.' She crossed to his trunk and took out his newly assigned uniform: slashed breeks and jerkin in Gutzmann's deep blue and white. Reiner splashed his face in the bowl of freezing water at his bedside and shivered in the morning chill. He almost longed for the comforts of Manfred's townhouse again. Almost.

'While I'm gone,' he said, as Franka helped him into his jerkin, 'your duties are to nose about and listen to the other valets, cooks and so forth. Rumour flies faster through the kitchen than the parlour, as they say. See what they are saying about Gutzmann and Shaeder and the rest. There's a struggle going on here and I want to know who has the winning hand. If you see any of our comrades, canvass them as well.'

'Aye, captain.'

'And give us a kiss.'

'No, captain.'

'Bah! Insubordination. Intolerable!'

AFTER BREAKFAST, WHICH he found he had a stomach for after all, he presented himself to Captain Vortmunder outside the stables, which were huge – three long wooden buildings – crowded with horses and swarming with knights, lancers and pistoliers.

The captain scowled at him, his moustaches like needles pointing at the sky. 'Sleeping late your first day, Meyerling? An excellent start.'

Reiner clicked his heels. 'Forgive me, captain. I am still a bit unfamiliar with the camp.'

'Then we will remedy that.' Vortmunder looked around at the men walking their horses out of the stables and fitting them with saddle and bridle. 'Hie! Grau! Here!'

A corporal saluted and trotted over. He was a square-jawed bantam-weight, lean and compact, with close-cropped blond hair and a neat beard. Reiner saw that many of the young cavalry officers sported the same look – an army of Gutzmann imitators – or perhaps worshippers. 'Yes, captain,' the corporal said, coming to attention.

'Light duty for you this morning, Grau. You will show Corporal Meyerling around the fort and familiarize him with his duties. Bring him to the parade ground after noon mess, in full kit and ready to ride. That is all.'

Grau saluted, beaming. 'Yes sir!'

Vortmunder turned to Reiner. 'Listen to him well, corporal. I don't care for slow starters. A keen mind is as important as a sharp eye to a pistolier.'

'Yes, sir,' said Reiner. 'Thank you, sir.' He saluted as well, then followed Grau.

When they were out of Vortmunder's earshot, Grau grinned and nudged Reiner in the ribs. 'I'm in your debt, old man. You've got me out of stable duty.'

Reiner raised an eyebrow. 'Pistoliers clean the stables? You have no squires?'

'Gutzmann wishes us to learn discipline. No soft berths here. No buying your way out of duty, no matter who your father is. I hated it at first. But I don't mind so much now. We're the best army in the Empire because of it. There's none to match us.'

'Aye?' said Reiner. 'You're not the only army to claim it.'

'But it's the truth with us. You'll see this afternoon.' He pointed to the big south wall. 'First things first. The great south wall. Thirty feet thick, fifty feet tall. It could probably stop most armies unmanned, but we man it anyway. Gives the foot something to do.' He lowered his hand to the gate. 'Oak doors. Two portcullises. Murder room above, with vents for pouring oil or lead on anyone who manages to get through the first gate. The walls can be reached through the gatehouse guardroom and each of the four towers.'

'And the only army likely to attack is that of a kingdom that has been friendly with the Empire for five hundred years?' said Reiner. 'No wonder you play so many games.'

'Oh, there's fighting, never fear,' said Grau. 'Nests of bandits in the hills. The occasional orc raiding party.

You'll know every goat track and rabbit trail for a hundred leagues before you're here a month.' He swung his arm to the keep. 'If an army breaches the south wall – not bloody likely, but if – we fall back to the keep. Armoury and main powder room are in there, as well as quarters for all the top brass and the barracks for their personal guard. The gate is like the south wall's in miniature. Oak doors. Murder room above, which also houses the winches that raise and lower the two portcullises. We've food, water and space to house five hundred men for three weeks.' He coughed. 'Unfortunately, there's two thousand of us at the moment, now that you lot have joined us.'

'Comforting,' said Reiner.

Grau turned to the other half of the fort. 'Stables. Smithy. Feed barn. Infantry drill yard. Barracks for the knights, lancers and pistoliers. Those new ones are for the infantry. Gutzmann built them when he doubled the garrison. And still there ain't enough. Hence the tents north of the fort.'

'Hence I'm sleeping under canvas.'

Grau grinned. 'Invigorating, ain't it?'

'I'll be happy to switch with you.'

Grau laughed. 'No fear.' He started back to the stables. 'Come, let's have a look at your kit. You brought your own horse?'

'Aye.'

'Well, we'll see if he's up to snuff.'

They found Reiner's horse and his gear and Grau looked it over while he explained Reiner's duties and what his days would consist of. Reiner grew tired just hearing it. Rise at daybreak every day, groom one's horse and clean one's tack. Then either drill, drudgery, or duty for the rest of the day. A third of the force was always on patrol, or escorting merchants to and from Aulschweig. A third was drilling on the parade ground, practising turns and wheels, shooting and swordplay from horseback. The last third was cleaning the stables or feeding the horses or mending tack or any of a dozen unpleasant but necessary chores. The more he listened, the more relieved Reiner was that he wasn't actually stationed here. He didn't know how long he would have to maintain his pistolier charade before he learned what Gutzmann was up to, but the sooner he could get away the better. Hard labour had never been his forte.

As Grau and Reiner led Reiner's horse to the smithy to be reshod – apparently Manfred's farrier did inferior work – Reiner heard raised voices coming from the far side of the privy shed, a low, stone building built against the canyon wall behind the stables.

'No man puts hands on me! I'll murder ye, ye clot!'

Reiner groaned. That could only be one man.

And as Reiner and Grau passed the shed, he was proved correct. Dag flew out of the door and fell across their path, his nose streaming red. He bounced back up into the face of a hulking crossbowman, who was cursing and shaking a filthy mop at him.

'Y'filthy little maggot, I'll shove you down the jakes and piss on you.'

'Touch me again and y'won't have nothing to piss from, y'great bullock!' shouted Dag.

'Hoy!' cried Grau. 'Stand down the both of you!'

The men looked up. The crossbowman stepped back, cowed by the presence of junior officers, but Dag, seeing Reiner, held out pleading hands.

'Captain Reiner, help me!' he called. 'This oaf tried to push me in the piss trough.'

Grau looked around at Reiner. 'You know this fellow?'

'Hardly.'

'I only bumped him, sirs,' said the crossbowman. 'The man's mad.'

'Mad!' Dag turned back to the crossbowman. 'Y'call me mad? I'll show ye mad! I'll eat yer liver!'

'Archer!' Reiner barked. 'Come to heel, curse you! What is the meaning of this!' He spun Dag around by the shoulder. Dag's eyes flared, but before he could speak, Reiner jabbed his finger in his face. 'You are mad, you horrible man! Starting fights for no reason! Calling on me as your captain! Do I look an archer? I am a corporal of pistoliers, footman! Your better in every way! And you would do well to remember it! Now stop this foolishness or you'll wind up in stir and be of no use to anyone! Do you understand me, cur?'

Dag hung his head, but Reiner was certain he saw a smile on the archer's lips. 'Aye, captain, er, corporal. I understand. Aye.'

'You will keep your fists, and your insults, and your liver eating to yourself, do you hear?'

'Aye, corporal.'

'Good.' Reiner stood back. 'Now be off, the both of you, and if I hear any more of this I'll string you up myself.'

He turned away with Grau and they continued towards the stables as Dag and the crossbowman slouched sulkily back into the privies, giving each other dirty looks.

Reiner breathed a sigh of relief. The damned madman had almost given the game away. Why had Manfred cursed him with command of such a fool? He shrugged as Grau gave him a questioning look. 'I did the fellow the kindness of letting him fetch me some water in exchange for a few coins one night on the march here, and now he thinks me his master. He's moon touched.'

Grau grinned. 'Well you gave him a proper scolding. You'll make parade corporal with that tongue. Strewth!'

NOON MESS FOR officers was served in the keep's great hall, where Reiner had supped the night before. This time, however, he did not sit on the dais with the captains, but mucked in with the other corporals on the long tables that ran the length of the room. It was a noisy affair, with much banter and horseplay once the oath to Sigmar had been pledged and the bread broken.

But the tensions he had felt elsewhere were here as well. There was very little mixing between the sergeants of the infantry and the corporals of the cavalry. They sat at separate tables and shot suspicious glances at each other. And under the cheery cacophony of insults and jokes he heard darker mutterings.

As he passed a table of sergeants he heard one say, 'We might lead 'em. But it's him and his cursed centaurs they love.'

One of the man's companions came to Gutzmann's defence. 'And why not? He's the best leader you've served under.'

'Aye, but where does he lead us? That's the question, ain't it?'

The question indeed. But though all around Reiner the cavalry officers exchanged sly glances and made veiled references to 'the future,' they were cagey in his presence. It maddened him. Their smug smiles and sly looks spoke of a conspiracy, but Reiner could learn nothing.

He could tell Grau itched to tell him what was afoot. After his lambasting of Dag, the corporal had decided Reiner was a good egg. He spent the whole of their meal cautiously feeling him out, trying to determine his loyalties, but afraid yet to betray himself, just as Matthais had the night before.

'But you've seen it close hand, haven't you, Meyerling?' he asked as they sat with the other pistolier corporals. 'How it is titles that win promotion not ability. That is the problem with the Emperor's army. Noble lackwits become generals while men with real talent can't rise above captain.' He sighed, perhaps a little too theatrically, 'If only a man like General Gutzmann ran things. We'd have professional soldiers leading us, men with experience in battle instead of politics.'

Reiner nodded sincerely, for he knew that was what Grau wanted him to do. 'Aye. That's how things should be. A modern, professional army, free of patronage. Too bad there's no chance of it happening in our lifetimes.'

Grau's eyes widened. He sat forward. 'You might be surprised, Meyerling. You might be surprised. Things might change quicker than you think. Perhaps not in the...'

The pistolier to Grau's left, a round-faced fellow named Yeoder, elbowed him in the ribs. Grau looked up and followed his gaze. A hush was falling on the cavalry tables as a company of men rose from their table near the dais and walked toward the hall's side door.

They were an impressive sight, twenty tall, stern greatswords, all in black, with snow white shirts showing at their cuffs and through their slashings. Their breastplates were black chased with silver and their kit matched down to the pommels of their swords and the buckles of their shoes. All had the twin comet stitched onto the right shoulders of their jerkins and silver hammers on a chain around their necks, which were smaller twins to the one that Shaeder wore. Their captain was a head shorter than the rest, but as powerfully built, with a magnificent square-cut white beard and eyes as blue and cold as a winter sky.

A circle of silence moved with them as they traversed the room, the conversations at the tables dying off and the cavalry officers turning to look at them over their shoulders after they had passed. Reiner could feel the hate emanating from his companions for the impassive men.

'Who are they?' he asked, when the men had at last left the hall and conversation had resumed.

Grau spit over his left shoulder. 'Shaeder's Hammer, we call 'em,' he said. 'They are Bearers of the Hammer, honour guard from Averheim's Temple of Sigmar, of which Shaeder was once a captain. Now they're his personal guard.'

'Gloomy lot,' Reiner said.

'Bah,' said Yeoder. 'Just stuck up. Think Sigmar is their personal property. Nobody else is good enough.'

'They'll find out,' said another pistol, darkly.

Grau gave him a sharp look and quickly turned the conversation to other things.

\* \* \*

THAT NIGHT REINER stumbled through the flap of his tent and collapsed onto his cot, utterly exhausted.

The afternoon had been one of the most gruelling of his young life. He had thought himself a veteran of the parade ground, having trained under Lord von Stolmen's master of horse, Karl Hoffstetter, considered one of the Empire's finest. But while Captain Vortmunder couldn't teach Reiner anything he hadn't learned already from Hoffstetter, what he did do was drill it into him until his limbs felt like lead and the blisters the constant repetition raised on his fingers, knees and thighs had burst and bled and burst again. No horse master back home had dared ride his pupils so hard. They were the sons of noblemen, used to being waited on and pampered. They would practise for a while and then they would retire to the taproom to boast about their prowess.

Not so with Vortmunder. He had no pity, and no deference to rank. He had his pistoliers ride and fire at targets again and again and again, until the actions became second nature and they hit the bull's-eye ten times in a row. He barked at them for the slightest failure of form. If a pistolier was ahead or behind his fellows as they wheeled, or he took too long to reload on the fly as he circled back from the target, Vortmunder was there, cantering beside him, ram-rod straight in his saddle, pointing out with his riding crop the pistol's offence.

And Reiner had felt the brunt of his attention. He had become the captain's target of choice.

'Let's have Gutzmann's favourite out again,' he would say when he was detailing the next exercise. 'Show us how they do it in the north, Meyerling.' Until Reiner thoroughly regretted his tent-pegging grandstanding the day before.

At the same time, even though by the end of the day he was cursing Vortmunder's guts with a vehemence he usually reserved for loan-sharks and officers of the watch, when the captain pulled up beside him as they were returning their horses to the stables and clapped him on the back with a 'Good work, corporal,' he felt a swelling of pride that almost made him want to do the whole thing over the next day.

Franka laughed at him as she helped him off with his jerkin, for he could barely lift his arms.

'Don't mock me, villain,' he said. 'Shall I tell you how weary I am?'

'Tell me,' said Franka.

Reiner looked over at Karel, who was already fast asleep in his cot, then leaned in to whisper in Franka's ear. 'Even had we the tent to ourselves, you would be as safe as if in a Shallyan convent.'

Franka's eyes widened. 'You are weary indeed, m'lord.'

FOR FIVE DAYS Reiner's routine continued the same. He was put in charge of ten men, and under Vortmunder's and Grau's guidance, learned the orders to give them, how to lead them in their turns and manoeuvres, and how to work with the other squads of pistols so that the entire company fought as a cohesive unit. It was exhausting, arse breaking work, but though he cursed it every night and every stiff-jointed morning, he found himself enjoying it more and more. He might almost be tempted to make it his life.

He had little time to seek out the other Blackhearts, and when he did they had little to tell him. Pavel and Hals had heard rumblings among the pikemen of some kind of revolt, but no details. Giano and Gert, attached to units of crossbowmen, heard similar whispers, but what shape the revolt would take they couldn't say. Dag had done two days in the brig for fighting and had heard nothing. Abel said he had heard that Gutzmann meant to storm Altdorf, but he said the fellow who had said it was drunk at the time, so he didn't credit it. Jergen said he had nothing to add, and Karel hadn't heard anything. Reiner wasn't surprised. The boy was so wide-eyed and guileless that no conspirator would trust him with a secret.

Of course he had done no better. Several times Grau had seemed to be on the verge of letting him in on the cavalry's secret, but something always made him hesitate at the last moment.

On the morning of the sixth day, as Reiner was saddling his horse outside the stables, Matthais approached on horseback and saluted Vortmunder.

'Begging the captain's pardon,' he said, 'but cavalry Obercaptain Oppenhauer accompanies the trade caravan to Aulschweig and requests an escort of pistoliers.'

'Very good, corporal,' said Vortmunder, and looked around at his men. His eyes lit upon Reiner. 'Ah. Take Meyerling. Time he rode further than the tilt yard and back.' He raised his voice. 'Meyerling, assemble your men and follow Corporal Bohm. He will give you your orders.'

And so, a short while later, Reiner rode out of the north gate at Matthais's side, their respective squads tailing behind them, accompanied by a unit of crossbowmen sitting on the back of an empty cart. The morning sun glanced blindingly off the neat rows of tents beyond the north wall, and glittered the dew on the tilting yard grass.

'Er, isn't Aulschweig south?' Reiner asked Matthais. Matthais grinned as they headed up the north road. 'Aye. But we're to the mine first to pick up some mining supplies before meeting the trade caravan. Every month we bring Empire goods to Baron Caspar at his castle just the other side of the border. In return we get grain, fodder, meat, and cooking oil. All for cheaper than carting it in from Hocksleten or Averheim, and better quality too. Very fertile valley, Aulschweig.'

Reiner raised an eyebrow. 'Aulschweig has a gold mine as well?'

'Er, no,' said Matthais. 'A tin mine. But, er, the tools are the same.'

'Ah, I see. And Obercaptain Oppenhauer comes with us?'

'Aye.'

'What's a cavalry obercaptain doing riding herd on a milk run?'

Matthais shot Reiner a hard glance. 'You are very astute, corporal. Er, well, there is another purpose for our visit. You remember I told you that Caspar has been eyeing his brother's throne?'

'I remember.'

'Well, apparently his grumblings have been getting louder of late, so Gutzmann sends Oppenhauer along to whisper soothing words in his ear. And also to remind him of our might.'

'Sounds a bit of a hothead, this Caspar.'

'You'll see.'

THE MINE WAS only a few hundred yards along a well-trodden path that branched westwards from the pass. Entry to it was guarded by fortifications that mirrored in miniature those of the fort – a thick, crenellated wall that blocked the canyon from wall to wall, with a tower on each side of a deep, portcullised gate.

Inside the wall were barracks, stables, and other out-buildings Reiner couldn't guess the purpose of. A system of pipes ran through one from a small aqueduct. Crowds of dust-caked miners trooped in and out of the mine entrance, a large, square opening in the mountainside framed with tree-trunks, carrying pickaxes and wheeling barrows. Almost as many pikemen and crossbowmen watched over them, patrolling the walls and every inch of the compound.

As Matthais called his party to a halt outside a low, weathered wood building, an overseer bustled out to greet them.

'Morning, corporal. Shipment ain't quite ready. A few minutes yet.'

'Very good.' The lancer turned to Reiner. 'Gives me an opportunity to show you around.'

Reiner sighed to himself. If he never went underground again it would be too soon. 'Certainly, corporal. Lead on.'

Matthais and Reiner dismounted and walked towards the mine. Matthais pointed out different buildings as they went, each of which was as busy as a beehive in the spring. 'That is the sluice room, where the raw ore is separated from the earth by means of a stream and a series of screens. There is the smelter, where the collected nuggets are melted and skimmed of impurities. This is the shakedown room, where the miners must strip and turn out their pockets before they leave the mine, to make sure they aren't absconding with any ore.'

'Very thorough of you.'

'One can't be too careful.'

Reiner shivered as he stepped into the mine. Memories of the last time he'd gone underground flashed through his head, but this cave was very different. It had none of the gloom and despair of the Kurgan mine. Nor the smell. Instead, all was bustle and industry. Two wide tunnels sloping away from the main entrance into the depths, and in and out of them went steady streams of miners, marching away with empty carts and picks on their shoulders, or trudging back with full carts and grime on their faces. Reiner found all this activity very interesting. If the mine was working at such a feverish rate, why was the stream of gold that reached Altdorf the merest trickle? It seemed as if Matthais's tale of difficulties in getting ore from the mine was less than the truth. Reiner didn't feel that now was the time to call him on it.

A third tunnel had no traffic. Its mouth was cluttered with broken equipment and stacks of supplies. Reiner pointed to it. 'Did this one run dry?'

Matthais shook his head. 'Structural problems. Had a cave-in recently. The engineers won't let the miners work it until it is safely shored up again.' He beckoned Reiner towards the left side of the entry chamber. 'This way. I want to show you something.'

As Reiner and Matthais dodged through the streams of miners, Reiner noticed that the men fell into a sullen silence as they passed, and then murmured under their breath behind them. Gutzmann must be driving them hard, Reiner thought. But then he thought there might be more to it than that. For as he looked around, he saw other signs of discontent. The miners had a haunted look, and glanced often over their shoulders. A group of miners had surrounded one of their foremen and were complaining vigorously. Reiner caught the words 'gone missing' and 'ain't doin' nothing about it.'

'Has there been some trouble?' Reiner asked.

Matthais snorted. 'Peasant nonsense. They claim men are disappearing in the mine. Running away, is my guess. There have been a number of village girls "stolen away" as well.' He shrugged. 'It doesn't take a magus to add that up. A few boys manage to steal a nugget of ore or two and off they go with their sweethearts to the flatlands where it doesn't snow eight months of the year.'

'Ah,' said Reiner. 'Like enough.'

They stepped through an open arch into a short hall.

'This is what I wanted to show you,' said Matthais. 'The first owner of this mine was a bit odd. Perhaps he wanted to be closer to his gold. But he decided that he would live in the mine, and so built his house underground. Here.'

He gestured before them to a beautifully carved wooden door that wouldn't have been out of place fronting some noble's Altdorf townhouse. Matthais pushed it open and peeked in, then beckoned Reiner to enter. The illusion continued inside. The entrance hall looked like a townhouse foyer, with a grand stairway curving up to a second floor gallery, and doors leading off to a sitting room on the left and a library on the right. That such a place existed at all so far from civilization was amazing in its own right, but what made it truly incredible was that everything, from the stairway, to the newel posts and banisters, to the statues of buxom virtues tucked into niches, to the moulding on the ceiling, to the oil lamp sconces that lit the place, was carved from the living rock. Even the tables in the library and some of the benches and chairs grew from the floor. And this was no crude cave dwelling. The ornamentation was exquisite, baroque columns wrapped in stylized foliage, heraldic beasts holding the wall sconces, gracefully curved legs on the stone tables and chairs. It took Reiner's breath away.

'It's beautiful,' he said. 'Mad, but beautiful. He must have paid a fortune.'

'Shhh,' said Matthais, as he followed Reiner into the sitting room. 'Not really supposed to be here. The engineers of the mine have taken it for their offices and kip. Gutzmann's had quite a time convincing them not to knock out some of the fixtures to make room for their infernal contraptions. No eye for beauty. If it ain't practical, they don't see it.'

A pair of wooden double doors at the far end of the sitting room opened, pinning them in a bar of yellow light. Shaeder glared out at them.

'What are you men doing here?'

Matthais jumped to attention, saluting. 'Sorry, commander. Just showing Meyerling our local marvel. Didn't mean to intrude.'

Behind Shaeder, Reiner could see a dining room, in the centre of which was a large round table, also carved from the rock. Around it sat a colloquy of engineers: grimy, bearded men in oil blackened leather aprons, many wearing thick spectacles, poring over a parchment spread on the table. Stumps of charcoal and ink quills were tucked behind their ears, and they held little leather-bound journals in their grubby hands.

'Well, now you've seen it,' said Shaeder. 'Be off with you.'

'Yes, sir.' Matthais saluted as Shaeder closed the door again. He shrugged at Reiner like a boy caught stealing apples.

As they tip-toed out through the door again, Reiner looked over his shoulder. 'Is the commander in charge of the mine?'

Matthais shook his head. 'Not officially, but Chief Engineer Holsanger was crushed in the cave-in and the commander has taken over his duties until Altdorf can send a replacement. Stretches him a bit thin. Makes him grumpy.'

'So I see.'

As they came into the mine proper again, Reiner heard raucous laughter and a familiar voice raised in protest. It was Giano, on duty with a squad of crossbowmen who watched the miners as they came and went.

'Is true, I tell you,' Giano was saying. 'I smell with my own eyes!'

'What's the trouble, Tilean?' asked Reiner.

'Ah, corporal!' said Giano. 'Defend for me, hey? They say I am be fool!'

A burly crossbowman chuckled and jerked his thumb at Giano. 'Forget him, corporal. The garlic-eater says there be ratmen in the mine. Ratmen!' He laughed again.

'Is true!' insisted Giano. 'I smell them!'

'And how do you know what a ratman smells like, soldier?' asked Matthais, condescendingly.

'They kill my family. My village. They come up under the grounds and eat all the peoples. I never forget the stinking.'

Matthais glared. 'Ratmen are a myth, Tilean. They don't exist. And if you don't want to spend some time in stir, you'll keep your foolishness to yourself. These peasants are superstitious enough already. We don't need them downing tools every time a rat squeaks in the dark.'

'But they here. I know…'

'It don't matter what you know, soldier,' snapped Reiner. 'Or think you know. The corporal has ordered you to be silent. You will be silent. Am I clear?'

Giano saluted reluctantly. 'Clear as bells, corporal. Yes, sir.'

Matthais and Reiner left the mine.

As the party rode back toward the fort with the loaded supply wagon, Reiner began to wonder why the armed escort had gone to the mine to pick up its cargo instead of waiting for the cart to come to the fort. Did Obercaptain Oppenhauer really think that a shipment of mining supplies was in danger in the short mile twixt the mine and the fort? Or was Manfred's order to sniff out suspicious activity causing Reiner to read nefarious motives into the most innocent of army procedures?

In any event, they reached the fort without incident. A train of wagons and carts joined them there, piled high with luxury goods from Altdorf, iron skillets from Nuln, wine and cloth and leather goods from Bretonnia, Tilea and beyond. As the party formed into march order, Oppenhauer trotted up on an enormous white charger that still looked small for his gigantic, barrel-chested frame.

'Morning, lads,' he cried in a booming voice. 'Ready for our outing?'

'Yes sir, obercaptain,' said Matthais saluting. 'Beautiful day for it.'

Reiner saluted as well, and they got under way, passing through the main gate into the pass to Aulschweig. The terrain was the same as that to the north of the fort. Steep, pine-covered slopes rising up to rocky, snow-capped peaks. The air was biting cold, but they still found themselves hot in their breastplates as the sun beat down on them.

'So, Meyerling,' said Oppenhauer. 'Getting used to our routine?'

Reiner smiled. 'I am, sir. My arse, however, is still a tenderfoot.'

Oppenhauer laughed. 'Vortmunder running you ragged, is he?'

'Aye, sir.'

They carried on in this merry vein for an hour or so, trading banter, jokes and good-natured insults. Reiner noticed that the lancers and pistoliers were more high-spirited here than in the camp. It was as if they were schoolboys who had run away from their tutor. He wondered if it was only that they weren't drilling and doing chores, or if it was the fact that there were no infantry officers around. He hoped that this relaxation might loosen their tongues, but whenever they started to talk about 'the future' or 'when Gutzmann shows Altdorf his mettle,' Oppenhauer 'harrumphed' and the conversation swung back to the usual barrack room subjects.

After a time one of the lancers began singing a song about a maid from Nuln and a pikeman with a wooden leg, and soon the whole company joined in, traders, draymen and all, inventing filthier and filthier verses as they went on.

But just as they were coming around to the sixth repetition of the chorus, an arrow appeared in the chest of one of the crossbowmen, and he fell off the supply cart. Before Reiner could comprehend what had happened, a swarm of arrows buzzed from the woods, targeting the other crossbowmen. Two more went down.

'Bandits!' shouted Matthais.

'Ambush!' boomed Oppenhauer.

All around Reiner horses were rearing and men were screaming. The surviving crossbowmen were returning fire at their invisible assailants. Reiner's pistoliers were drawing their guns.

'Hold!' Reiner cried. 'Wait for targets!'

A lancer fell, clutching his neck.

Oppenhauer stood in his saddle. An arrow glanced off his breastplate. 'Forward! Ride! Do not stand and fight!'

The crossbowmen hauled their wounded onto the carts and the draymen and traders whipped their carthorses into a lumbering canter. Reiner's and Matthais's squads flanked them. As the party surged ahead, ragged men in tattered buckskin leggings and layers of filthy clothing ran out of the woods after them, spears and swords in hand.

'Now, lads!' called Reiner. He and his squad drew their pistols and fired left and right. Bandits dropped, twisting and screaming. Vortmunder's constant drilling showed in the steadiness of the pistoliers as they used their knees alone to guide their horses, while reloading and firing behind them.

'Meyerling!' bawled Oppenhauer. 'Guard the rear. 'Ware their ponies.'

'Aye, sir. Rein in, lads. Double file behind the last wagon. Fire as you can.'

Reiner looked back as he and his men let the wagons slip ahead. More bandits were bursting from the woods, but these were mounted on wiry hill ponies, half the size of Reiner's warhorse. They raced after the company. The pistoliers could have outdistanced them easily, but the heavily laden carts were too slow. The bandits were gaining.

Reiner reloaded and fired, adding his shots to the ragged volley of his men. Only a few found a mark, but one was a fortunate hit, catching the lead pony in the knee. It screamed, leg buckling, and went down on its neck, throwing its rider. Two more ponies crashed into it from behind and fell. The rest leapt the carnage and kept coming. They closed with every step.

The road jogged sharply around an outcropping of rock. The crossbowmen and traders clung desperately as the carts bumped and fishtailed. Reiner hugged his horse's neck as he leaned into the turn. The cart full of mine supplies hit a stone, bucked, and came to earth again with a bang. One of the smaller crates jumped and slid. A crossbowman made a grab for it, but it was too heavy. It tipped off the back of the cart and bounced a few times before coming to rest on its side. The rest of the carts swerved around it.

'Obercaptain!' cried Matthais, as the box rapidly fell behind them. 'We've lost a crate!'

'Sigmar curse it!' Oppenhauer growled. 'Turn about! Turn about! Defend that crate!'

'Turn about, lads!' Reiner called. He and Matthais reined up and wheeled in tight circles with their men behind them as the traders' carts began lumbering around. Oppenhauer swung around to take the lead.

Reiner was baffled. Was the obercaptain so concerned
with picks and shovels that he would endanger his men's
lives, and his own, to rescue them? What was in that
crate?

As Reiner's and Matthais's squads rode back round the
bend ahead of the carts, Reiner saw that some of the bandits had stopped. Four of them were trying to carry the
crate into the trees. The others were on guard. The four
with the crate could barely lift it.

Oppenhauer shouted back to the draymen over the
thunder of their hooves. 'Stop your carts left and right of
the crate! We shall need their cover while we load.' He
pointed at Reiner and Matthais. 'Clear the men at the
box, then take cover behind the carts.'

Reiner and Matthais saluted, then raised their arms.

'Pistols ready,' said Reiner.

'Lancers ready,' said Matthais.

The pistoliers held their guns at their cheeks. The
lancers pointed their lances at the sky.

'Fire!' cried Reiner.

His men levelled their guns and fired into the cluster of
bandits. A few dropped, a few fired back. The rest ran to
their ponies, trying to remount.

'Charge!' cried Matthais.

The lancers lowered their lances and spurred their
horses into a thundering gallop. Oppenhauer charged
with them.

'Sabres!' Reiner called.

His men drew their swords and followed the lancers
and Oppenhauer as they ploughed into the bandits,
impaling them and running them down. The rest scat-
tered, on foot or on horseback, racing for the woods as
the carts pulled up around the crate. More bandits were
running up the road, most on foot – stragglers from the
ambush – but when they saw the situation they too
melted into the woods.

Reiner and Matthais circled back quickly with their
squads and dismounted behind the cover of the carts as

the crossbowmen began firing bolts into the trees. They were answered by a storm of arrows that thudded into the wagons and cargo.

'Lancers!' bellowed Oppenhauer, jumping off his horse. 'Help me with the crate!'

Matthais and three of his men stepped to the crate and grabbed the edges. Even with Oppenhauer joining them, they strained to lift it. Reiner's questions were becoming suspicions. He saw that the lid had pulled up at one corner and stepped forward.

'Let me give you a hand.'

'We have it, Meyerling,' grunted Oppenhauer, but Reiner ignored him and helped lift. As they edged it up on the cart, next to another just like it, Reiner got a glimpse under the lid. It was filled with small rectangles of yellow metal that shone like...

Gold.

Before he could be sure of what he had seen, Oppenhauer pounded the lid shut with the heel of his hand.

'Now, ride! Ride!' he called.

Reiner glanced at the obercaptain as he hurried back to his horse, but Oppenhauer's face was unreadable. Did he know Reiner had seen the gold? Had he been hiding it, or just closing the lid?

The carts turned clumsily about as arrows whistled around them. The crossbowmen returned fire, shooting randomly into the woods until they got under way. Oppenhauer, Matthais and Reiner and their squads fell in behind, but the bandits didn't follow, only stole out after the crossbowmen no longer had their range, to collect their arrows and see to their fallen.

The train of wagons continued on toward Aulschweig with four dead and ten wounded. Reiner rode in silence, oblivious to his men's nervous post-battle chatter. He had discovered where Manfred's missing gold was going, though why it was crossing the border he had no idea. More important was its mere existence. The crate he had seen held enough gold to make a man one of the wealthiest in the

Empire. And there were two of them, tucked amidst the rest of the cargo. Two fortunes. More than even Karl-Franz himself might spend in a lifetime.

Reiner smiled. He wasn't greedy. He didn't want them both. He needed only one. One would be more than enough to pay a sorcerer to remove the poison from the Blackhearts' blood – to buy their freedom.

The only question now was, how did he get it?

# SEVEN
## A Man of Vision

THE CASTLE OF Baron Caspar Tzetchka-Koloman sat hunched above the fertile Aulschweig valley like a wolf looking down at a hen-house. It had been built to guard the mouth of the pass from the Empire, when in the wild days of long ago there had been danger of invasion from that quarter – a small, but sturdily built keep that seemed to grow out of the crags that surrounded it. The valley below was like a dream of how the Empire might have been, if not for so many years of war – a bright green jewel of wheat fields not yet ripe and orchards of apple, pear and walnut. Tiny stone and shingle villages nestled in the gentle folds of the land, the spires of their country shrines sticking up above pine spinneys.

Baron Caspar was a restless young man a few years older than Reiner, but a child in temperament. A pale, sharp-faced fellow with jet black hair and dark eyes, he twitched and squirmed in his seat all through the generous dinner he laid before his guests in the high, banner-hung hall of his chilly keep.

'So General Gutzmann is well?' he asked as he mashed peas onto the back of his fork with his dagger. He spoke Imperial with a lilting mountain accent.

'Very well, my lord,' said Oppenhauer between mouthfuls. 'And your brother, Prince Leopold? He is in good health?'

'Oh, fine, fine. Never better, last I heard. Though it's precious little news I get here on the edge of nowhere. From my brother, or General Gutzmann.' He stabbed his meat with more force than necessary.

Oppenhauer spread his hands. 'Are we not here, my lord? Did we not bring the mining supplies you requested? Did I not convey the general's heartfelt greetings?'

'Yes, but no news. No answer.'

Oppenhauer coughed and shot a look at Reiner. 'Let's not spoil a good meal with matters of state, shall we? When we let poor Bohm and Meyerling go back to their men, you and I will speak of other things.'

Caspar pursed his lips. 'Very well. Very well.' But Reiner could see his leg jumping under the table as he bounced his foot nervously up and down.

Reiner waited for Oppenhauer or Matthais to make polite conversation. When they didn't, he cleared his throat. 'So, baron, your mining goes well?'

Oppenhauer and Matthais froze, forks halfway to their mouths.

Caspar looked up at Reiner sharply, then snorted. 'Ha! Yes. My mining goes well, indeed. We have been able to recruit many more men for the work, and with your new shipment of supplies we will be able to expand our operations even more. It is a great cure for my enforced idleness here, mining. I am looking forward to the day that I will be able to show my brother the steel we are bringing from that mine.'

Reiner struggled to keep his face straight. Steel from a tin mine. Interesting.

* * *

WHEN THE MEAL came to an end, Matthais invited Reiner to join him and his men in Caspar's guardroom for a game of trumps, but though the temptation to shear these yearling lambs of their golden fleece was strong, Reiner instead pleaded weariness and an upset stomach and retired to his room. He did not, however, stay there long.

Caspar and Oppenhauer had taken their after-dinner schnapps to the library to discuss 'matters of state' by the fire. Reiner wanted to hear that conversation, and so as soon as the footman who had guided him to his room had departed, Reiner stepped back into the corridor and began making his way back to the lower floors. The castle was nearly deserted. Caspar had no wife or children, and only a few knights lived there with him – and those were playing cards with Matthais – so reaching the library meant only avoiding a few servants. Finding a way to hear what went on behind the thick carved-oak door was another matter.

He pressed his ear to the wood, but heard nothing but a low murmur and the roar of the fire. Perhaps there was a balcony window he could listen at if he could get outside. He crept to the next door along the hallway and listened. He thought he could still hear fire, but there were no voices, so he risked opening it.

There was indeed a fire, tightly penned inside an iron grate, and Reiner hesitated momentarily, fearing that the room was occupied after all. But though numerous eyes glittered back at him, they were in the heads of a silent jury of hunting trophies that stared accusingly at him from the walls. Deer, elk, bear, wolf and boar all were represented.

Reiner gave them a mock bow as he closed the door behind him. 'As you were, gentlemen.'

He crossed to tall, velvet-draped windows on the far side of the room and opened one. There was no balcony, only an iron railing to keep one from pitching headlong down the cliffside the castle was built upon. Reiner leaned out and looked to his right, towards the library.

There were similar windows there. An agile man, with nerves of steel, might possibly climb over the railing, edge along the narrow ledge that ran between the windows, cling to the library window and listen. But even then he might not hear anything. The windows were tightly closed against the night's chill and the heavy curtains drawn. Still, this was the sort of conversation that Manfred would most want him to overhear. Reiner looked down the cliff, where jagged rocks poked up at him. He swallowed.

With a shrug that hid a shiver, he swung his leg over the railing. A booming laugh erupted behind him. He flinched and almost lost his footing. He looked back. He could have sworn the laugh had come from within the room. Another laugh burst forth, and this time he pinpointed its source. The fireplace.

Reiner pulled his leg back over the railing and closed the window, then stepped quietly toward the fireplace. Muffled voices came from it. He peered into it, and was surprised to find that beyond the flames, he could see into the library. In fact he could make out Caspar's booted feet tapping nervously as he sat in a high-backed leather chair. Reiner had seen such fireplaces before, cleverly constructed to warm two rooms at once, but in intrigue-riddled Altdorf, where privacy was at a premium, most of them had been bricked up.

'But when?' came Caspar's voice. 'Why won't you tell me when?'

Reiner leaned in as close as he dared. The heat from the fire was intense, and its roar nearly drowned out all other sound, but if he held his breath he could hear Oppenhauer's rumbling reply.

'Soon, my lord,' the obercaptain said. 'We have just recruited the last men we need, but it will take some while to train them, and to discover which are sympathetic to our aims.'

'But curse it, I'm ready now! I tire of this waiting. Rusting here in the wilderness while Leopold sleeps through his reign. To think what could be made of this land if there was a man of vision on the throne!' He slapped the arm of his chair with his palm.

'It will happen,' said Oppenhauer. 'Never fear.'

Reiner leaned in closer as the obercaptain's words got lost in the crackling of the fire. His cheek felt aflame. His left eye was as dry as paper.

'The general is as eager as you, my lord. You know his history. He too has had his ambitions thwarted. Wait only a little longer and you and he will sweep your sleeping brother from his throne and place you upon it instead. Then with you as king and Gutzmann as the commander of your armies, Aulschweig will become all you want it to be. The other border princes will fall before your might, and you will unite the Black Mountains into one great nation. A nation that might one day rival the Empire itself.'

'Yes!' cried Caspar. 'That is my destiny! That is as it will be. But how soon? How soon?'

'Very soon, my lord,' said Oppenhauer. 'Very soon. Two months at the most.'

'Two months! An eternity!'

'Not at all. Not at all. By next month, when I return with more "supplies", I will bring you the general's final plans. And the month after that we will slowly ease our forces into position so that we may spring our trap without losing the element of surprise.'

Reiner stepped back from the fireplace, rubbing his stinging face. So that was the plan. If it were true, then it certainly met Manfred's criteria for 'removing' Gutzmann. Reiner could kill the general and get out of these freezing mountains as soon as they returned to the fort. On the other hand, there were some very good reasons to wait. Some golden reasons.

It was time to have a talk with the old Blackhearts.

# EIGHT
## Manfred's Noose

IN THE MINING town of Brunn the next night, Reiner strolled into Mother Leibkrug's house of joy like a man coming home. The look of the low ceilinged, dimly lit tap room, with the forms of men and women huddling in its dark corners, the smell of lamp smoke and cheap scent, the sounds of laughing harlots and dice in the cup, were a balm to his soul.

From the time he had left his father's home to attend university in Altdorf, until the day Archaon's invasion had made it impossible for even the least patriotic of Imperial citizens not to answer the call of honour, Reiner had lived his life in brothels such as this. In their salons had he and his friends argued points of philosophy, while bare-bottomed bawds served them beer and fritters. In their boudoirs had he lost his innocence and gained the bittersweet knowledge of lust, love and loss. In their card rooms had he learned and practised his preferred trade, and paid for his lodgings and his tuition with money won from rubes and rustics. He had been away from these hallowed halls so long it nearly brought a tear to his eye to enter them once again.

Franka, however, hesitated on the threshold.

Reiner looked back. 'What's the matter, young Franz? They don't bite unless you ask.'

Franka's eyes darted about the dark room. 'Are you certain you couldn't find a more suitable place to meet?'

'There is none better,' Reiner said. He put an arm around her shoulders. 'A brothel is a place where all soldiers can go, regardless of rank. And a place where one can buy some privacy. Name another place within a hundred leagues that offers as much.'

'I understand. Nevertheless…'

Reiner stopped and turned, a look of amused shock on his face. 'You've never been in a brothel before.'

'Of course not,' said Franka, disgusted. 'I'm a respectable woman.'

'You were. Now you're a soldier. And soldiers and brothels go together like… like swords and sheathes.'

'Don't be vulgar.'

'Beloved, if you removed my vulgarity, there would be precious little left of me.'

As he and Franka crossed to the bar he saw Pavel, Hals and Giano at a table, deep in conversation. He waved, and they rose and joined them.

'Here, barman,' Reiner called. 'I want a private room for me and my lads.'

'Certainly, sir,' said the barman. 'Would you care for company?'

'No, no. Just a bottle of wine for me and beer for the rest. As much as they want.'

'Very good, sir. If you will just follow Gretel.'

A serving girl led the party down a narrow hall and let them into a cramped room with a round table in the centre and grimy tapestries hiding bare-plank walls through which the wind whistled. Two oil lanterns provided more smoke than light and made their eyes water. But there was a brazier for cooking sausages in the middle of the table that kept the room warm. Giano was still arguing with Pavel and Hals as they sat down.

'Is ratmen!' he said. 'I smell their stink!'

Pavel sighed. 'There ain't no ratmen, lad.'

'Something down there,' said Hals. 'That's certain. Plenty of the lads have seen shadows moving where there shouldn't be none. And the boys what pull graveyard duty say the ground shakes under their feet late at night.'

'You see!' said Giano. 'Is ratmen! We must fight!'

'Lads, lads,' said Reiner, holding up his hands. 'It matters not what it is. And with luck we won't have to fight anything. With luck we'll do a quiet month here and be off to Altdorf with enough gold in our kit to win our freedom and be rid of Manfred and his intrigues once and for all.'

All heads turned his way.

'What's this?' asked Hals.

'Is this why you didn't want the others?' asked Pavel.

'Aye,' said Reiner. 'I think I've found our salvation at last.' He leaned forward eagerly. 'Here it is. Gutzmann means to desert to Aulschweig and help Baron Caspar usurp his brother, Prince Leopold, where he will become commander of Caspar's armies.'

'Bold dog,' said Hals, laughing. 'Won't that teach Altdorf to leave its bright sparks at loose ends, hey?'

Pavel nodded. 'Thought it might be some such.'

'What concerns us,' said Reiner, 'is that he helps to fund Caspar's army with regular shipments of gold.' He turned to Pavel. 'I escorted a shipment of it to Aulschweig yesterday, disguised as "mining equipment". And there will be another shipment of "shovels" next month. Which, with some luck, will be ours.'

The others stared at him.

Giano grinned. 'This good plan, hey? I like!'

'Aye,' said Hals. 'I like, too!'

'Free of Manfred's noose at last,' said Pavel.

'But can we do it?' asked Franka.

'Well, it will take some work, that's certain,' said Reiner.

'We can't just cut and run. We'll have to finish the job Manfred's set for us, or he could kill us before we find someone who will take our gold and remove the poison. We'll have to return to Altdorf and pretend...' He paused. Pavel and Hals's faces had fallen. 'What's wrong?'

'We still kill Gutzmann?' asked Pavel slowly.

Reiner nodded. 'Aye. We'll have to.'

Hals grimaced unhappily. 'He's a good man, captain.'

Reiner blinked. 'He's won you over, too? He means to betray the Empire.'

'Ain't that what we mean to do?' asked Pavel.

'We just want to save our own lives. He's leaving our border unguarded and taking his whole garrison with him.'

'Yer starting to sound like Manfred,' grunted Hals.

'None of that.' Reiner sighed. 'Listen, I agree. Gutzmann's better than most. He loves his men, and they love him. But is he worth dying for? For that's your option. If we don't kill Gutzmann, Manfred kills us. It's one or the other.'

Pavel and Hals continued to hesitate. Even Giano was looking glum.

Franka was frowning, thinking it over. 'But what if the poison is a lie? A ruse to keep us tame. What if he never poisoned us at all, only said he did?'

Reiner nodded. 'Aye, I've thought of that as well, and it might be. But since we can't know, we have to act as if it is, don't we?'

'There must be some way we can get away without killing Gutzmann,' said Hals, chewing his lip. 'Yer clever, captain. Cleverest man I know. Y've thunk us out of all sorts of messes, haven't ye?'

'Aye, captain,' said Pavel, brightening. 'Ye'll think of something. Y'always do! There must be some way, hey?'

'Lads, lads, I may be clever, but I'm no sorcerer. I can't just wish it better. I...'

There was a knock on the door. 'Captain Reiner, are you within?'

Reiner and the others froze, hands on their daggers, as the door opened. It was Karel. The new Blackhearts were behind him.

# NINE
## Is Someone There?

ABEL PEERED OVER Karel's shoulder. 'You see. Didn't I say they'd snuck away together? They hide things from you, corporal.'

Karel stepped into the room, the new men pushing in around him. 'What is this, captain?' he asked. He looked hurt. 'What is the purpose of this meeting?'

Reiner scowled. 'I don't see what business it is of yours, any of you, how we spend our off hours, but if you must know, we were reminiscing, talking over old times.'

'Without us?' asked Abel accusingly.

Reiner gave him a withering look. 'You weren't there for the old times, Halstieg, that I recall.'

There were a few chuckles at that.

Reiner motioned around the table. 'We five have bonds forged in blood and battle. Do you find it strange that we sometimes seek each other's company?'

Dag pushed Abel angrily. 'Told ye ye were a fool! The captain's a good 'un. He'd not play us false.'

'Easy, Mueller,' said Karel. He inclined his head to Reiner. 'Forgive me, captain. Quartermaster Halstieg said he saw you and the others sneaking away and thought you had a suspicious air about you. I see now he was overstating things.'

'It is suspicious,' insisted Abel. 'They told none of us!'

'And they'd no reason to, boy,' said Gert, laying a heavy arm across Abel's shoulder. 'We ain't their minders. Leave it be. Jawing about old battles is the right and privilege of every soldier.'

Abel shrugged and glared at the ground. 'Aye. Fine. Fine.'

'Not to worry, Halstieg,' said Reiner. 'I don't blame you. We none of us like our situation. Death if Gutzmann discovers our purpose. Death if we fail Manfred. New companions and a proven rogue for a commander. It isn't any wonder we're all wary of each other, but if we start fighting amongst ourselves, we're lost before we're begun.' Reiner tipped back in his chair. 'I, for one, want to survive this little job, and the only way to do it is to stick together. Agreed?'

He looked around at the others, questioning.

The men all grunted their ascent, though not all of them wholeheartedly.

Reiner nodded and sat forward. 'Good. Now that's settled, and since we suddenly find ourselves all together, I've a bit of news to share with you all.'

All eyes turned to him.

'Some of you won't like to hear it,' he continued, 'but I've the proof Manfred wanted that Gutzmann is planning to leave the Empire with his men. Which means we must kill him.'

The new men took the news silently, but Reiner saw a few hard looks among them, and Hals stared at the table top, fists clenched.

'I know,' said Reiner. 'He's a fine leader, but he's also a traitor. He plans to help Baron Caspar of Aulschweig snatch the throne from his brother, Prince Leopold, and then accept the post of commander of his armies.'

Karel's jaw dropped. 'By the holy hammer of Sigmar!'

Reiner nodded. 'So we've a job to do.'

'A dirty job,' muttered Hals.

'Yes,' said Reiner, giving him a look. 'A job for black-hearts, to be precise.' He looked up at the others. 'But worry not. Your warm berths are safe for the moment. It will take some time to work out the how and when and where of it. It must look like an accident, and I for one want to be able to walk away if it goes awry. So it will be a month or more before we're ready to begin.'

Reiner pushed back his chair. 'In the meanwhile, I ask you to continue watching and listening. I want to know more of who hates whom, who sides with whom. It may be the key to our puzzle. Report back to me as you can, and be ready to move on the moment. But tonight...' He stood, smirking, and fished in his belt pouch. 'I still have a little of Manfred's travelling money left, and we are in a knocking shop.' He began flipping gold coins at each of them. 'Let us live while we can. Enjoy the night, lads. I know I will.'

The men caught the coins, grinning – at least most of them did. Jergen plucked his out of the air without a change of expression, and turned to the door while the others were still thanking Reiner and making dirty jokes.

As they began filing out into the hall, Reiner put a hand on Franka's shoulder. She looked back. He motioned for her to wait.

When the rest had left, Reiner whispered in her ear. 'We could easily be alone here. Truly alone.'

'For what purpose, besides the obvious?'

'Why, merely to be alone. To enjoy each other's company uninterrupted. To talk, to hold hands...'

'To take advantage of my weak nature,' Franka said, wryly.

'Beloved, I assure you...'

'Don't,' she said sharply. 'Make no promises you cannot keep. I don't want to be disappointed in you.'

Reiner sighed. 'So you won't?'

Franka hesitated, then sighed in turn. 'I know I am a fool, but… I will.'

Reiner pulled her to him for a quick hug.

'Do you start already?' she asked, laughing and holding him away.

'No, no, my love,' said Reiner. 'Mere exuberance.' He looked toward the door, then leaned in to her. 'Now, this is what we will do.'

AFTER DRINKING FOR a short time with the others in the taproom, Reiner approached Mother Leibkrug and hired a girl, as both Hals and Abel had done before him. But unlike them, when he got his girl upstairs, he dismissed her, tipping her lavishly and telling her that he was meeting a secret lover there and only needed the room. Happy to make twice her usual fee, the girl agreed to closet herself above stairs for a while so that all would think she was still with Reiner.

A few minutes later, there was a knock at the door. Reiner opened it cautiously, but when he saw that it was Franka, alone, he pulled her in and held her close. They kissed for a long moment, then Franka pulled away with a sigh.

She straightened her jerkin. 'So,' she coughed, 'conversation?'

'Er, yes, of course. Conversation.' Reiner turned and flopped down on the ridiculously ruffled and beribboned bed. Like all the furniture, it was too big, too elaborate, for the tiny, shabby room – the overstuffed chaise, the wildly curved and carved vanity with the flaking gold paint, the voluminous curtains over rickety windows, the armoire so pregnant with clothes the doors couldn't close.

Franka didn't seem inclined to sit. She paced the room, examining the frilly furnishings and fidgeting. There was a blonde wig on a wig stand. She stroked it absently.

'So what do we talk about?' asked Reiner after a long silence.

Franka shrugged, then chuckled. 'Strange, isn't it? Now that we are free to talk, we're at a loss.'

Reiner tucked a pillow under his head. 'That's because you don't allow me my favourite topic.'

Franka laughed and pulled the wig off the stand. 'Seduction? Are you so limited?' She sat at the vanity. She lowered her head and pulled the wig on, then flipped it back. 'And you claim to be a man of the world.' She turned to him, looking though the blonde tresses. 'Go on. Speak to me of poetry, art. Or, what was your subject at university? Literature?'

Reiner gaped, open-mouthed, at her. 'You're... you're beautiful.'

'Am I?' Franka looked over her shoulder at the mirror, a cracked, poorly silvered glass. She smoothed the wig. 'It looks strange to me now. I have become so used to living as a boy.' She looked up at his reflection. 'Do you like me better like this?'

'Better?' Reiner blinked, transfixed. 'Er, I wouldn't say better. But it makes a change.' He sat up for a closer look. 'A very nice change.'

Franka began searching through the harlot's powders and paints. She found some rouge and smoothed it into her cheeks, then applied a thicker coat to her lips. She looked up at the glass from under her lashes. 'You aren't speaking. I thought you were going to declaim about literature.'

Reiner swallowed. 'You are being disingenuous, you little wench. You tell me we mustn't touch. That you are weak and I mustn't tempt you, but you are tempting me! Deliberately!'

Franka looked down, blushing behind her rouge. 'I suppose I am. And I apologize. It's just that... that it has been so long since I have looked like this. Since I have been able to flirt and be pretty.' She turned to face him. 'It is hard to resist.'

Reiner licked his lips. 'It certainly is. Try on a dress.'

Franka raised an eyebrow. 'And have you accuse me of provocation?'

'I don't care. I want to see it.'

Franka smiled. 'Are you sure it won't act like a red rag to a bull? Are you sure you won't go mad?'

'I... I will be a perfect gentleman.'

Franka laughed and stood. 'That will be interesting. I have never met one before.'

She crossed to the bursting armoire and began sorting through the dresses. She stopped at a deep green one – not as clean as it might have been, and a little frayed at the hem and cuffs, but well cut. She pulled it out and unlaced the stays at the back, then threw the whole thing over her head and tried to tug it down around herself.

'Help me,' she said with a muffled laugh.

Reiner sprung from the bed and began tugging and straightening. 'My lady is used to a lady's maid?'

'My lady is used to doublet and breeks,' said Franka as her head popped out. 'And has forgotten the intricacies.' Her wig was askew. She straightened it, and began pulling the dress into place.

Reiner laughed. 'And I'm afraid I have more experience getting women out of dresses than into them.'

Franka's smile froze, then fell. 'You needn't remind me.'

Reiner's heart lurched. He went down on one knee and took her hand. 'Lady, forgive me. You see I am as confused as you are. I forget if I speak to Franz or Franka. I will not mention it again.' He kissed her fingers.

Franka laughed and ruffled his hair. 'Forget it, captain. I have no illusions about your past. I don't love you for your virtue. Now stand and tell me how I look.'

Reiner stood and stepped back. The illusion wasn't perfect. Her jerkin and man's shirt stuck up above the low cut collar of the green dress. But in all other respects Franka had become the woman she truly was.

Reiner stepped forward. His arms encircled her waist. 'You are beautiful. Heartbreakingly so. When we are free of our chains, I shall buy you a hundred such dresses, each more lovely than the last.'

Franka giggled and bumped her head against his chest. 'A hundred dresses? Do I want so much trouble and fuss? I think perhaps I've grown used to my breeches.'

Reiner pulled her wig off and kissed the back of her neck. 'As have I. I like knowing there's a woman inside them. I like knowing your secret.'

Franka purred. 'Do you?'

'I do. In fact, it maddens me!' Reiner crushed her to him. Their lips met, then their tongues. Franka's hands ran down his back.

There was a scratching from the window. They leapt apart, afraid they were spied on. Reiner's heart thudded. If they were caught, explanations would be difficult.

'Is someone there?' asked Franka.

Reiner stepped closer, hand on his dagger. 'I see nothing. Just mice, I suppose.' He turned back to Franka. 'Where were we?'

Franka smiled sadly. 'A place we should not have come to, and to which it would be better not to return...'

The window flew open, knocking the curtains to the floor, and figures in dark robes, with burlap sacks over their heads, dived in with inhuman agility. There were at least six of them, though Reiner found it hard to count, they moved so quickly.

'What's this?' Reiner cried, backing away and drawing his sword and dagger.

Franka reached for her weapons as well, but they were trapped beneath the dress. She rucked at her skirts in frustration. The intruders swarmed her, ignoring Reiner in order to grab her arms and legs.

'Reiner!' she screamed.

'Unhand her!' Reiner kicked one and jerked another back by the collar. They were small men, not much taller than Franka, and Reiner was surprised at how easily he booted and threw them across the room. But he was even more surprised by how quickly they sprang up again, seeming to bounce rather than fall, and turning on him with feral snarls.

Franka clubbed one of her captors with the wig stand and kicked another in the head. The man fell back, upsetting the chair, and crashed to the floor. But the other two continued to drag her towards the window.

'Reiner, help me!'

'I'm trying…'

The two Reiner had knocked down attacked him, and another joined them, daggers like curved fangs in their tiny hands. He blocked and parried desperately. They were blindingly fast. And their smell was an attack of its own. The reek was overwhelming. Perhaps it came from the filthy fur shirts they wore under their robes.

Reiner backed away, bleeding from a handful of cuts, and tripped over the chamber pot, left by the door. He kicked it at his attackers. They ducked, and the tin pot smashed the vanity mirror behind them. Glass shards rained to the ground.

One of the robed figures looked back at the noise, and Reiner ran him through. He fell, hissing. The others only pressed Reiner all the harder. Their thrusts rang off his sabre like clanging bells.

'No, you little daemons!' Franka shrieked. 'Let me go!'

Reiner risked a look her way and saw three of the men trying to drag Franka out of the window. She grabbed one by the burlap mask and pulled it askew so that the eye-holes were on the side of his head. The villain let go and fumbled at the sack, blinded.

'Franka!'

Reiner threw his dagger as Franka looked up. It stuck, point first, into the window frame beside her. With a grateful look, she snatched it up and began stabbing indiscriminately at all who held her. They fell away, shrieking thinly.

Suddenly the door slammed open and Hals shouldered in, bare to the waist and dagger drawn. 'What's all the noise?' he bellowed.

Abel and a few other half-dressed brothel patrons stood behind him, harlots peering over their shoulders.

A robed man launched himself at Hals and the pike-man defended himself. Reiner called to the men in the hall as he fought. 'Hurry! Stop them! They're trying to take…' His voice fell off as he remembered who the attackers were trying to take, and how she looked. And as if to confirm his fears, he saw Hals goggling at Franka in her dress. He almost took a curved dagger in the belly before he recovered and returned to the business at hand.

No one else entered the room. Abel backed out, wide-eyed. 'I… I shall protect the women!'

But it seemed the three Blackhearts wouldn't need the help. Hals clubbed his man to the ground with a fist. Reiner kicked his back with a well placed boot, and they were advancing on those grabbing at Franka when one of them looked around, then drew something from its sleeve and threw it at the ground.

Reiner got the briefest glimpse of it before it smashed on the bare floorboards – a small glass ball. But then great billows of smoke erupted from the shards and the room was quickly filled with an impenetrable, acrid cloud that had them choking and their eyes tearing.

Reiner threw an arm over his face. It did no good. He heard scrabbling at the window. 'They're retreating!' he shouted, and stumbled forward, blind.

'Come back, y'wee villains!' coughed Hals.

But at that moment there was a piercing scream from the hallway and Hals stopped so suddenly Reiner bumped into him. 'My girl!' cried the pikeman. 'They're taking Griga!'

He charged back out of the door.

Reiner followed. 'Franz! Hurry!' he called over his shoulders. 'I want to talk to one of these assassins.'

'I'll protect the women,' said Abel again as they ran past him.

Hals and Reiner burst into another dingy boudoir, but they were too late. The window was open, frilly curtains blowing in the breeze, and the rumpled bed was empty.

Reiner looked up as he heard feet scritching across the roof above.

'Hals,' he said, turning back to the door, 'you and Abel go up from this window, Franz and I will…' He stopped. Franka wasn't there. He grunted. But of course not. She was still in her dress. She wouldn't have dared join them. Unless…

Reiner swallowed.

He started back down the hall, terror dragging at his guts. 'Franka?' he called. 'Franka?'

Hals followed behind him, and they entered Reiner's room together. The smoke had thinned enough to see that the room was empty, but for the corpse of one of the mysterious attackers. Franka wasn't there.

'Sigmar,' hissed Hals. 'Look at his hands!'

Reiner glanced down at the body as he ran to the window. What he had thought a fur shirt looked now like furry arms, and the hands at the ends of them were scaly, long-fingered claws. But even this unsettling curiosity couldn't distract Reiner from his fear. There was a scrap of deep green velvet caught on a nail in the window sill. He stuck his head out. 'Franka!' There was no response. He climbed out onto the shingled roof, from which rose the second storey, and began pulling himself up the stone wall.

'Who the devil is Franka?' grunted Hals as he ducked out after Reiner.

'Franz, I meant,' said Reiner, and then realized he shouldn't have. He should have said that Franka was the name of his whore, and he was afraid she was taken. Now Hals would associate the names Franka and Franz, and likely draw unfortunate conclusions. But it was too late to call back the words.

He pulled himself up onto the cedar-shingled roof and clambered up the steep slope to the peak. 'Franz!' There was no sign of the robed men, or Franka, or Hals's harlot. He turned in a circle, peering out over the low roofs of Brunn.

'Captain…' said Hals, struggling up the wall.

'There!' said Reiner, pointing. A tangle of shadows slipped around a corner a few blocks away. In the midst of them Reiner had seen a flash of pale flesh. He leapt down to the first floor roof, then slipped and bounced down the shingles on his posterior before pitching over the edge and landing on his ribs on a pyramid of kegs of finest Averheim ale. He slid down this, groaning and wheezing, and ended up sitting in an icy puddle of what he hoped was water.

Hals dropped down beside him in a more controlled fashion. 'Captain…'

Reiner staggered up. 'No time. We can't let them get away.' He ran for the street in a half crouch, clutching his bruised ribs and limping. As they came around the front of the brothel they were met by men and harlots spilling out of the door, including Pavel, Giano, Dag, Abel and Gert. Only Jergen and Karel were absent.

Reiner waved to them. 'Follow us, lads. They've got Fra… Franz!'

Reiner started off as quick as his laboured breathing would allow, Hals at his side, in the direction the robed men had gone.

As they wound through the streets, Hals coughed uncomfortably. 'Er, captain…'

'I know, Hals. I know,' Reiner interrupted, thinking desperately. 'I know what it looked like, but I assure you, nothing could be further from the truth. You see, we… er, we meant to play a trick on Karel. The poor boy. I don't think he's ever had a woman, so Franz and I thought it would be a good joke to rile him up a bit. Franz would dress up like a woman, you see, and… and make advances, then, when Karel got all hot and bothered, Franz would pull off his wig and we'd see what shades of crimson young Karel could turn. Amusing, hey?'

'Aye,' said Hals, flatly. 'And did you mean to dress up as well?'

'What?' said Reiner. 'No, of course not. Who in their right mind would ever mistake me for a woman?'

Hals nodded, his face a blank. 'Then you might want to be wiping yer lips. Y've rouge all over 'em.'

# TEN
## They Were Not Men!

REINER AND THE Blackhearts found no trace of Franka, Hals's harlot, or the robed men, though they searched Brunn from end to end. The kidnappers and their prey had disappeared utterly. Even eerier, when the search party returned to the brothel to see if anyone else had seen anything, they found that the corpse with the furry arms was gone, vanished when no one was looking, though patrons and whores had been in and out of the room constantly. The only evidence that the whole incident hadn't been some mad fever dream was a small glass ball that Reiner spied under a chair. It looked like the one that had filled the room with smoke, but this one was unbroken, and churned within with a greenish murk. Reiner pocketed it. Combined with the vision of the robed man's clawed hand, it began to stir memories of things he had read in forbidden books while at university.

He stepped out of the brothel and joined the other Blackhearts, who were huddled in a circle before the door.

'We must return to the fort at once,' he said. 'I want to tell Gutzmann of Franz's kidnapping and the new evidence we have about the disappearances.'

It was obvious to Reiner that Abel had told the others all he had seen when he and Hals had burst in on Reiner and Franka, for none of them would meet his eye, and they answered him with surly grunts and mumbles.

Reiner cursed inwardly all the long cold walk back to the fort. Foolishness on top of tragedy. Just when he needed them most, when the life of one of their number was in deadly peril, his men had become suspicious, nearly mutinous. The maddening thing was that if he could tell them the truth all would be well again – at least with him. Things would be much worse for Franka. Only Reiner and Manfred knew the girl's true sex. If it were revealed to anyone else, her usefulness as a soldier would be over, and the count might have her killed. And this didn't take into consideration the reactions of her comrades. Franka loved Hals, Pavel and Giano like brothers. If they turned their backs on her, it would break her heart.

REINER DEMANDED TO see Gutzmann as soon as they returned to the camp, but the general was sleeping, and so Reiner must go up the chain of command, telling his story first to Captain Vortmunder, then to Obercaptain Oppenhauer, both of whom would have dismissed his story out of hand if not for the corroboration of his fellows and the strange glass orb. At last, and very reluctantly, they brought him to Commander Shaeder, who was called from his bed, yawning and cross.

'What is such an emergency that you must wake me at this ungodly hour?' the commander asked as he sat down behind his desk, wrapped in a heavy robe. Vortmunder and Oppenhauer stood on either side of Reiner looking nervous.

'My lord,' said Reiner, bowing. 'Forgive me, but a soldier has been kidnapped, and I fear there are inhuman agents involved that might be a danger to the fort and the Empire.'

Shaeder pinched the bridge of his nose and waved a weary hand. 'Very well, captain, tell your tale.'

Reiner clicked his heels together. 'Thank you, commander. Er, earlier this evening, I and some others, including my valet, Franz, were entertaining ourselves in Brunn….'

'Whoring and drinking, you mean.'

'I was indeed visiting with a young lady, commander,' Said Reiner. 'But before any, er, business, had occurred, the window flew open and we were attacked by men in masks and robes. My valet, Franz, hearing my calls, ran to my aid, and we fought the men. Patrons of the house came at the noise and helped, but just as we were on the brink of victory the men threw some sort of grenade and we were choked by thick smoke.'

Reiner thought he saw Shaeder frown at this, but the tic was gone before he could be sure.

'When the smoke cleared,' Reiner continued, 'the men were gone, as was Franz.' He coughed. 'One of the ladies of the house was taken as well.'

'Most distressing, certainly,' said Shaeder, though he didn't look distressed. 'But in what way is a kidnapping in a brothel a danger to the Empire?'

'I was coming to that, sir,' said Reiner quickly. 'One of the masked men was killed in the fight, and I was shocked to see that his hands weren't hands at all, but claws. Like those of a rat. And his arms…'

'A rat?' Shaeder guffawed. 'A rat did you say? The size of a man?'

'A little smaller, sir. He…'

'Do you mean to suggest that you were attacked by, what do the old women call them? By ratkin? By wives' tales made flesh?' He turned to glare at Oppenhauer and Vortmunder. 'What do you mean bringing this nonsense before me? Are you mad?'

'His story was seconded by several others, commander,' sad Oppenhauer. 'And he has evidence.'

'Evidence?' asked Shaeder. 'What evidence?'

Something in the commander's voice made Reiner reluctant to bring the orb out of his pouch, but there was nothing for it. Shaeder wouldn't be convinced without it. Reiner took out the glass ball and placed it on his desk.

'What is this?' asked the commander, picking it up with reluctant fingers.

'One of the smoke grenades, my lord,' said Reiner. 'The ratmen threw one at the floor and smoke poured out of it when it shattered.'

Shaeder scowled. 'This is a grenade?' He looked up at Oppenhauer. 'You let him convince you this was a grenade? This bauble from a harlot's dress?' He set it on a stack of parchment. 'A paperweight, perhaps.'

'Commander,' said Reiner, getting angry. 'I fought them hand to hand. They were not men!'

'And how do you know? Did you look under their masks? You had a body, did you not? Why are you showing me a marble instead of a body?'

'Er,' Reiner flushed. 'We left the body behind while in pursuit of the others, who were getting away with Franz. When we returned to the brothel again, it... it was gone.'

'Gone?'

'Aye, sir.'

Shaeder paused for a long moment. It seemed almost that he relaxed. Then abruptly he burst out laughing, a loud, derisive bray that had him wiping his eyes. When he had recovered himself he waved a hand at Reiner. 'Go to bed, corporal.'

'Beg pardon?' said Reiner, confused.

'Go to bed, sir. Sleep it off.'

Reiner pulled himself up, indignant. 'You don't believe me sir?'

'I believe that you are one of those remarkable rascals who shows no outward sign of inebriation while being completely pie-eyed drunk.'

'Commander,' Reiner protested. 'I am telling the...'

'I'm sure something happened,' Shaeder interrupted. 'A brawl, perhaps even a kidnapping. Y've wounds enough.

But it's just as likely you fought your reflection in some whore's mirror and cut yourself on the glass. Whatever happened, I will not muster the Emperor's might to rescue some Altdorf dandy's valet, no matter how well he polishes your boots. If the boy doesn't show up in the morning, I will assign a detail to look for him in the gutters of Brunn, but until then, I'm for bed, as you should be.'

Reiner balled his fists. 'Commander, I do not think this is a threat that should be ignored. I demand to see General Gutzmann. I demand to put my case before him.'

'You demand, do you?' asked Shaeder. 'The next thing you demand will be a week in the brig for insubordination. Now go to bed, sir. I am through with you.' He turned to Vortmunder and Oppenhauer. 'And in the future, you will think twice before waking me with such foolishness.'

'Aye, commander,' said Oppenhauer, saluting. 'Thank you, sir.'

He and Vortmunder turned with Reiner between them. Oppenhauer gave Reiner a sympathetic shrug as they walked out the door.

'I believed you, lad,' he said.

REINER DIDN'T SLEEP that night. All he wanted to do was ride out in search of Franka, but searching in the dark would have been fruitless, particularly on his own, particularly if Franka had been taken where he suspected she had. When dawn finally came, he reported again to Shaeder, begging to be allowed to join the search detail the commander was sending out, but he had refused, telling Reiner to leave the search to men who better knew the town and the pass.

Reiner couldn't leave it at that. Shaeder's men wouldn't find Franka. They wouldn't look in the right place. And so, though he knew it might compromise Manfred's mission to do so, he had failed to report to Vortmunder for his morning duties, and instead sent word through Hals to the others to meet him behind the parade ground stands where they had watched Gutzmann tent-pegging on the first day. This mass dereliction of duty was sure to arouse comment, but the alternative was to leave Franka to her fate, and that was no alternative at all.

As the men arrived, slouching up in ones and twos, Reiner knew he was in trouble. The suspicion of the previous night hadn't cleared. In fact it seemed to have grown deeper. Their faces were closed and grim. Even Karel looked troubled.

'Here it is,' he said when they'd all gathered in the shadow of the viewing stand. 'I've turned it over in my mind and I believe I know where Franz was taken.' He nodded at Giano. 'As much as we've ribbed our Tilean friend for smelling ratmen under every rock and cellar floor, I think this time he's right. Hals and Abel, you saw the body in the brothel last night. I can find no way to deny its nature. Can you?'

Abel said nothing.

Hals shrugged. 'Not sure what I saw now.'

Reiner groaned. That didn't bode well. 'Well, what of the glass orb? Every fairy tale I've ever heard of ratkin speaks of them using bizarre weapons. What of the stories the miners have been telling about men disappearing? And Giano smelling them in the tunnels?'

Giano's eyes glowed. 'You believe now?'

'I don't know what I believe,' said Reiner. 'But be it ratmen or some other horror, I think something lurks in the mine, and I mean to go down and look for Franz.'

There was a silence. Abel broke it.

'To look for your beloved, you mean.'

Reiner's head snapped up. 'What do you say?'

'Shut yer trap, y'clod,' growled Hals.

'You speakin' ill of the captain?' asked Dag, menacingly.

Karel glared at the man. 'You are out of order, quartermaster.'

Abel looked at them disbelievingly. 'Do you still have loyalty to this... this invert? How can you trust him when he's been hiding his true nature from you all this time?'

The Blackhearts looked at the ground, uncomfortable.

Abel sneered. 'You saw him last night, with red all over his mouth. We all did. He'd been kissing his "boot boy"'.

'Enough, Halstieg!' cried Karel. He looked to Reiner pleadingly. 'Captain. Tell them they're mistaken!'

Pavel shifted uncomfortably. 'Captain's a good leader. He ain't led us wrong.'

'Hasn't he?' asked Abel. 'Are you happy to be walking around with poison in your veins? Dancing at the mercy of some cagey jagger. Who led you to that?'

There was a simmering silence.

'Listen...' said Reiner, but Abel cut him off again.

'And he certainly ain't leading you right this time; thinking with his stem instead of his head, asking us to go into some dirty hole that'll most likely cave in on us. For the good of the mission? Because it will get us home quicker? No. It hasn't anything to do with what we came here to do. He's afraid for the life of his precious catamite, and he'll lead us all to our deaths to save him.'

'Enough!' barked Reiner. 'I'll not waste time arguing and explaining. I am afraid for Franz, as I would be for any of you.' He shot a glance at Abel. 'Even you, quartermaster. And I want to try to find him before he comes to harm. As I would with any of you.' He shrugged. 'I won't order you. I never have. But I'm going down there whether or not you accompany me.' He stood and shouldered the pack of pitch torches he'd gathered. 'Who's with me?'

'I!' said Giano immediately. 'I want all my life to be fighting ratmens.' He stepped to Reiner's side.

The rest didn't move. Reiner looked from one to the other. They hung their heads. He sighed. He hadn't expected the new men to come with him. They hadn't fought through the bowels of the Middle Mountains with him. They hadn't faced down Valnir's Bane and Albrecht's mindless army by his side. But when Hals and Pavel wouldn't meet his eyes it felt as if some giant crushed his heart in his hands.

'Sorry, captain,' said Gert.

Dag muttered something under his breath.

Karel hung his head. 'It isn't part of our mission, captain.'

Reiner shrugged, then glared at Abel. 'The poison with which Manfred cursed us is naught compared with that which you wield.' He turned toward the pass road. 'Come, Giano. Let's be off.'

As REINER AND Giano walked north toward the mine in the cold morning light, Giano jerked a thumb over his shoulder. 'Fella want you job, I thinking.'

And he might get it, thought Reiner, nodding. A tricksy cove, Halstieg. A way with words when he wanted, and a streak of ambition that one might miss at first glance. And no heart at all. Reiner was certain Abel cared not a whit if he loved men, women or goats. He only used the issue to drive a wedge between him and the others, so that he might step in and lead them. The quartermaster was smart enough to know that his survival depended on pleasing Manfred, and if that meant betraying Reiner and proving he was the better man, so be it.

THE MINE WAS as busy as ever, and Reiner and Giano had little trouble in wandering through all the chaos to the closed tunnel. The first hundred feet or so were still open, and were used as a storage area for cartwheels and rail ties and supplies. Reiner and Giano wound around the clutter until they came to the barricade, a wall of planks and cross braces that reached from wall to wall and floor to ceiling. It was dark this far from the entrance. Reiner pulled a torch from his pack and lit it from his tinder box. He and Giano examined the wall. A rough door had been cut in it, locked with an enormous iron padlock.

'Can you pick?' asked Giano.

'I'm afraid not. My burglar's tools are cards and dice.' He began pushing on the planks around the door. 'But I don't think we'll have to.'

'Hey? For why?'

'Well,' said Reiner, as he walked down the wall. 'If the ratmen are in there, and they come out through here, then they wouldn't use a door that locked on this side, you see?'

'Ah! Si. Captain damn smart.'

'Or perhaps not,' grumbled Reiner as he reached the end of the wall without finding a board that gave. He started back along the wall, looking at the boards once again. There had to be something. He couldn't allow himself to believe he was wrong. The ratmen had to be here.

He stopped, frowning. The left edge of one of the boards was grimier than the rest. He reached out and touched the grime. It was oily. He sniffed his finger. It reeked with an animal stench – the same stench the robed men had given off. Reiner's heart jumped. He took another step down the wall. The next plank was clean, but the one after that had corresponding grime on its right edge. He stepped back. Filthy fur pushing through a narrow opening would leave just such marks.

He pointed to the plank between the begrimed planks. 'This one.' He pushed on it. It didn't move. But of course not. It would push from the other side. He looked for some way to pull it. There was no handle, or string. But there was a hole – a knot hole near the floor.

Reiner stuck his finger in the hole. It was greasy as well. He pulled. The board came up easily, revealing utter blackness.

Giano grinned. 'Knock, knock, hey?'

Reiner swallowed. 'Aye. Er, after you.'

Giano ducked eagerly through the gap. Reiner followed more cautiously, sticking his torch through first, then squeezing in afterwards. The board banged down behind him. Inside was a bit of an anticlimax. It looked exactly like the outside – a high, wide tunnel sloping away into darkness.

'No sign of a cave-in,' said Reiner.

'Maybe further down.'

'Or maybe not at all.'

They started down the tunnel, travelling in a small sphere of light through a universe of black. A hundred yards on, they almost tripped over two small crates piled against one wall. Reiner held the torch low. The crates looked familiar.

'What is?' asked Giano.

Reiner snorted. 'Mining tools.'

As they continued on, Reiner's heart thudded with excitement. Now they need not wait for the next shipment to Aulschweig. They could kill Gutzmann whenever they wanted and take the gold from here instead – a much easier proposition than stealing it en route. This was excellent news – at least it would be if Franka still lived.

Shortly after that the tunnel stopped at a rough rock face, and for a moment Reiner's heart sank. But then he saw a small opening in the face. It was a tunnel so narrow that he and Giano had to walk single file. Ten paces in, Giano stopped suddenly and raised his hand.

'Light,' he said.

Reiner put his torch on the ground behind him and they crept forward.

Three yards further the tunnel opened up into a large space, lit with a wan purple light. Giano peeked out then gasped and flinched back. Reiner followed his gaze and jumped back as well, heart thudding. Looming over them was a monstrous insect the size of a house. Huge sabre-like mandibles jutted from its maw. It took a moment of deep breaths to realize that the insect wasn't moving, wasn't alive, wasn't in fact an insect. It was a giant machine. And it wasn't alone.

Giano and Reiner stepped cautiously into the tunnel, looking up at the four massive metal monstrosities that sat on man-high wooden wheels to the left and right of the narrow hole. A thrill of fear ran through Reiner as he divined their purpose. They were digging machines. Mad, skeletal contraptions of iron, wood, leather and brass. The mandibles were giant steel picks meant to chew at the workface. They were attached by a series of axles, gears and belts to an enormous brass tank, green with corrosion, fitted with all manner of valves and levers. Broad leather belts led from beneath the mandibles to the backs of the contraptions, where strings of wooden mine carts were lined up, ready to take the chewed rock away.

The scale of the enterprise made Reiner's head spin. Not even the Empire built machines this large. What were they digging? Did the ratmen mine gold as well? Was there something else of value in the rock? Or...

It came to him with sudden clarity and dread, and his blood turned to ice in his veins. The ratmen were building a road – a road high enough and wide enough to allow an army to march to the surface. And they were only twenty paces from connecting with the mine tunnel, which was just as high and wide. Their work was almost done.

Giano swallowed. 'This bad, hey?'

'Aye,' said Reiner. 'Bad is a word for it.'

As he and Giano crept around the towering machines, weirdly lit by the pulsing purple light that came from glowing stones set high in the walls, Reiner saw movement in the shadows and jerked his dagger out of its scabbard. Rats – of the small, four-footed variety – swarmed over piles of bones and rubbish that cluttered the floor, ample evidence that this wasn't some long abandoned endeavour. Some of the bones looked human. Reiner moaned in his throat. Were the ratmen kidnapping women for food?

There was a small side passage in the left wall, and more dotted the tunnel on both sides as far as they could see. The openings made Reiner nervous. At any moment a ratman could pop out of one, and then where would they be?

He and Giano started forward, looking warily around. A few moments later, distant structures began to emerge from the gloom. At first Reiner thought they were battlements of some kind – the walls and towers of some underground town – but as they got closer, he saw that they were siege towers, mounted on wheels and laid on their sides. They were surrounded by other giant engines of war, catapults, ballisti, and battering rams.

'Blood of Sigmar,' he breathed. 'They mean to take the fort.'

Giano nodded, wide-eyed.

They crept forward at a snail's pace, hugging the wall and keeping low, and at last reached the jumble of machines, Giano sniffing like a bloodhound. As they came around a prone tower, they saw, further on, an encampment of sorts, though to one used to the regimented order of an Empire camp, it was an offence to the eye. Low structures that looked more like piles of blankets than tents hugged the walls of the tunnel and shadows wormed in and out of them like… well, like rats.

Giano stopped, his hand on the hilt of his sword. He was trembling. 'Ratmen!'

'Easy, lad,' said Reiner, as Giano began to draw. 'We ain't here to fight 'em all.'

Giano nodded, but it seemed a supreme act of will for him to return his blade to its scabbard.

As they stepped back behind the tower, an overpowering stench overcame them. They clapped their hands over their noses and looked around. Against one wall was a pile of furred bodies – dead rat men, discarded like old apple cores. There was movement on the pile – the four-legged feeding on the two-legged – and it reeked like a slaughterhouse, an odour equal parts animal filth and diseased death. Some of the bodies were bloated with fat black boils.

Reiner was turning away, nauseous, when he saw a white arm among the mangy limbs. His heart froze, and he stepped, trembling, to the pile, the rats scattering at his approach. Giano followed, covering his mouth with his handkerchief. Reiner reached out toward the arm, then stopped when he saw that it possessed a man's hand, callused and thick. He looked for the rest of the body, and found, half hidden among rotting ratman corpses, and grinning, partially fleshed ratman skulls, the face of a pikeman, his right cheek and temple gnawed away.

'Poor devil,' said Reiner.

Giano made the sign of Shallya.

They returned to their vantage point and surveyed the ratmen's camp. It was not an encouraging sight. The whole place seethed with motion: ratmen darting in and out of the holes in the tunnel walls, ratmen swarming around the tents, rat men crawling over the line of carts in the centre of the tunnel, loading and unloading spears and halberds and strange brass instruments that Reiner feared were weapons as well, ratmen arguing and fighting.

Giano shook his head. 'How we finding boy in all these?'

'I don't know, lad,' said Reiner. His heart was sinking. He wasn't by nature a coward, but neither was he a fool. He wasn't the sort of stage-play hero who charged a horde of Kurgan armed only with a turnip. He was a follower of Ranald, whose commandments stated that one shouldn't go into any situation without the odds clearly in one's favour. Walking into this mess was a sure way to incur the trickster's wrath.

And yet, Franka was in there somewhere, if she wasn't already some ratman's dinner. And he couldn't just turn around and leave without trying to find her.

'Damn the girl,' he growled.

'Hey?' said Giano, puzzled. 'Girl?'

'Never mind.' Reiner pulled himself up onto the prone siege tower. The view was no better. The ratmen were everywhere at once. No area of the camp was ever vacant long. There was no little-used corridor for Reiner and Giano to sneak down – no catwalk high above. They would be discovered at once, and that would be the end.

Unless…

Reiner looked at the tower he clung to. Its timber frame was stretched over with a patchwork of leather and furs. Reiner blanched when he saw that some of the skins had tattoos, but he couldn't be squeamish now.

'Giano,' he said, drawing his dagger. 'Help me cut down some of these skins. They walked robed among us. We shall walk robed among them.'

Giano obediently started cutting but he looked doubtful. 'The rat, he have damn good smelling, hey? He sniffing us even hiding.'

Reiner groaned. 'Curse it, yes. I'd forgotten. They'll smell us for human in an instant.' He sighed deeply, then nearly choked on the stink of the pile of corpses as he inhaled again. An idea brought his head up and he looked at the pile, eyes shining. 'There could be a way…'

Giano followed his gaze, then moaned. 'Oh, captain, please no. Please.'

'I'm afraid so, lad.'

BEHIND HIS POINTED leather mask, and beneath his makeshift leather robes, sewn together with lengths of rawhide unwound from binding that held the siege machines together, Reiner's heart beat as rapidly as a hummingbird's. He and Giano were picking their way through the ratmen's camp, tails cut from the ratmen's corpses tied to their belts and dragging behind them, and with every step, retreat became more impossible and discovery more likely. Though they tried to hug the line of carts, where there were the fewest ratmen, still the beasts were all around them, and a mere skin was all that shielded them from their ravenous fury. If he or Giano revealed their hands or feet they were lost, for the ratmen's appendages looked nothing like theirs. If they were

challenged they were lost, for the ratmen's speech was a
chittering gabble of hisses, chirps and shrieks that
Reiner's throat couldn't possibly have reproduced even if
he had understood it. Fortunately, the ratmen hardly gave
Reiner and Giano a second look – or to be more accurate,
a second sniff – for they were covered in an almost visi-
ble reek of rat musk and death, and as such, blended in
with the general atmosphere of the tunnel.

Over Giano's piteous protestations, Reiner had ordered
the Tilean to follow his example and roll like a pig in
mud within the pile of corpses. Reluctantly, they had
rubbed themselves and their makeshift robes and masks
against the oily fur and decaying flesh and diseased
wounds of the bodies and caked their boots and gloves
with their excrement. It had been a foul, gut-churning
experience, and was continuing to be. Being trapped
inside the hooded mask with the stench was like drinking a sewer. If it hadn't been for the distraction of the
wonders and horrors he was seeing through his eye-
holes, Reiner would undoubtedly have vomited.

There were so many ratmen, so closely packed together
– hundreds, perhaps thousands – within his range of
vision, it made his head swim. And the camp continued
around the curve of the tunnel with no apparent end.
They were loathsome creatures, their long, narrow faces
covered in filthy, lice-ridden fur, their mouths slackly
open to reveal great, curving front teeth. But it was their
eyes that truly repulsed Reiner – vacant black orbs that
glittered like glass. They seemed utterly empty of intelli-
gence. If it hadn't been for the scraps of rusty armour that
covered their scrawny limbs, and the earrings that dangled from their tattered ears, and of course the weapons
that they carried, Reiner would not have believed them
thinking beings.

Their filth was indescribable. They seemed not to have
separate places to dispose of their refuse and droppings;
instead, they appeared to nest in them. Their tents were
filled with bones, rags and filth shaped into crater-like

depressions in which they slept. Some of the ratkin appeared to be deathly ill, yellow mucus weeping from their eyes and black lesions covering their scaly hands, but the other ratmen made no effort to avoid their diseased fellows. They shared their food and drink and rubbed past them in the narrow byways of the camp without a second thought. Did they wish to get sick? It came to Reiner with a shudder that perhaps they did. Perhaps disease was only another weapon to them.

Some of the weapons Reiner saw them carrying he couldn't even begin to understand: bizarre pistols and long guns that sprouted weird brass piping and glass reservoirs filled with phosphorescent green liquid. On the carts in the centre of the tunnel larger weapons were stored; great spears that hummed as they passed them, handheld cannon connected by leather hoses to large brass reservoirs.

What Reiner did not see was any sign of Franka, or any humans at all. The camp seemed only tents and carts and rats as far as the eye could see. After walking a few hundred yards into it, Reiner's steps began to slow. It was hopeless, pointless. If the myths of the ratmen were correct, their tunnels ran under the whole wide world. Franka might be halfway to Cathay by now. Or he might have passed her bones in one of the piles of garbage that were heaped everywhere. At last he stopped, overcome. He tapped Giano on the shoulder, and motioned him to turn around, but before the Tilean could respond, Reiner heard, very faintly in the distance, an agonized scream – a human scream!

The men froze, listening with their whole beings. The scream came again. It was behind them, back the way they had come – a cry of terror and unbearable pain. Reiner and Giano turned and hurried back through the camp as quickly as they could, listening for further cries. What a bitter irony, Reiner thought. The screams were so pitiful it made him wish the man who uttered them a quick death, and yet, if he was to find their source the man must cry again and again.

They had almost returned to the edge of the camp before the cry came again, and this time it was words. 'Mercy. Mercy, I beg you!'

Reiner turned. The voice came not from before or behind them, but to one side – from one of the branching passages.

'In the name of Sigmar, have you no…' The voice broke off in a bone chilling shriek. Reiner winced, but at least he had pinpointed the passage. He touched Giano's arm and they moved toward it.

The passage was short and opened up at its far end into a room that glowed brightly with the purple light. It was hard to determine the room's dimensions, for it was so cluttered that Reiner couldn't see the walls. Machines from a poppy eater's nightmare loomed on the left: a thing like a casket surrounded by metal spider's legs, each tipped with a scalpel or pipette, a chair with straps to pinion the arms over which dangled a helmet ringed with sharp screws, a rack that seemed to have been constructed to stretch a creature with more than four limbs, a charcoal brazier that glowed with red heat, a contraption of glass bulbs and tubes through which coloured liquids bubbled and dripped.

On the right, piled up like so many children's blocks, was a jumble of small iron cages, none more than four feet high, but all containing at least one, and sometimes three or four, filthy, dung- and blood-smeared humans. Reiner's heart leapt at this sight – foul as it was – for Franka might be among them. He wanted to run forward and check them all, but he daren't. The room wasn't empty.

In the centre was a tableau Reiner had been avoiding looking at directly, for it was from there that the screams came. Now at last he faced it. There was a table, and a man on the table, shackled to it, though so weak now the fetters were no longer necessary. It was extraordinary to Reiner that the man still lived, for his torso had been laid open like a gutted fish, the skin of his belly pinned back with clips so that his organs were exposed. They shone wetly in the purple light. The fellow had the rough hands and hard-lined face of a miner, but he was begging for mercy in the high whimper of a little girl.

Hovering over him like a cook making a pie was a plump, grey-furred ratman, scalpel and forceps held high in gloved hands. He wore a blood-drenched leather apron with a belt full of steel implements slung at his waist, and a leather band circled his brow, attached to which were articulated arms, all fitted with glass lenses of various thicknesses and colours that could be pulled down in front of the creature's beady black eyes. It already wore thick spectacles, which it balanced on its broad furred snout. It was such a caricature of the short-sighted scholar Reiner might have thought it comic, had it not been for the horrible vivisection it was engaged in.

What made the situation even more horrible was that the ratman was speaking to his victim, and not in the chittering gibberish of his kind, but in high-pitched and broken Reiklander. 'Does read Heidel?' it asked, then tsked sadly when the man didn't respond. 'Wasted. Wasted. You Reik-man. Finest books. Finest lib… lib…' It snarled in frustration. 'Book places! And you no read, no think. Just to drink, to mate, to sleep. Shameful.'

The sound of Giano muttering furiously in Tilean beside him snapped Reiner out of his horrified trance. The crossbowman's hand was reaching for his sword. Reiner touched Giano's arm and pulled him out of the doorway behind the bulk of a great black-iron cauldron. Giano patted his shoulder gratefully, recovering himself.

'Here me,' the rat-surgeon continued, sighing. 'Down below. Book come garbage and sewer. But know I more of out world than it.' He severed some membrane in the man's belly. The miner groaned. The ratman ignored him. 'Does know Volman's *Seven Virtue*? History of beer-making in Hochland? Poem of Brother Octavio Durst? I know this. And so more. Many more.'

He set his implements aside, pulled a lens in front of one eye, and began to paw through the man's organs with delicate claws. 'This me confuse. Why man? Why man so big? Why win so many battles? Why so brave?' He shook his head. 'First think, maybe man stupid. Too stupid to be scare. But skaven stupid too, and always scare. Run away, all time run. So not that.' He scooped out his victim's intestines with both hands and set them on the table beside him. 'So now think something new. Fix the moulder way! Pinder say brave in spleen. So I try if man with no spleen will scare. Then, I try if skaven with man-spleen will brave. Ah, here is.' He tugged at an organ with one hand, then cut it from its mooring with his scalpel.

The man convulsed and gasped. Blood welled from the cavity of his belly and his hands began to clutch and grasp. The grey ratman tsked again, then tried to stem the flow with a clamp. He was too slow. Before he had successfully applied it, the table was awash with blood and the man lay still and silent.

The rat-surgeon sighed. 'Another. Too bad. Well, we try again.' He raised his voice and chittered over his shoulder. Two brown rats in leather aprons came out of a further room. The surgeon directed them to remove the body and bring another from the cages.

Reiner and Giano watched queasily as the two ratmen piled the man's intestines on his chest and carried him out of the room by his arms and legs as the surgeon swept miscellaneous body parts off the table. Giano was muttering again. Reiner put a hand on his shoulder. The crossbowman lowered his voice but didn't seem to be able to stop cursing.

The ratmen returned and crossed to the stacked cages. The first opened one at random, with a key from a ring on his belt, and pulled out a small figure.

Franka.

# ELEVEN
## Black Death Take You

REINER NEARLY SHOUTED out loud. The poor girl was so battered and dirty that, had he not known her so intimately, he wouldn't have recognized her. The dress she had been taken in was gone, as was much of her uniform. Only her breeks and shirt covered her, and they were shredded and caked with filth. Her face was bruised and blank, and streaked with dirt and blood. She looked around dully, as if she had been sleeping, but when she saw where her captors were taking her, she began to scream and fight, kicking at them and trying to wrench her arms from their grasp.

'Unhand me, you vermin!' she cried. 'I'll kill you! I'll cut you to ribbons. I'll...' Her threats dissolved into sobs of fury. The ratmen threw her at the table and she crashed against its metal edge, gasping.

The surgeon chittered angrily at his assistants, motioning for them to hold Franka still while he opened a vial he had taken from a table behind him. 'Quiet, boy. Stop...'

Reiner could take no more, the voice of self-preservation that normally stopped him before he launched himself into deadly danger drowned out by Franka's pitiful moans. He charged forward, screaming inarticulately as he drew his sword. Giano followed, roaring.

The ratmen looked up, startled. Perhaps the hoods Reiner and Giano wore confused them, but for one crucial second they stood frozen, staring. Reiner cut his down before it could pull its cleaver from its belt. Giano evaded the other's wild slash and ran it through the ribs. Franka fell with her dying captors.

The grey-furred surgeon scrabbled backwards, squealing. Reiner leapt after him, but he squirmed behind a giant contraption like one of his four-legged kin. Giano dived to block the back door. The ratman was too swift. He dodged around him and disappeared into the dark hallway beyond. Reiner and Giano gave chase, but the hall quickly split into three curving corridors and they couldn't tell which one he had taken.

Reiner skidded to a stop and turned back. 'Forget him. Let's fly.' He re-entered the room and crossed to Franka, holding out his hand. 'Franz…'

The girl crabbed backward, looking from him to Giano in terror. She snatched up a fallen scalpel and held it before her. 'Back, monsters!'

'Franz?' Then Reiner remembered. He pulled off his mask. 'It's only us.'

Giano pulled his off too. 'See? Nothing to be afraid!'

Franka blinked for a moment, then her face crumpled and she began to sob. The scalpel clattered to the ground. 'I thought… I didn't think… I never…'

'Easy now, easy now,' said Reiner, helping her up and clapping her roughly on the shoulder. 'Be a man, hey? Lad?'

Franka swallowed and sniffed. 'Sorry, captain. Sorry. Forgot myself. You…' she managed a weak grin. 'You certainly took your time.'

'Blame the damned vermin, lad,' said Reiner. What he wanted to do was draw Franka into his arms and hold her, but for Giano's benefit he played at manly heartiness. 'Damned inconsiderate of them, living so far underground. Now...'

'Save us,' said a weak voice.

Reiner, Franka and Giano turned. The men and women in the cages were staring out at them. They were thin, haggard creatures. Some of them had obviously been there for weeks. The skin hung from their bones like wet muslin. Others were hideously deformed, strange growths sprouting from their faces and chests. Still others had extra arms and hands stitched onto them in bizarre places. Reiner groaned. There were at least a dozen of them – probably more. How could he possibly get them all out?

'Please sir,' said a peasant girl with hands like purple mittens. 'We'll die otherwise.'

'You must, captain,' said Franka. 'You've no idea what they do.'

'I saw enough,' said Reiner, swallowing. 'But... but it's impossible. We'd never make it.'

'Y'can't leave us,' said a gaunt miner, gripping the bars. 'Y'can't let 'em have their way with us.'

Faint noises came from the far door: chittering rat-speech and the click of many rat feet.

'They coming,' said Giano.

'Captain,' Franka urged. 'Reiner, please.'

'It's too late. I...' With a growl of frustration, Reiner stepped to one of the dead ratmen and cut a ring of keys from his belt. 'Their weapons,' he said. 'And the scalpels.'

Giano and Franka began stripping the dead ratmen of their cleavers and swords and daggers as Reiner tried a key in a lock. They gathered up all the surgeon's scalpels, chisels and saws as well. The key didn't fit. Reiner tried another. It wouldn't turn.

The rat-voices were getting closer.

Reiner cursed. 'Give them the weapons.' He was sweating.

Franka kept a sword for herself, then helped Giano pass the rest of the blades through the bars to the prisoner's eager hands. Reiner tried another key. Still no luck.

The rat-voices were clear now. Reiner could hear the jingle of weapons and armour.

'Damn damn damn!' He thrust the keys at the man who had spoken first. 'I'm sorry. We must go. Good luck to you.'

'What's this?' said the man, taking the keys by reflex. 'You're leaving?'

Reiner backed to the door, pulling on his mask. 'We must.' He turned to Giano and Franka. 'Hurry.'

'Reiner, you can't...' said Franka.

'Don't be a fool. Do you want to live?'

He pushed her towards the door. She looked like she was going to protest again, then turned on her heel and started into the corridor, her face twisting with emotion. Giano pulled on his mask and followed her.

'Black death take you, you bastards!' cried a woman.

Reiner flinched as he Franka and Giano ran down the narrow corridor to the main tunnel.

'How we take with no face on?' asked Giano, gesturing at Franka.

Reiner closed his eyes. 'Curse me for a fool. Should have made three disguises. Give me a moment to think.'

They stopped just before they reached the tunnel, crouching in the shadow of the opening. They heard cries of rattish dismay behind them as the ratmen found the dead guards.

'No moment left,' said Giano.

'I don't know!'

'Carry me!' said Franka.

'Carry you?' asked Reiner.

'The surgeon sells his mistakes for food. I saw ratmen carry bodies out this way all day.'

'Perfect!' said Reiner. 'Hold tight, lad.' He hoisted Franka over his shoulder like a sack and started into the tunnel. 'And mind you play dead.'

'Or we be dead,' added Giano.

Reiner and Giano crossed quickly to the far side of the tunnel, putting the line of carts between them and the side passage, then hurried for the edge of the camp, hunching low. Before they had got twenty yards they heard their pursuers burst into the tunnel behind them, screeching orders and questions at their brethren. Reiner picked up his pace. Franka bounced slackly on his shoulder. He heard her retch.

'They come,' she whispered. 'Others point the way.'

'Shut up!' Reiner hissed.

He looked back, pulling his mask close with his free hand to see better through his eye-holes. The ratmen were indeed coming; a squad of guards with long spears and steel helms that stretched down their long snouts like horse's barding. They spread out across the width of the tunnel and jogged through the tents and carts, looking high and low – and sniffing.

Reiner pulled Giano around a high mound of garbage, his heart pounding. If the rat-guards had their scent, it didn't matter how well they hid, their sensitive noses would find them.

And just as he thought it, a rat squealed in triumph in the distance. Reiner moaned. The guards had sniffed out their man scent, even under all the rat-filth they had rolled in. It wouldn't be long now. He had to do something to throw them off the trail, to draw their attention. He looked around. The tents and the garbage would make perfect tinder except there was no fire. The rats didn't seem to use it. They ate their meat raw and slept clustered together for warmth, which made sense for a race that lived underground. He considered firing his pistols into one of the wagons loaded with the curious hand cannon and brass tanks, but he had no idea how big a blast they would make, if any.

The ratmen were closing in, following their trail through the camp like dogs after a fox. If Reiner and Giano broke into a run they would be spotted instantly.

The sweat was pouring down Reiner's sides. Franka, who had weighed nothing when he picked her up, now felt heavier than an ox. He crossed his fingers and sent a prayer to Ranald. Alright, ye old charlatan, he thought, if ye get me out of this fix I'll trick a thousand men before next I touch wine, and that's a promise.

He dodged around a large tent and tripped over a small, fiercely hot forge, where a ratkin smith was pouring lead into bullet moulds. Reiner swallowed a curse and swerved drastically to avoid crashing into another rat who was busy folding measures of black powder into square gauze packets. Damn fool rats, not enough sense to keep blackpowder away from a...

Reiner stopped dead in his tracks. Giano crashed into him. Franka yelped. Idiot, thought Reiner, cursing himself. His prayer instantaneously granted and he'd nearly dismissed it as an obstacle. He dumped Franka unceremoniously to the ground, whispering, 'Stay dead,' then stepped up to the powder rat. The creature was scooping the powder out of a small wooden cask with what looked like a soup spoon from a nobleman's banquet table. Reiner kicked him off his haunches, caught up the powder keg in both hands, stepped back, and before the rat smith had begun to comprehend what was happening, hurled it at the forge with all his strength.

The cask smashed to pieces on the bricks and the powder caught with a great whump. A huge ball of fire erupted, almost enveloping Reiner in its billows. His mask and robes were smoking as he hurried back to Giano and Franka. The rats around them shrieked. The tent was ablaze. The smith was wreathed in fire and screaming as he scampered in careening circles, setting on fire everything he touched.

'Hurry!' cried Reiner. He scooped Franka up again, then ran on with Giano at his side. The ratmen they passed paid them no mind. They were too busy staring at the spreading fire with blank expressions or pushing forward with blankets and skins of water. The whole tunnel's attention was taken by the fire. Ratmen craned their necks over Reiner and Giano as they ran by. Reiner crossed his fingers again. A thousand men, ye mountebank, he thought. A thousand men.

They reached the edge of the camp and dodged through the jumbled ranks of siege towers and war machines, then stopped with the broad tunnel before them. Reiner set Franka down with a grunt of relief and tore off his mask and robes.

'You take robes off?' asked Giano, worried.

'I don't care,' said Reiner. 'I can't stand another moment.'

'Good.' Giano pulled his off too.

'We'll be sitting ducks,' said Franka looking at the wide open space before them.

'We'll have to risk it,' said Reiner. 'The side tunnels could go nowhere, or double back.'

'So we run, hey?' said Giano.

'Aye,' said Reiner. 'We run.'

RANALD'S GIFT OF luck must have been holding, for they jogged the length of the tunnel without seeing or hearing any signs of pursuit. Reiner hoped their hunters were caught in the fire – or even better, that the whole ratman encampment had gone up in flames. Though even that would not have been enough to ease his mind. The faces of the men and women he had left in the iron cages bobbed in front of him as he ran. Their pleas rang in his ears.

As they neared the end of the tunnel, where the digging machines faced the wall, Franka put a hand on his arm and nodded ahead.

'Torchlight,' she said quietly.

Reiner stopped and peered forward. Beyond the monstrous contraptions, the tunnel's omnipresent purple light was pushed back by a warm yellow glow. Reiner frowned, trying to remember if they had left a torch burning there. No. They had not. They had ground it out.

A shadow appeared on the tunnel wall, grossly distorted, but recognizably the shadow of a ratman.

Reiner froze, his heart pounding. Was it their pursuers? Had they circled around somehow and beaten them there? Were they waiting to kill them?

But then another shadow pushed into the light next to the ratman's. It was human.

'What this?' whispered Giano. 'Rat and man?'

Reiner didn't care to find out. He looked around at the few side passages piercing the tunnel's walls. Was there a way around? He doubted it, and even if there was, which one should he take? They could wander lost down here forever. Had they the luxury of waiting, whoever it was that was blocking their way might go away, but they couldn't wait. Their pursuers might come up behind them at any moment. They had to move.

Reiner put a finger to his lips and motioned Giano and Franka ahead. They crept forward, drawing weapons and keeping the bulk of the massive diggers between them and the torchlight. Reiner began hearing voices, an alternating hissing and rumbling. He paused. He could swear he recognized that rumble. Another few steps and the rumble turned into words.

'But I tell you you can wait no longer. You must attack as soon as you can. Tomorrow if possible!'

A cold snake of dread began to stir in Reiner's guts. It was Commander Volk Shaeder speaking.

A voice like a knife on slate answered. 'Tomorrow no. Many days cutting from skaven-tunnel to man-tunnel. War machiness not get out unless cutting.'

Reiner almost choked. Giano was growling in his throat. Franka put a hand on his arm to calm him.

'But you don't have days,' continued Shaeder. 'Look. This was left in the brothel. If Gutzmann saw this all would be lost. You must act before your carelessness exposes you!'

The harsh voice hissed, distressed. 'My armies all not here. I half strong only.'

'You needn't worry about that. The fort will be lightly defended. I'll make sure of it.'

There was pause, then the rat-voice spoke again. 'This trick?'

'Why would I trick you when we want the same thing? You want Aulschweig for a grain farm. I want the gold we've shipped to Caspar. All that stands in our way is Gutzmann and the fort. Then I will be away to Tilea with more gold than the richest man in Altdorf, and you will have food for your people for all time.'

The ratman practically crooned his answer. 'Yes. Yes. Grain farm, man-slaves to work, and make strong us with they flesh. No more we eat you garbage. Now we grow strong.'

Reiner could almost hear Shaeder biting his tongue. 'A grand dream, to be sure.'

'This you do,' said the ratman. 'Close mine. Say no safe. We dig all day and night and day again. Ready tomorrow moonrise.'

'Excellent,' said Shaeder. 'I will…'

Giano spat, drowning out the rest. 'Traitor! Traitor to man! He die! I must–'

Reiner clapped a hand over the Tilean's mouth, but it was too late. There was silence from beyond the digger. And then a harsh slither of syllables from the ratman.

Clawed feet skittered toward them and Reiner could hear swords scraping from sheaths. He backed away, pulling Franka with him.

'Sorry, captain,' said Giano. 'I carry away myself…'

'Shut up and move, you fool,' Reiner growled. 'Out from under these things.'

They ran out of the shadow of the diggers, and not a moment too soon. Black shapes swarmed around the big machines, slipping under them, over them and through their skeletal structures like eels.

'Against the wall,' said Reiner. 'Don't let 'em encircle us.'

They ran to the left wall and turned, swords at the ready. Reiner drew his pistol. From the diggers came ten of the biggest ratmen Reiner had yet seen: tall, lean warriors with glossy black fur and gleaming bronze armour. Their swords were rapiers, long and thin. They flickered like heat lightning in the purple gloom.

# TWELVE
## The Honour of Knights

As THE RATMEN closed in, Reiner saw, behind them, Shaeder running into a side passage, and a tall black-furred ratman in burnished armour watching from a safe distance. Then there was no time to pay attention to anything but the blades slashing toward him. Reiner fired his pistol into the eyes of the closest ratman, and it flew back, its face a red crater. Another lunged at him savagely, though its shiny black eyes betrayed no emotion. Reiner threw his pistol at it and blocked with his sword while drawing his dagger.

Beside him, Franka and Giano were parrying and dodging like mad. Nine blades poked and chopped at them, and the ratkin were no mean swordsmen. Though not a match for Reiner or Giano in strength, they more than made up for this deficit with their terrifying speed. The three humans had no chance to counter-attack. They were too busy keeping the ratmen's blades at bay – or at least trying to. They were failing miserably.

Reiner barked as a ratman cut him across the forearm. He heard Franka and Giano gasp as they too were pinked.

Another ratman sliced Reiner's forehead, and blood trickled into his left eye, half blinding him. A third blade slid across his ribs.

A ball of rage and despair welled up in him. The scriptures of Sigmar told one that dying in battle against the enemies of mankind was the noblest destiny a man of the Empire might attain. Well, it was a lot of bunk. Reiner wanted to die of his excesses at a ripe old age, surrounded by fabulous riches. Instead he was going to die here in a filthy tunnel, pointlessly, shoved through the gate of Morr with his whole life ahead of him.

Any notion that dying beside his beloved was in some way romantic was bunk as well. It was the cruellest of jokes. There was so much they hadn't done. They hadn't danced together or lived together. They hadn't made love together. And worst of all, they hadn't been free together. For the entire time Reiner had known her, he and Franka had been prisoners, under the thumb of the Empire or Manfred or his brother. Reiner had never been able to take her where he liked, show her his old haunts, explore new places with her, or even stay in and forget the world with her.

He could feel his arms growing heavier as he fanned them this way and that to catch all the steel stabbing his way. A blade pierced his leg. Another nicked his ear.

'Franka. I–'

The girl flicked a look his way between ducking and blocking. Her eyes shared his sadness. She grinned crookedly. 'Should have broken my vow, hey?'

Reiner laughed. 'Well yes, damn ye, y'should have. But–' A blade nicked his shoulder. 'Curse it! What I wanted to say–'

'Hoy!' came a cry, and one of the ratmen Reiner was facing suddenly had a crossbow bolt sprouting from his neck. It fell, choking and screeching.

Both the ratmen and the humans looked around. Running through the giant diggers and drawing their weapons were Karel and Hals and Pavel, as well as Dag, Jergen and Gert. Only Abel was missing.

Despite what the rat-surgeon had said about his kind having no spleen, the ratmen did not break, but met the new threat in good order. Three locked up with Pavel and Hals, one forced Gert back, besting the reach of his short-hafted axe with its long blade. Their leader, who had previously hung back, lunged at Karel, pressing him strongly. Dag windmilled wildly at another with a short sword and dagger, screaming his head off but doing little. Reiner, Franka and Giano, freed to fight one ratman apiece, continued on the defensive while they recovered their strength.

Jergen, as silent as ever, once again made all the other Blackhearts look like children waving sticks. He cut down the first ratman he faced with a single stroke, and before it had collapsed, had stepped past another and beheaded it with a backstroke. A third, seeing him with his sword arm stretched behind him, lunged at his exposed chest. Jergen swayed slightly to the left, allowing its sword to pass by his ribs, then trapped the blade under his arm and chopped down through the ratman's clavicle to the heart.

'Would you look at him work,' breathed Franka.

This sudden butchery at last unnerved the other rat-men. Their attacks faltered as their comrades screamed and spouted blood. Their leader sprang back from Karel and cried the retreat.

The ratmen scampered away towards their encamp-ment, so quick that not even Jergen got in a last lick as they disengaged. Their wounded cried after them piteously, but they never looked back.

Franka stepped forwards to dispatch these with her dagger as the others started after the retreating rats.

'No!' said Reiner. 'There's a whole army down there.'

And just as he said it, he noticed shadows moving on the tunnel walls beyond the retreating rats. Their pursuers had finally resumed the chase.

'We must fly,' he said. 'There's more coming.'

The men reluctantly turned back, wiping down their weapons and sheathing them.

'Walking vermin,' said Gert wonderingly. 'Just as y'said.'

As the men started to crowd into the hole, Dag made a face. 'That you what stinks, captain? Thought it was the rats.'

'We had to disguise our scent.'

'Ye did that well enough,' said Pavel covering his nose.

Reiner looked around for Franka. 'Franz?'

She was sitting on the chest of one of the fallen ratmen, mechanically plunging her dagger into its chest over and over again, her eyes streaming tears.

'Franz.'

She didn't respond.

He crossed to her. 'Franz!'

He caught her wrist.

She looked up, snarling. Then blinked. Her face relaxed. 'I… I'm sorry. You didn't see…'

Reiner swallowed. 'No need to explain. But they're coming.'

She nodded and stood, and they followed the others into the hole.

As they emerged into the mine tunnel, Reiner caught Hals's eye. 'Changed your mind, did you?'

Hals scowled and looked away. 'We… we couldn't let y'die. But yer safe now, so, uh, we'll be on our way.'

'Fair enough,' Reiner said.

Pavel and Hals and the others turned and started hurrying up the slope. Reiner snorted as he pressed his kerchief against the cut above his eye. It was ridiculous. They were all travelling the same way, but Reiner allowed them to pull ahead for appearance's sake.

Franka shot him a questioning look.

'Hals and Abel saw you in your dress,' Reiner said softly.

Franka groaned. 'So they know my secret?'

Reiner chuckled. 'No, no. They think I have one.'

'They…?' Franka's eyes widened. 'Oh, no!'

The divided party continued on in uneasy silence, but after a while, Pavel looked over his shoulder. 'So, what do ye know of these rat-things.'

Reiner cocked an eyebrow at him. 'You're speaking to me?'

'We only ask as it concerns the safety of the garrison,' said Gert.

'Ah.' Reiner hid a smirk. 'Well, they mean to take the fort, and Aulschweig after that. Shaeder's in with them, betraying Gutzmann for the gold in the mine.'

Hals stopped and turned. 'Is this the truth?'

'Ask Giano. He heard him too, talking to their leader.'

Pavel looked at Giano. 'Tilean?'

'Aye. Is true. He tell them attack tomorrow.'

Pavel gaped. 'Tomorrow!'

Hals spat. 'Chaos take Shaeder. Jagger's more rat than these vermin.'

'Worse than Gutzmann,' said Pavel. 'That's certain.'

'Aye,' said Gert. 'Filthy turncoat. Ought to be fed his own guts.'

Karel shook his head. 'I can't believe that a knight of the Empire would do this. Is honour dead?'

The Blackhearts laughed. Karel looked baffled.

'You forget the company you keep,' said Reiner. 'We are all too well acquainted with the honour of knights.'

'This is bad,' said Hals. 'We've to warn the fort.'

Gert laughed. 'And will you be the one to tell 'em rat-men are coming to kill 'em? They'll lock you up.'

'Why warn 'em at all?' asked Dag. 'They be no mates of ours. Let's put these cursed mountains behind us and find someplace warm to hole up.'

'Forgotten the poison in our blood, lad?' asked Pavel. 'We've still a job to do, ratmen or no. And it may take longer than a day to finish it. We have to warn 'em.'

'Someone does,' said Hals.

The pikemen slid another glance toward Reiner.

Hals coughed. 'Er, captain…'

'Is it captain now?' Reiner drawled.

'You think you can trust him?' asked Gert.

'I trust him to save his own skin,' said Pavel, cold. 'He always looks after that.'

Reiner grunted. 'All right. I'll speak to Gutzmann. But it would serve you right if I lit out on my own.'

'But... but we're to kill Gutzmann,' said Karel, frowning. 'Gutzmann is a traitor to the Empire.'

'Who else would you have us tell?' asked Franka. 'Shaeder?'

'Shaeder's a traitor to mankind,' said Gert.

Karel was upset. 'So we ask Gutzmann to save us one moment, and then kill him the next?'

'It ain't all roses is it, laddie?' said Hals.

'Blame your future father-in-law if you don't find it to yer liking,' said Pavel.

'Manfred couldn't have known what we would find here,' said Karel defensively.

'There is a way Gutzmann might be spared,' said Gert. 'We're to kill him only as a last resort, aye? Maybe he gets a chance to fight for the Empire for once, he might think twice about leaving.'

'Aye,' said Pavel, brightening. 'That's true. He might.'

Hals nodded at Reiner. 'All right, captain. You tell him. Let's go.'

'As you wish.'

IN THE MAIN entry chamber of the mine all was chaos. The Blackhearts heard it before they saw it: bells ringing, horns braying, guards bellowing orders. As they crept out of the closed tunnel, they saw miners streaming from the two open ones, picks on their shoulders and worried expressions on their faces. The guards herded them towards the exit with shouts and shoves.

'What's all this?' asked Reiner of a guard as they joined the crush.

'Commander Shaeder's orders. Engineers say the lower tunnels could collapse at any moment. Mine's to be closed until further notice.'

'Shaeder ordered this? When?'

'A few minutes ago, sir. Now on your way.'

Reiner frowned. The last he had seen of Shaeder he had disappeared down a side passage in the ratmen's tunnel. It must come out somewhere up here. He wondered where.

IT WAS DUSK when they at last reached the fort, wheezing and gasping from the long run.

The gate guard saluted Reiner and stepped in his way. 'Pardon, sir,' he said, covering his nose. 'But Captain Vortmunder asks that you see him immediately about absenting yer duties all day.'

Reiner dodged around the man. 'My regards to Captain Vortmunder, and tell him I will see him as soon as I am able.'

'Ye might have a bath first!' the guard called after him.

Reiner made directly for Gutzmann's quarters, the rest of the Blackhearts trailing behind him. Reiner kept a weather eye out for Shaeder or his guards, the Hammer Bearers, but they didn't appear.

Two of Gutzmann's personal guard stood outside his door, chatting together. They came to attention as Reiner and the rest rumbled down the hall.

'Easy now, sirs,' said the first, holding up a hand. 'What's all this?'

Reiner saluted, breathing heavily. 'Corporal Meyerling reporting, sir. I wish to speak to General Gutzmann about danger within the mine and treachery within the camp.'

The guard stepped back, hand over his nose. His mate gagged. 'You must take it through the proper channels, corporal.'

'This is an emergency, sir,' said Reiner, drawing himself up. 'It cannot wait to go through channels.'

'Sorry, corporal. I got my orders...'

The door opened behind him and Matthais looked out. 'What's the trouble, Neihoff...?' He broke off as he saw Reiner. He sniffed, frowning. 'Meyerling. What are you doing here? And what's that horrible stink?'

'Never mind the stink. I've something to tell the general. What are you doing here?'

'Er, a fellow made a disturbing report to me. I brought him to Gutzmann.'

'Well, what I've to say is disturbing as well. Can you ask him if he'll see me?'

'I, er, yes. I will. Wait here.'

Matthais closed the door, and there was a wait, during which Reiner and the others caught their breath, and the guards held theirs. Reiner wondered what was troubling Matthais. He was far from his sunny self.

After a minute he reappeared and held the door open.

'All right, he'll see you,' he said. 'The rest are to wait in here.' He indicated the general's ante-room.

Reiner and the Blackhearts filed in as Matthais spoke to the guards. He then beckoned Reiner into Gutzmann's inner office and followed him in.

Gutzmann sat in a deep chair by the fire with his booted feet up on the fender. He waved as Reiner saluted. 'Ah, Hetsau. You wished to see me?'

'Yes, sir. I…' Reiner froze as he realized that Gutzmann had called him by his real name. 'Er…'

'I believe you know my guest?'

There was another chair at the fire, which faced away from Reiner. Its occupant leaned forward and looked around.

It was Abel.

Reiner cursed inwardly. A damned neat trick. He would have applauded if it hadn't been directed at him.

'My lord, I don't understand.' He spoke automatically, his mind racing. What was Abel's game? Why betray him when he was betraying himself as well? He would hang from Gutzmann's battlements right beside Reiner.

Gutzmann snorted. 'Don't be tiresome, Hetsau. You understand perfectly well. Quartermaster Halstieg has told me everything. How you were commanded by Count Valdenheim to assassinate me. How you joined my army under false pretences to do so. How you spied on my officers to discover my plans. How you attempted to recruit Halstieg and others to help you in your plot.'

'I beg your pardon, my lord?' Reiner's heart thudded in his chest. Now he was beginning to see. He'd underestimated Halstieg. The quartermaster was cleverer than he looked. He had found a way to at once betray Reiner and clear himself. This way he could remove Reiner, take Manfred's job for himself, and win his way into Gutzmann's confidences all at the same time.

Gutzmann scowled at him. 'Do you deny the charges?'

Reiner hesitated. He might try to brass it out and deny everything; try to use his powers of persuasion to convince Gutzmann that Halstieg had made it up out of the whole cloth, but there was little chance of success that way. Reiner had already condemned himself out of his own mouth. He cleared his throat. 'I do not deny that I was sent by Valdenheim, but not as an assassin. Halstieg and I and the others of my group were ordered by my lord Valdenheim to travel here and discover who was taking the Emperor's gold, and then to stop those responsible. Execution of the culprit was not beyond the purview of our brief, this is true, but neither was it our only option. We might have found a way to convince you…'

'We? Our?' cried Abel. 'Don't try to tar me with the brush of your guilt, deceiver. I had nothing to do with it.'

Reiner looked at Gutzmann. 'Is that what he has told you, my lord?'

'Hetsau came to me here, my lord!' said Abel. 'The first day he arrived! He approached a number of us, trying to turn us against you.'

'My lord,' said Reiner. 'Halsteig has been with us from the beginning. There are ten of us. We came, all of us, from Altdorf. We…'

'And the others wait in my ante-room?' asked Gutzmann. 'Have you decided that I am your culprit? Did you come to kill me?'

Reiner pursed his lips. 'My lord may accuse me of treachery, but I hope he doesn't think me unsubtle.'

Gutzmann laughed. 'Then why did you come? Other than to foul my offices with your odour. Sigmar, Matthais, you warned me, but I had no idea.'

Reiner paused. Caught flatfooted by Abel's betrayal he had almost forgotten why he had come. But now...

He sighed. He had been close to convincing Gutzmann that he was a more honest villain than Abel; and given time, he might have found a way to salvage the situation, but now, now he must mention the ratmen, and all his credibility would wither away in a storm of laughter.

Unfortunately, ridiculous as it sounded, the danger was real. The camp would be overrun, the garrison slain, Aulschweig enslaved – and most distressing of all, he and Franka and the other Blackhearts might be caught in the middle of it. Someone had to do something. He only regretted that that someone appeared to be him.

He licked his lips. 'Know, my lord...'

Muffled cursing and shouting came from the ante-room. Reiner could hear the sounds of a scuffle. He looked at the door.

'Pay it no mind, corporal,' said Gutzmann. 'It is merely your men being arrested. Pray go on.'

Reiner groaned. He was beginning to think that, poison or no poison, Manfred or no Manfred, he and the Black-hearts should have turned north when they ran out of the mine, and just kept running. 'Yes, my lord.' He took a deep breath. 'Know that when I speak you will call me mad. But if you are wise, you will see that its very lunacy is proof of the truth of my warning. For only a terrible danger would cause me to squander what little goodwill you feel toward me at such a delicate moment.'

'What are you babbling about?' said Gutzmann, confused.

Abel laughed, a high nervous giggle. 'He's about to tell you about the ratmen!'

'The...?' Gutzmann looked at Abel.

'The ratmen,' Abel repeated, still chuckling. 'It was the tale he meant to tell to lure you away. Ratmen in the mine. He would, er, lure you there and then bury you in a rock fall, claiming an accident.'

Gutzmann frowned. 'You said nothing of this before.'

Abel shrugged. 'Can you blame me, my lord?'

Gutzmann turned to Reiner, an eyebrow raised. 'Is this true? Is this the ruse you meant to use?'

Reiner cursed inwardly. Abel had twisted his words before he had even said them. But he had no choice but to go on. 'Except that it is no ruse, my lord. There are rat-men mustering in tunnels below the mines. And they mean to attack the fort.'

Gutzmann laughed and looked at Abel wonderingly. 'You were right. He prates the stuff of fairy tales. It is beyond understanding.' He turned to Reiner. 'Come sir, why do you persist? Ratmen? Could you think of nothing better?'

'They exist, sir. I have today seen them with my own eyes. We fought them. I have their blood on my clothes. The odour that offends you is theirs.'

Gutzmann stared at him with his bright blue eyes, as if trying to see into his soul. 'You don't seem mad...'

'There is worse to come, sir. But still I must tell it.' Reiner coughed and continued. 'While returning from their tunnels, we came upon a party of these ratmen talking to a man. We crept forward and discovered that it was Commander Shaeder.'

'What!' Gutzmann banged his hand on the arm of his chair. 'Sir, your foolishness goes too far. How dare you malign the commander's name?'

'He betrays you, my lord. It seems that the ratmen mean to take Aulschweig for a grain farm, and Shaeder has promised them an easy victory over you so they might cross over the pass. In exchange, they promised him all the gold from the mine. The reason...'

Gutzmann laughed uproariously. 'Now I know you are mad.' He raised his voice and called through the door. 'Neihoff!'

After a moment, the guard poked his head in the door. 'General?'

'Fetch Commander Shaeder here. He must hear this.'

The guard ducked his head and disappeared again.

Gutzmann tipped back in his chair. 'You've betrayed yourself, for you don't know Shaeder. There isn't enough gold in the world for that old Sigmarite to turn his back on the Empire. He loves it more than life itself. If he were to betray me, it wouldn't be for gold, it would be to stop me from leaving.'

'I only repeat what I heard, sir,' said Reiner. 'The cave-ins are a lie. The reason he shuts the mine is so that the ratmen may use their digging machines, which they have heretofore used only at night, all this day and night to widen their tunnel to the mine in order to bring up their siege engines and attack the fort tomorrow after dark.'

Gutzmann was red in the face. 'Enough sir, enough. Digging machines? Siege engines? It is already madness to believe in ratmen, but to credit them with the ability to build machines of such complexity?'

'My lord, please!' Reiner held out his hands. 'Think for a moment. Why would I put myself at such great risk to tell you a foolish lie? I have found already the proof Manfred asked me to seek out. I know you intend to desert the Empire and help Caspar usurp his brother's throne. I know of the shipments of gold.'

'You...!' Gutzmann's eyes bulged. 'Quiet, you fool!'

Reiner ignored him. 'If I had wanted to betray you, I would have found a way to kill you and escaped north with the gold you hide in the crates in the third tunnel.'

Reiner saw Abel's head come up at that.

Veins were throbbing in Gutzmann's temples. 'You know all this?'

'And yet,' said Reiner. 'Still I came here to warn you, when a fortune and Manfred's favour were within easy reach.'

'But...' said Gutzmann. 'But, ratmen?'

There was a knock at the door and Shaeder entered. 'You wished to see me, general?'

'Shaeder, come in,' said Gutzmann. He wiped his brow and composed himself. 'I... I thought you should face your accuser.'

Reiner thought he saw Shaeder pale a little as he turned and saw him. The commander had recognized him in the tunnel then – and undoubtedly thought him killed by the black rats. He recovered instantly, however. 'Corporal Meyerling? Of what does he accuse me?' His nose wrinkled. 'And why does he smell so?'

'He says that you conspire with ratmen who live in tunnels below the mine to overrun the fort and make of Aulschweig a, what was it you said, sir? A grain farm? And that you did all this for the gold in the mine.'

Shaeder laughed, long and loud. But stopped when he realized that Gutzmann hadn't joined him.

He frowned. 'I'm sorry, general. It is no laughing matter. For whether the man is mad, or has some more sinister purpose in spouting this nonsense, he is dangerous, and should be locked up before he tries to do you injury. You can't possibly believe him?'

Gutzmann shrugged. 'I don't know what to believe now.'

Reiner swallowed. 'My lord, I don't ask you to believe me. Only go to the end of the closed tunnel and see what you find. If after that you find nothing, you may do with me what you will.'

'You see, general,' said Abel, 'he seeks to lure you to a cave-in. Hang him.'

Reiner thought he saw a sly smile flick across Shaeder's lips as he turned to Gutzmann, chuckling. 'No no, my lord. I could not live with your suspicion hovering over me. I insist that you come to the mine and see for yourself the falseness of Meyerling's story. Merely allow the engineers tomorrow morning to make sure that he hasn't planted some vile trap and I will have them escort you down to the cave-in that blocks the tunnel.'

Gutzmann nodded. 'I will. I have meant to see it for myself anyway.' He turned to Reiner, his face sad and

hard. 'I can pity a madman, sir, but I do not care for liars.
As you will discover.'

Reiner cursed himself as Gutzmann motioned for
Matthais to take him away. What a fool he was. He had
played directly into Shaeder's hands. He had given him
the perfect excuse to deliver Gutzmann to his doom. He
didn't resist when Matthais took his arm, or notice when
he gave him a hurt look. He didn't even spit at Abel as he
passed. He was too absorbed in flagellating himself.

# THIRTEEN
## Do You Still Say I Lie?

THE REST OF the Blackhearts were sitting in sullen silence when Matthias and two guards threw Reiner into a dank, straw-strewn stone cell deep beneath the keep. He could barely see them as they raised their heads, just their eyes glinting in the dim torchlight that found its way through the oak door's heavily barred window. Franka nodded to him, but said nothing. She sat apart from the others.

Only Karel brightened at the sight of him. 'Captain, you're here! The others thought you might have betrayed us.'

Reiner shot a look at Hals and Pavel. 'The others will think anything of me, it seems.' There was little room left to sit. Much of the floor was studded with heavy iron bolts from which the chains had rusted long ago. No one seemed inclined to make room for him. He sighed, then crossed deliberately to Franka and sat down beside her. No one spoke. 'It wasn't I who betrayed us,' he said at last. 'It was Abel. He named us assassins.'

'Hey?' said Giano. 'For why?'

Gert snorted. 'So he can get us out of the way and claim the credit of killing Gutzmann for himself. Always thought that boy was a mite too smart.'

'Aye,' said Reiner, pointedly. 'There's a fellow who truly cares only for his own skin.'

There was an uncomfortable silence after that. In the darkness, Reiner could see Pavel nudging Hals. Hals shoved back, angry, but after a moment he sighed.

'All right, all right.' He looked up at Reiner, his mouth pulled down into a bulldog frown. 'Captain, I'll ask ye plain what we all been wondering. What went on in the room in the brothel before the ratmen attacked?'

Reiner shook his head. 'We are locked in a cell, with our true purpose exposed and the noose getting nearer by the second, and this is what concerns you?'

'I no care,' said Giano. 'Is they who is caring. Love is love, hey?'

'That weren't an answer,' said Gert.

'Then I'll give you one,' Reiner snapped. 'What happened in that room is no business of yours. Now, have any of you any ideas for escaping this pit?'

'But it is our business! How are we to follow ye when ye keep secrets from us?' asked Pavel. 'How can we trust ye when y've lied?'

Reiner snorted. 'Don't be ridiculous. We're all of us liars. We've every one of us secrets. You and Hals still haven't told what really happened with your captain, to name an instance.'

'We have, though,' said Hals.

'And t'ain't the same anyway,' Pavel said, shaking his head. 'The secrets we keep don't make us unfit to lead.'

'Nor does mine.'

'Captain,' said Karel, pleadingly. 'Just deny it plainly and have an end to it.'

Pavel sneered. 'Being a lover of men may not matter in Altdorf gambling houses, but t'ain't right in the army, where we all live, er, cheek by jowl, so to speak…'

'Captain ain't an invert, curse you!' cried Dag. 'And I'll kill the man who says so!'

'Then y'll be killing all of us, I think,' said Gert.

Reiner sighed. 'And that's what it comes down to, isn't it? It's not the secrets. It's not the lies. Well, let me set your minds at ease. Dag is right. I am not a lover of men.'

'You see!' cried Dag. 'You see.'

'Though if I was,' continued Reiner, 'I wouldn't be the first or the last to lead men...'

He stopped when he saw Hals's and Pavel's faces. They were almost comically downcast.

'What now?'

'We hoped at least that ye wouldn't lie,' said Pavel.

Hals clenched his fists. 'Captain, I saw ye!'

'What you saw wasn't what you thought it was,' said Reiner. 'You were mistaken.'

'Then what was it?' asked Pavel.

Reiner's eyes slid to Franka, then away. 'I cannot say.'

'T'ain't good enough,' said Hals.

'Pikeman,' said Karel, angry. 'You have no right to harass a superior officer this way. Captain...'

Reiner waved a hand at Karel. 'Forget it, lad, forget it.' He sighed and looked back to Hals. 'And if I were to say I am, would you trust me again? Would you follow me?'

There was a long pause. Everybody looked at the floor.

At last Reiner chuckled. 'You see, I was right. The lies and secrets don't matter. It's only who I bunk with that concerns you. Something that matters not the slightest...'

'So you admit it?' said Hals.

'No, I do not,' said Reiner scornfully. 'You put words in my mouth.'

Gert sneered. 'Better than what you put in your mouth, captain.'

Dag shot to his feet, fists balled. 'Y'filthy dog. Y'll die for that!' He leapt at Gert, swinging blindly. Gert lurched aside, absorbing most of the punches with his bulk, then grabbed the archer's legs and pulled him down. They rolled about on the floor in a chaos of flailing arms and legs. Everyone but Reiner and Jergen shouted at them and tried to pull them apart.

Franka jumped up, furious. 'Stop it, you fools! Stop it! You're all mad! Captain Hetsau isn't a lover of men!' she cried. 'And I should know better than any of you!'

Reiner's heart banged against his ribs. 'Frank – Franz! Don't be a fool!' He tried to pull her back down.

She wrenched her arm away. 'The reason I was wearing woman's clothes, and the reason Captain Reiner was kissing me…'

'Franka! Stop!'

'…is because I am a woman!'

Reiner groaned. The secret was out. Franka would be a soldier no more. Manfred would send her away from him. The other Blackhearts would shun her.

The other Blackhearts hadn't heard her. They were too busy trying to separate Gert and Dag. She grabbed Pavel and shook him by the shirt-front.

'Listen to me, curse you! I'm a woman!'

'Hey?' Hals blinked. 'What d'ye say, lad?'

'I'm not a lad,' Franka screamed. 'Are you deaf?'

The others were turning now. Even Dag and Gert were slowing their punches.

'Not a lad?' said Pavel, confused.

'No,' said Franka, struggling for patience. 'I am a woman. I disguised myself as a boy so I could fight for the Empire.'

The men stared at her. Dag and Gert gaped at her from the floor.

'Is true?' asked Giano.

'Of course it ain't,' said Hals. He shook his head sadly. 'Lad. I know why y'do this. Ye wish to protect the captain, and 'tis a noble thought. But it won't wash. We've seen y'fight. Lasses don't fight.'

'I do,' said Franka. 'Come, have you never wondered why I've never bathed with you? Why I always tented alone? Why I said I'd kill any man who touched me?'

'Y'might have been afraid of, er, temptation,' said Pavel.

Franka laughed. 'Do you think yourself so irresistible, pikeman?'

'Why don't y'ask her to show ye proof,' said Gert.

Dag laughed. 'Aye. Aye, give us a show.'

'No!' cried Reiner. 'I forbid it. Get away, you filthy jackals!'

Franka shrugged. 'I think I must, captain. There seems no other way to convince them. But not to all of you, curse you!' she shouted, catching their looks.

She turned from one to the other, then at last came to a decision. 'Hals, stand in the corner.'

She pointed to the far end of the cell. Hals looked embarrassed. The others chuckled.

'Come on, come on,' said Franka. 'Let's be done with it.'

With dragging feet Hals trudged to the corner and faced out. Franka stood in front of him and began unlacing her jerkin.

The company waited in silence. Dag's eyes gleamed. Reiner wanted to kill them all for forcing Franka to this indignity. How dare they not take her at her word? Then he recalled that she had had to do the same for him in order to convince him.

Hals shifted uncomfortably as Franka opened her jerkin and began undoing her buttons. He didn't seem to know where to look. At last Franka pulled aside her shirt and tugged down the bandages with which she bound her chest. 'There,' she said, glaring. 'Do you still say I lie?'

Reiner and the others couldn't see Franka's nakedness, but the look on Hals's face told them all they needed to know. Reiner laughed in spite of himself. The veteran pikeman was gaping like a gaffed trout. He looked like the cuckolded husband from an innyard farce.

'Yer... yer a lass!' he said, blinking.

Franka pulled up her bandages and closed her shirt. 'Aye,' she said dryly. 'So now you've no reason to distrust the captain, yes?'

'But this is no better!' cried Pavel, stepping forward. 'We, we've cursed in front of you. Told barracks stories in front of you.'

'We've pissed in front of you, for Sigmar's sake!' roared Hals, outraged. 'Y've seen us naked.'

'Not to worry,' said Franka. 'I took no pleasure in it.'

Gert laughed. 'The lass has wit, at least.'

Karel turned to Reiner, very stiff. 'Captain, you have known this girl's secret for some time?'

'Since the caves of the Middle Mountains,' said Reiner.

'And you have allowed her to fight, to put herself in danger?'

'Aye.'

'And you still call yourself a gentleman?' The boy was red in the face.

Reiner sighed. 'First, lad, I have never called myself a gentleman. Second, you try stopping her. She won't listen to me.'

'But this won't do,' said Hals. 'A lass can't fight. It ain't right. We've to tell Manfred. Send her back to her husband.'

Franka shuddered.

Reiner put his hand on her shoulder. 'You can be sure Manfred already knows. His surgeons had their way with her as they did with us.'

Karel choked. 'Count Manfred lets her fight?'

Reiner smiled. 'After all this time you still find yourself shocked by your future father-in-law's behaviour? To him Franka is only another criminal, whose imposture is another sword he holds over her head to force her to do his bidding.'

'Well, damn Manfred and damn you,' said Hals. 'I won't have it! Never let it be said that an Ostlandman stood by and let a lass fight while there was still life in his limbs!'

'Hear hear!' said Pavel. And Gert and Dag echoed him.

A sudden sob from Franka stopped them. They looked at her.

'I knew it would be like this!' she moaned. 'I knew it!' She balled her fists at her sides. 'Is this one thing enough that you turn against me? Am I not your friend?'

'We don't turn against you, lass,' said Pavel softly. 'We want to keep you safe from harm.'

'But it's not what I want! I want to be with you! I want to be a soldier!'

'But y'can't be,' said Hals. 'Yer a lass now.'

'As I always have been! All that has changed is that you know it.'

Hals shook his head. 'And I can't unknow it. I'm sorry, girl.'

Gert shrugged. 'What matters it one way or t'other? Likely we die swinging before we've a chance to fight again anyway. Either Gutzmann hangs us for spies, or Shaeder feeds us to his furry friends.'

The others sighed, returned by this unwelcome reminder to the reality of their situation.

'True enough, boy,' said Pavel. 'But still, she shouldn't be here, should she?'

'Nor should any of us,' said Reiner. He straightened up. 'And if we turn our minds to getting free, we might be able to continue this fascinating debate later in more pleasant surroundings. Like the Griffin in Altdorf. What say you?'

After some sullen reluctance, the others agreed to try to think of some way out of their predicament, but the day had been long and filled with running and fighting and uncertainty, and once they had returned to their places against the walls and wrapped their arms around their knees, the talk quickly devolved into mumbles and grunts, until at last, one by one their heads nodded and dropped.

Just as he was drifting off, Reiner felt Franka slump against him. He put his arm around her and pulled her close. At least there is that, he thought. At least there is that.

* * *

THEY HAD NO idea how long they had slept or what time it was when they woke. Neither noise nor light penetrated this far underground, so they couldn't tell if it was morning or afternoon or still the middle of the night, or what might be happening in the fort above. Frustrated, Reiner tried to puzzle it out from what he had learned the previous night, but it was so cold that he found it hard to concentrate. Would Gutzmann discover Shaeder's treachery and come down to free them with profuse apologies and praise, or would a flood of ratmen pour down the stairs and tear them to bloody shreds? After a while his thoughts became a muddle and he could do no more than lean against Franka and stare at the opposite wall, numb with boredom and despair. The others were no better. They had tried at first to invent an escape plan, but all started, 'Once we get out of this cell…'

Reiner had thought he might be able to accomplish something by engaging their guards in conversation. For if he could make friends with them he might trick them into relaxing their guard, but they must have been warned of his powers of persuasion. He could get nothing out of them but grunts and curses.

Sometime later he woke panting from a nightmare of pleading voices and twisted hands reaching from iron cages to tug at his clothes, to find that Franka was shaking him.

'What's the…'

She shushed him, pointing to her ear. There were voices outside the cell. He sat up and listened. Karel was crouched at the door.

'But we're not to be relieved until evening mess,' said one of their guards.

'You're relieved now,' said a new voice. 'Commander Shaeder's orders.'

The Blackhearts looked around at each other.

'That's us done then,' whispered Hals.

Reiner cursed. 'How many are there?'

Karel rose up to peek through the window then dropped back down again. He held up four fingers. His eyes were wide. 'Shaeder's greatswords!'

The light increased as boot heels clopped closer to the door. Reiner slapped at his belt, but of course his sword wasn't there. They had all been disarmed. 'On your feet!' he hissed. 'Be ready.' He wished he knew for what.

The Blackhearts pulled themselves up, stiff and groaning, trying to shake feeling into their numb limbs. Karel shifted away from the door.

The key turned in the lock.

# FOURTEEN
## May Sigmar Speed You

REINER'S MIND RACED, trying to think of some way to overcome the greatswords. It was impossible. They were proven veterans. They had seen everything. They were ready for any trick, and they were armed to the teeth. What could he possibly do to throw them off their stride, to shock them?

The door was swinging open. He could see the four Hammer Bearers standing beyond it, swords out. The leader held a lantern at his side. They had the look of witchfinders on the hunt, seeing sin in everything.

His heart banged against his chest. He had it!

'Franka!'

He grabbed the girl's wrist and dragged her before the door just as the four greatswords stepped in, raising their swords.

'Your time has come, villains,' said the leader.

Reiner pulled Franka into his arms, crying, 'Kiss me, beloved!' Then put action to his words and mashed his lips against hers with all the passion he could muster.

The greatswords gaped, paralyzed with shock. The tip of the leader's sword hit the stone floor with a clank. 'What abomination is this? Inverted degenerates…'

As quick as an eel, Jergen darted forward and kicked the lantern from the leader's hand, then ripped his sword from his slack fingers as the cell was plunged into darkness.

'Rush 'em!' Reiner shouted.

He dived at the second man's knees as Franka head-butted him in the chest. The fellow hit the floor. Around him, Reiner could hear, but not see, swords clanging as the others charged forward, screaming battle cries. Fists smacked into skin. Men grunted and yelped. There was a sharp gasp, and the unmistakable sound of steel chunking into flesh.

Reiner flailed for his greatsword's sword arm, trying to catch it before the man could swing. He caught the sword instead and razored open the base of his thumb. Reiner wrapped the blade in his arms and hugged it as the man tried to pull it away.

'Sit on him!'

'I am!' came Franka's voice.

Reiner fought the man's hands and kneed for his groin as shouts and thumps and clanks came from all over the cell. There was a sickening crack nearby. His man convulsed. A second crack and all the strength went out of the fellow's limbs. Another and he let go of his sword.

'Franka! Enough.'

'Oh.'

Reiner grabbed the Hammer's sword and stood, but the sounds of the other conflicts were trailing off except for one last thrashing fight in the centre.

'Is me you have!' came Giano's voice. 'Get he…!'

Reiner groped around in the darkness and found the lantern. He righted it and fumbled in his belt pouch for flint and steel, but the flame had not gone out, only guttered, and now came to life again.

Reiner looked around. Giano was fighting a disarmed greatsword, and Dag was fighting Giano, trying to punch him in the kidneys. Around them the other Blackhearts were rising to their feet. Their opponents remained motionless.

'Dag!' Reiner called. 'Leave off! Get the greatsword! I want to…'

Dag sprang up as he saw the greatsword was still alive. As the others stepped forward to help, he jumped on the man's chest, snatched his dagger from its scabbard and plunged it into his eye up to the hilt. He laughed like a child with a pin-wheel as the man spasmed and jerked, then lay still.

'Got him, captain,' he said, looking up. 'What'd ye want?'

Reiner balled his fists. He had never in his life come across a fellow who was in more need of killing. He forced himself to speak slowly. 'I wanted… to speak… to him. To find out if Shaeder had put his plan into action yet.'

Dag looked at him blankly. 'Oh. Well, too late for that now, hey?' He giggled.

'Aye,' said Reiner. 'Too late.'

The rest of the greatswords were dead as well. Gert had crushed the windpipe of one with his thumbs while Pavel and Hals held his arms and legs. Jergen had accounted for another, with the help of Karel, who had held the man by the ankles. The life poured out of his neck in a red flood. Franka sat on the chest of the last. The back of his head was a crimson crater, and hair and brains slicked one of the iron rings that stuck up out of the floor. Franka held clumps of the man's beard and hair in her clenched fists. She shivered with revulsion when she saw what she had done, and flung the tufts away.

'Well done, lads,' said Reiner, wrapping his cut thumb with his handkerchief. 'Rohmner, check the guardroom.'

Jergen stepped to the door and looked out. He gave the all's well sign.

Gert laughed as he stood up. 'What in Sigmar's name inspired you to kiss the lass?'

Reiner shot a chagrined look at Franka. 'It worked, did it not?'

'Almost didn't,' said Hals, scowling. 'Ye surprised me near as much as ye surprised them.'

'Aye,' said Pavel. 'I nearly pissed m'self.' He blushed and looked at Franka. 'Beggin' yer pardon, lass.'

'Stop that!' Franka barked.

The others laughed.

Reiner took the sword belt, keys and gloves from his man and gave Franka her dagger. The others looted the rest, sharing out swords and daggers as best they could.

'So,' said Gert. 'What's yer plan, captain?'

Reiner smirked. 'Captain again, is it? Well, I...' He hesitated. He knew what he wanted to do. He wanted to get Gutzmann's gold out of the mine and scurry off back to civilization before the ratmen poured out of their hole. But he couldn't do that until he knew Gutzmann was dead. The fact that Shaeder's greatswords had come to kill them suggested he was, but Reiner couldn't be sure. He sighed. 'Well, I suppose we should go up and see what's in the wind first.' He glared at Dag. 'Since we've no one to ask.'

He stepped out of the cell with the others behind him. A stairway ascended into darkness on the far side of the square guardroom. They took it, swords at the ready. As they turned up the last flight they saw at the top a guard with his back to them, standing on the far side of a locked gate.

Reiner motioned them back down around the corner. 'Any of you recognize that fellow? Or recall his name?'

Gert frowned. 'I need another look.' He crept up to the landing, peeked around, then came back down. 'Herlachen, I think,' he said. 'Or Herlacher. Some such. His tent's by mine. We did wall duty together t'other day.'

Reiner shrugged. 'It will have to do. Now back down a bit, then come up marching.' He looked to Jergen. 'When he opens the door, you run up and pull him in. You understand?'

Jergen nodded.

The Blackhearts backed down another flight, then Reiner dropped his hand and they began marching up, kicking the stairs with their boot heels.

Just before they reached the last flight again, Reiner called out, gruff and loud. 'Herlachener! Open the gate!'

The guard's voice echoed down to them. 'Yessir! Right away, sir.'

Reiner listened to the jingle and clank of the guard putting key to lock. He held up his hand and the Blackhearts marched in place. It wouldn't do to come around the corner before the fellow had opened the door. At last he heard the scrape of the key and the squeal of the door swinging open.

'Now, Jergen!'

Jergen darted around the corner as Reiner and the rest resumed marching.

They mounted the last flight just in time to see him springing up at the surprised guard. Jergen punched him in the nose as he tried to draw, then caught him around the back of the neck and flung him down the stairs, where Reiner and Giano caught him and clamped hands over his mouth. Reiner held his breath as the swordmaster took the keys from the lock, pulled the gate closed and slipped back down the stairs. He expected shouts and challenges, but none came. He exhaled.

'Right,' he whispered. 'Tie him up and leave him downstairs.'

'Better to kill him, hey?' said Dag.

'We ain't at war with the army, lad,' growled Reiner.

As Hals and Pavel tied the guard's wrists and ankles with the laces of his jerkin, Reiner craned his neck to look through the gate. The soldiers who wandered through the hallway beyond it seemed calm, which told Reiner that the ratmen had not yet attacked, and Gutzmann had not been reported dead or missing. Daylight streamed into the hall from the courtyard door. It looked to be late afternoon.

He waited for the hall to empty, but it never did. The armoury was the first door on the right, the barracks where Gutzmann's retinue of knights slept the second. On the left were the tall doors that led to the main hall – usually locked – and beyond them, the door to the courtyard. The hall was in constant use.

'We'll have to brass it out, lads,' Reiner said. 'With luck, our fall from grace isn't common knowledge. We'll just stroll out like naught's the matter.'

'You forgetting you and Ostini and the lass smell like a latrine, captain?' asked Gert.

'And look like ye fell in one,' added Pavel.

Reiner sighed. 'Curse it, I had. Well, I'll think of something.' He hoped he wasn't lying. 'If anyone challenges us, let me do the talking. If they call guards, run for the north gate.' He took a deep breath. 'Right. Off we go.'

Reiner mounted the steps and pushed open the gate with the others behind him. He tried to keep his breath steady, but every soldier who stepped into the hall made him jump. They all wrinkled their noses as the Blackhearts passed.

At last a knight stopped, scowling. 'Sigmar's oxter! What happened to you, corporal?'

Reiner saluted. 'Sorry for the smell, sir. Floor of the guardroom latrine caved in. Some of us got banged up a bit. Going to clean off now.'

The captain made a face. 'Well be quick about it.'

Reiner saluted again and they continued to the courtyard door. Reiner looked out, then pulled back, heart thudding. Shaeder was on the steps before the keep's main door, talking with Obercaptain Nuemark.

'Shaeder,' said Reiner over his shoulder. 'Curse the luck. We'll have to wait a moment...'

Before he could finish there was a commotion at the gate, and a lance corporal galloped into the courtyard on a lathered horse. 'General Gutzmann,' he called, reining up. 'I have urgent news for General Gutzmann.'

Shaeder stepped to the lancer as he dismounted. 'General Gutzmann is called away to the mines, corporal,' he said. 'Tell me your news.'

Everyone in the courtyard turned to listen as the lancer saluted. 'Yes commander. My lads and I were patrolling the southern pass, bandit hunting, when we saw a column coming from Aulschweig.'

'A column?' asked Shaeder, frowning. 'What do you mean, man?'

'Commander, it was Baron Caspar at the head of an army. We crept forward to observe and counted six company of horse, eight hundred pike and musket, and siege engines.'

'Siege engines?' Shaeder sounded shocked. 'What is he about? Does he mean to take the fort?'

'My lord,' said the corporal. 'I believe that is exactly what he means to do.'

There was uproar in the courtyard as everyone within earshot began talking at once. Lancers began pushing past Reiner and the Blackhearts into the courtyard. It was a perfect opportunity. No one, not even the guards at the gate, would look at them now.

'Around the edge, lads,' Reiner murmured. 'And keep your heads down.'

They shuffled out in the midst of a crowd of lancers. Shaeder had mounted the steps and was issuing orders to the assembled troops. 'Daggert, ride to the mine and ask General Gutzmann to return at once. I will take command until he can be found.' He turned to Nuemark. 'Obercaptain, assemble a force of three hundred pike and a company each of pistoliers, knights, lancers, swords and handguns, then march south to Lessner's Narrows and hold it for as long as you are able so that we may have time to prepare. In the meantime, all other captains are to have their troops make the fort ready to receive an attack. And someone find Obercaptain Oppenhauer and ask him to see me in my offices at his earliest convenience. Now go, all of you, and may Sigmar speed you.'

The courtyard erupted into confusion as men ran hither and thither while officers shouted questions and bellowed for horses.

Above it all, Infantry Obercaptain Nuemark called out his orders in a clear, calm voice. 'I will have Knight Captain Venk, Lance Captain Halmer and Pistolier Captain Krugholt report to me as well as Pike Captain...'

The rest was lost as Reiner and the Blackhearts dove into a stream of men rushing out of the gate. No one stopped them as they passed into the fort. In fact, they gave them a wide berth.

'Aulschweig attacks now?' cried Karel as they hurried along. 'What rotten luck!'

'Don't be a fool,' said Reiner. 'Couldn't you see? That little scene was more staged than one of Detlef Sierck's murder plays.'

'Staged?' queried Karel. 'What do you mean?'

'It's a trick,' said Franka, answering before Reiner could reply. 'There is no attack from Aulschweig. Shaeder only pretends there is to draw the fort's attention south while the ratmen attack from the north.'

'And he sends away half the fort to make it even easier for them,' said Gert. 'By the time Nuemark's forces return from their wild goose chase they will be locked out, and at the mercy of our cannon in the hands of the rats.'

Reiner motioned to the others, and they pushed out of the flow of men into a narrow alley between two cavalry barracks.

'But... but it can't be,' said Karel, catching his breath. 'The man who gave the warning was a lancer. The lancers are loyal to Gutzmann.'

'I'm sorry to be the one to break it to you, lad,' said Reiner. 'But even a cavalry man can be bought.' He sighed and leaned against the wall. 'Lads, I've a feeling there's nothing left for us to do here. If Shaeder makes his move, then Gutzmann must be dead. I think our best play is to head home and report the commander's treachery to Manfred.'

'And leave the fort to the mercy of the ratmen?' asked Karel, aghast.

'What would you have us do, lad?' asked Reiner. 'We nine can't stop an army of monsters, and we've tried warning the brass already. Twice.' He looked around at the others. 'I am, of course, open to suggestions.'

The Blackhearts looked unhappy, but said nothing.

'Right then.' Reiner pushed away from the wall. 'We go. I want to return to the mine to be sure Gutzmann is dead first. Then we head north.'

The others nodded, glum. Franka shot Reiner a sharp look.

# FIFTEEN
## They Knew

THE BLACKHEARTS SPLIT up briefly to return to their various tents and barracks and arm themselves. Though time was of the essence, Reiner took a moment to strip out of his befouled uniform, rinse himself off, and put on fresh clothes. There really was no other option.

His pistols had been taken by his jailers and he hadn't a second pair, so for weapons he had to make do with the sword he had taken off Shaeder's man – a greatsword much too big for him. When he was ready, he borrowed a spare horse and pulled Franka up behind him. Her bow was slung across her back. They met the others again at the edge of the tent camp. They had commandeered a hay cart. Reiner was relieved to see that Giano had taken the time to clean himself as well.

There was no one to stop them leaving. The camp was nearly empty, as captains and sergeants bullied their troops into their armour and then herded them into the fort. As they rode into the pass, a bitter wind whipped up and clouds began to race across the sky. Their fat shadows slid across the jagged sunset peaks above the treeline like slugs across rough gold. Reiner cursed as he looked north. An armada of clouds was bearing down on them. The weather would be less than ideal for travelling, and he wanted to be far away before they stopped for the night.

Franka hugged Reiner's waist and leaned into his back. 'What are you up to, my lord?' she whispered. 'It isn't like you to ride into danger. You know Gutzmann's dead. There's no reason to go back to the mine.'

Reiner whispered in turn. 'Gutzmann's gold.'

She cocked an eyebrow. 'You intend to mine it yourself?'

He shook his head. 'On our way to rescuing you I discovered where the general holds it for shipment to Aulschweig. There are two crates in the closed tunnel.'

'So why lie to the others?'

'You forget the spy?'

'Isn't Abel the spy?'

Reiner shrugged. 'And if he ain't?'

'Then how do you intend to get it out without the others knowing what you do? Will the boxes fit in your pockets?'

Reiner laughed. 'I'm still working on that.'

THE WIND MOANED through the ravine as the Blackhearts approached the mine's defensive wall. The light had faded to a bruised purple as the sun dropped behind the mountains and the clouds spread across the sky. Reiner's nerves were so on edge that he was seeing ratmen in every murky shadow and patch of scrub. The vicious vermin could pour out of the mine at any moment and slaughter them all. And he was leading his companions closer to them with every step.

Reiner shivered as they entered the compound. What a contrast to the bustling industry of yesterday. The place felt as if it had been deserted for decades. The mine's heavy iron gates hung open and squealed like doomed souls as the wind pushed at them. The shutters of the outbuildings banged open and shut. Dust devils fought in the alleys and pebbles rattled down the piles of waste rock, making the Blackhearts jump and turn.

The square black entrance of the mine looked like the maw of some great fish, a leviathan of legend, into which they were being inexorably drawn. The wind moaning across it sounded like the beast's mournful cry. Reiner and Franka dismounted as the others stepped down from their cart. Though there was no threat apparent, they all drew their weapons. Franka, Giano and Gert set arrows and bolts to their strings.

'Come on, then,' said Reiner.

Inside, the wind's moan became a roar. Reiner couldn't hear his own footsteps. The entry chamber was lit by a single flickering lantern hung from an iron hook to the right of the entrance. Its light was not enough to touch the far walls, but the mine was not entirely dark. As Reiner's eyes grew accustomed, he could see a faint glow of torchlight coming from the mouth of the third tunnel.

Pavel noticed it too. 'Is it the rats?' he asked nervously.

Reiner shook his head. 'It's torchlight. The rat light is purple.' That the source of the light was human was to some extent comforting, but it was also frustrating. Who was it? What were they doing down there? Why were they in his way? The gold was down that tunnel. Was someone else after it? 'Let's find some torches and have a look.'

But as the men stepped further in, a clash of steel and a hoarse cry cut through the wind. They froze in their tracks and looked around, weapons at the ready. It had come from within the mine, but where was hard to tell.

'A fight,' said Giano.

'That was Gutzmann's voice,' said Hals. 'I swear it.'

Karel nodded. 'I heard it too.'

The cry came again, and more clang and clatter. This time the direction was clear. The sounds were coming from the engineers' quarters – the strange subterranean townhouse.

Reiner snatched the lantern off its hook and ran for the passage that led to the house. The others pounded after him. It took a few strides for Reiner to realize that he wasn't sure what exactly he meant to do. Was he hurrying to save Gutzmann or to kill him?

As they entered the passage the sounds of fighting became clearer – grunts and cries and the clash and slither of swordplay. The beautifully carved door was half open, and the lamps within threw a hard-edged bar of light into the hall. Reiner skidded to a stop and held up his hand. The others peeked over his shoulders as he tilted his head around the door.

The beautiful stone foyer was lit with a massive marble chandelier. The parlour to the left was dark, but the dining room beyond it glowed with lamplight, and Reiner gaped at the scene revealed there. It was like a painting done by a poppy fiend in his madness. The table was set as if for a state dinner, with fine porcelain plates and goblets and flatware of silver glinting in the mellow light. Bottles of wine were open, and rich platters of meat, fish and game surrounded a central candelabrum. Each plate was filled with a half-eaten meal.

As strange as the dinner was, in the light of current events, the diners were stranger. Seated around the table was a number of ratmen, all dressed in armour and holding bloody daggers in their gnarled claws. Each of them was stone dead, hacked and pierced with horrible wounds. But what tipped the scene into lunacy was the sight of General Gutzmann, bleeding and exhausted, fighting a handful of Shaeder's Hammer Bearer greatswords around and across the table. The greatswords were comically hampered by a strange disinclination to disturb any of the particulars of the scene. They checked their swings so as not to smash any of the plates or goblets, and straightened the dead ratmen in their chairs when they bumped into them. It was this, more than any dazzling feats of swordsmanship, that was allowing Gutzmann to hold his own in such an unequal contest.

'Sigmar's beard!' whispered Karel. 'What madness is this?'

Reiner shook his head. 'I've never seen the like.' He slipped into the entryway for a better look. The others eased in behind him, hiding behind the massive granite urns and ornate stone furniture. It was hard to turn away from the scene. What did it mean, Reiner wondered? What was Shaeder up to?

'At least we haven't to sweat killing him ourselves,' chuckled Dag. 'Those lads'll do for him.'

'Are y'mad?' said Hals. 'We have to help him. Gutzmann's the only one who can save the fort!'

Pavel turned to Reiner. 'We help him, captain. Don't we?'

'We…' Reiner hesitated. What did he do? Here indeed was the salvation of the fort, but also the best opportunity yet to fulfil Manfred's orders and kill the man who was stealing the Emperor's gold, or at least see him dead. Of course, if they saved Gutzmann now, they might kill him later once he had beaten the ratmen. But the general knew their orders now. He would protect himself. Such a chance wouldn't come again. 'We…'

He looked at Franka. Her soft brown eyes had somehow grown sharp as daggers. They lanced his soul. 'We…'

There was a clatter of boots in the passage behind them. The Blackhearts turned as the front door flew open and six engineers burst in, faces flushed.

'They're coming!' cried the first, slamming the door behind him. 'Hurry! Let's be…' He stopped short as he saw who he faced.

Reiner glanced back to the dining room. Gutzmann and Shaeder's greatswords were looking into the foyer as well. For a long moment the tableau held, as each side sorted out who was who and what was what.

It was Gutzmann who broke it, by leaping up and running across the table, sending plates and goblets flying, then charging through the parlour to skid to a stop at Reiner's side.

'Kill them!' called one of the Hammers. 'They mustn't expose the plan!'

Gutzmann grinned, though it was obvious he was in pain from a dozen wounds. 'So, Hetsau. Right in all particulars. I owe you an apology.'

Reiner was embarrassed by the general's trust, for he had been thinking that he could stab him in the neck and fulfil Manfred's orders then and there. But the engineers were drawing swords and hammers and axes and advancing on them on one side, and Shaeder's greatswords were coming through the parlour on the other. Reiner needed Gutzmann's sword more than he needed him dead. And more than that, he didn't want him dead. He felt a kinship with him. They were both bright men. They shared a wry humour. And they had both been manipulated and betrayed by Altdorf. Perhaps he wouldn't have to kill him after all? Gert's foolish notion that if the Empire was threatened here, Gutzmann would reconsider deserting, suddenly became very attractive.

'Back the way we came, lads,' said Reiner. 'Jergen, Karel. Help me hold the swordsmen. The rest, break through these ditch diggers.'

The men shifted around so that Reiner, Karel and Jergen faced the Hammer Bearers while the others jabbed at the engineers with spears, swords and axes.

Gutzmann stood shoulder to shoulder with Reiner as the Hammers closed with them. There were six of the black-clad giants. Reiner's wrist nearly snapped as he parried a cut from one. Gutzmann blocked another and riposted with ease. Wounded as he was, he looked like he could fight all night.

'I never thought I'd be glad to see anyone break out of my brig,' he said.

'Four of this lot came to kill us,' said Reiner. 'We turned the tables on them.' He ducked a slashing blade and pinked his opponent in the leg. 'We thought they'd done for you.'

Gutzmann grinned. 'They meant to. But when they took me down into the mine I started to suspect, and ran away. We've been playing hide and seek in the tunnels since.'

The engineers were falling back. Though armed and schooled as soldiers, they were not used to hand to hand combat. Hals stabbed one in the arm and he dropped his mallet. Gert brained him with his axe. Franka ducked a hammer, and was about to run her man through when Pavel pulled her back.

'Behind me, lass,' he said.

'What!' Franka shoved him. 'Don't be an ass!' She tried to squirm back around him, but he and Hals closed ranks.

Gutzmann blinked. 'Lass?'

'I'll explain later,' said Reiner.

The Blackhearts forced the engineers back while Gutzmann, Jergen, Karel and Reiner protected their rear. They could do little more than block and retire, for even Jergen was reduced to playing a defensive game against so many skilled blades. At last the engineers broke and fled out of the door. Pavel, Gert, Franka and Giano ran after them.

Hals stopped at the door. 'Clear, captain. Disengage.'

'Fall back!' shouted Reiner.

Jergen, Karel and Gutzmann jumped back from the Hammers with Reiner, and ran for the door. The greatswords lunged forward, stabbing at them as they darted through. Hals slammed the door in the Hammers' faces.

As they ran down the short hall Reiner frowned, for at the end, the rest of the Blackhearts and the last few engineers stood together, not fighting, but instead staring into the entry chamber.

'Go! Go!' called Reiner. He pushed through them, dragging at Franka, then froze as he saw why they had stopped.

'Sigmar's balls,' said Gutzmann, beside him.

The greatswords came roaring down the passage, swinging at the Blackhearts' backs.

Gutzmann spun on them, hissing. 'Quiet, you fools, or we're all dead!'

And such was his aura of command that they skidded to a stop before him.

Gutzmann pointed. 'Look.'

They looked.

It seemed, in the dark, a muddy river, flowing through the mine – a river at full flood that carried branches and trees and wagons with it. It was ratmen – so many, so densely packed, and so fleet of foot that it was difficult to see them as separate bodies. They poured out of the third tunnel in an unending tide, spears and halberds bobbing above their heads, and disappeared out of the mine entrance without break or pause. They didn't march as men. They kept to no formations. There were no ranks and files, no order, just a pulsing, fevered rush. The carts, overloaded with odd brass contraptions and strange weapons, careened through it all, pulled by scrawny, filthy rat-slaves that were harnessed to them like oxen. More frightening than the weapons were hulking, half-seen shapes, taller and more massive than men, that lurched along, roaring, as ratmen in grey robes guided them with whips and sticks.

Reiner could feel the vibration of the army's passage through his feet, like an avalanche that never stopped. And the smell was overwhelming. They seemed to push it out of the tunnel before them. It filled the entry chamber like a solid thing – a reeking, animal stink mixed with the stench of illness and death. Reiner covered his mouth. The others did the same.

Fortunately, the ratmen seemed so intent on their purpose that they looked neither left nor right, and so hadn't yet seen the men at the side of the chamber, but there were outrunners – sergeants perhaps – who loped along beside the river of rat-flesh, and it was inevitable that one of them would eventually look their way.

'Back into the house,' whispered Gutzmann. 'Quietly.'

The men backed away, Blackhearts and engineers and greatswords together, too awed by the horror before them to remember to fight each other.

As they tiptoed back into the stone house, Gutzmann turned on the Hammer Bearers, who looked sick with shock. 'You disgust me! To deliver your fellows into the hands of such monsters! How can you stand to live?'

'You have it wrong, general,' said their sergeant. 'Commander Shaeder has a plan.'

'A plan?' Gutzmann sputtered. 'What kind of plan allows these vermin to take the fort unawares?' He pointed his sword at the sergeant, then hissed and pressed his elbow to his side 'You, Krieder. You will... You will escort me. We will take the hill track back to the fort as quickly as we may.' Below his breastplate his jerkin was red and damp. He was more wounded than he had let on.

'We cannot allow that, general,' said Krieder.

The greatswords raised their swords.

Gutzmann, Reiner and the Blackhearts went on guard as the Hammer Bearers began to close with them again. The engineers hefted their weapons again as well, but seemed reluctant to return to the melee.

A greatsword lunged at Reiner, slashing at his head. Reiner parried and dodged away, but before he could counter, a bang and a muffled shriek from the parlour made everyone jump. Reiner looked beyond the Hammers, who had stepped back again. The parlour fireplace was moving, the mantle splitting in the middle and opening out with a grinding of stone on stone, revealing a secret door.

Out of the black opening staggered an engineer, his face bloody and his clothes shredded. He dragged another, whose arm was over his shoulder, but the man was obviously beyond help. Half his skull had been blown away and his brains were spilling down his neck.

The living engineer threw out a hand to the Hammer Bearers, his eyes wild. 'Save us. We are lost. They knew!' He tripped over his friend's slack legs and fell.

Krieder ran to him and pulled him up. 'What do you say, man?' He shook him. 'Speak, damn you!'

The Hammer Bearers joined him. Gutzmann, Reiner and the rest followed them into the parlour.

The engineer's lower lip trembled. 'They knew! They swarmed the cart before we could loose it! The tunnel remains open!'

'Bones of Sigmar,' breathed the greatsword sergeant. 'This is…'

Before he could finish, a crowd of ratmen swarmed out of the secret door, looking around with darting black eyes. They stopped when they saw the men and snarled, brandishing curved swords and halberds.

'So Shaeder had a plan, did he?' said Gutzmann as the men edged back from the rats.

Sergeant Krieder dropped the dying engineer and joined his fellows. 'It wasn't to be like this.'

'I'm sure it wasn't.'

The ratmen charged, flowing around the Hammers, the Blackhearts and the engineers in a brown flood. The men slashed at them in a terrified frenzy. One of the greatswords went down immediately, a halberd in his neck. The others closed ranks. An engineer fell, screaming, pierced by two blades. Gutzmann killed a ratman, then grunted and stumbled into Reiner, his leg bleeding. Before Reiner could help him he stood again, and renewed his attack on the squirming wave of fur that surrounded them. These were not the tall black-furred killers Reiner and the others had faced before. They were of the smaller brown variety, but there were more of them.

'Protect the general!' cried Krieder, the Hammer sergeant.

His men pressed forward to form a wall around Gutzmann. They hacked down the front line of ratmen like so much underbrush.

'Bit of an… an about face hey, Krieder?' said Gutzmann. He was having trouble breathing.

'My lord,' said the Hammer sergeant, without looking around, 'we have doomed the fort through our intrigues. If we must die so that you can save it, so be it.' He decapitated a ratman. Its head spun across the room. Two more took its place.

Though the Hammer Bearers were in the thick of it, there were plenty of ratmen to go around, a seething jumble of slashing, screeching monsters. Reiner fought three, and all around him he could see the Blackhearts and the engineers kicking and hacking and stabbing. An engineer threw down his hatchet and tried to run away. The ratmen chopped him to pieces.

Franka's voice raised above the fray. 'Let me fight, curse you!'

Reiner looked around. Franka was shoving Hals and trying to dodge around him. The butt of a ratman's spear caught her in the temple. She fell.

'Franka!' Reiner cried. He fought to her and stood over her, blocking a spear that stabbed down at her.

'Sorry, captain,' said Hals. 'She won't stay back.'

'And will you let her die to keep her from fighting?'

Franka staggered to her feet as Reiner held off the rats. 'I'm all right, captain,' she said. But her hands shook as she lifted her sword.

Reiner stepped back as he parried a halberd. His calf touched an obstacle. He looked back. A stone bench.

'Draw your bow, lass,' he said. 'Get up. Gert, Dag, Giano. You too.' The four eased back and stepped onto the bench as Reiner, Gutzmann, Karel and the Hammer Bearers protected them, then wound their crossbows and nocked arrows. Pavel, Hals and Jergen took up positions behind the bench and guarded their backs. There were no engineers left standing. The bowmen fired over their protector's heads into the crowd of ratmen and loaded again.

Another Hammer Bearer went down. Only three remained, but each fallen greatsword had accounted for a handful of ratmen. The vermin lay in mounds around the survivors, but more rats stood on their dead to fight them.

Gutzmann stumbled into Reiner again, and narrowly missed being spitted by a ratman's spear. Reiner pulled him out of the way.

'My thanks,' Gutzmann said, gasping. 'Just need to catch my breath.'

'Yes, general.' But Reiner was afraid it was more than that. Gutzmann was pale and shaking.

The tide was turning. The fire of bow and crossbow was thinning the back ranks of the remaining ratmen as the Blackhearts and the Hammers cut down their front lines. But just as Reiner thought the worst might be over, Gutzmann collapsed entirely, and this time sprawled across the floor before the ratmen, utterly exposed. A rat halberdier raised his heavy weapon to stab down at him.

'No!' Krieder leapt forward and gutted the ratman, but two more ratmen gored him with swords. The Hammer sergeant vomited blood and fell across Gutzmann's body.

With a roar of anger, the last two greatswords charged into the thick of the ratmen, swinging their swords with an utter disregard for defence. One took a sword in the groin, but their opponents fell back in pieces, arms, legs and heads severed. It was too much. The ratmen broke in terror, filling the room with a horrible sweaty musk as they tried to flee back to the secret passage. They didn't make it. Franka, Gert, Giano and Dag shot them down, while Jergen, Karel, Pavel and Hals caught the ones they missed.

As the last rat fell, everyone stopped where they were, sucking air and staring around at the heaps of brown-furred bodies. Reiner felt numb, as if he had been battered by a hurricane. He wasn't yet recovered from the surprise of the ratmen's initial attack and already it was over.

'Sigmar,' said Hals, snatching up an unbroken wine bottle from the floor. 'What a dust-up!' He took a drink and held the bottle out to Reiner. 'Captain.'

Reiner reached for the bottle, then stopped. He'd almost forgotten his vow to Ranald. He let his hand drop. 'No. No thank ye.'

Hals shrugged and passed the bottle to Pavel.

As his head stopped swimming, Reiner felt again the steady throbbing vibration of the ratmen on the march. He cursed and looked for a living engineer. There were none. Only one Hammer Bearer still lived. He was rolling Krieder's body off Gutzmann. Gutzmann was wheezing wetly. The greatsword's eyes glistened with tears.

Reiner squatted beside them. 'Pardon, general,' he said, nodding to Gutzmann, then put a hand on the Hammer's shoulder. 'What was that about closing the tunnel? What was your plan?'

The Hammer Bearer looked up at him blankly.

Reiner shook him. 'Quickly, damn you!

'The–' the man swallowed. 'The engineers filled a mine cart with explosives and hid it in the secret passage where it slopes down to the ratmen's tunnel. All they had to do was light the fuse and cut the rope, and it would roll down into the tunnel and explode, bringing down the roof and trapping the ratmen inside. But they…'

'Yes. They knew. This passage?' Reiner pointed to the open fire place.

The greatsword nodded. 'At the bottom.'

Reiner looked at Gutzmann. He was very pale. 'General, can you travel?'

'I'll have to, won't I?' He said it through gritted teeth.

Reiner stood and looked around. The Blackhearts were looking a bit worse for wear. Franka had a cut on her leg, as did Hals. Dag had a bump the size of a goose egg over his temple and was weaving slightly. Jergen was wrapping his hand in strips torn from the tablecloth, and Pavel had apparently lost most of his left ear. He was wrapping his head with a strip cut from the dining room tablecloth.

Reiner sighed. 'Bind up your wounds, lads. We're not done yet. Karel. Stay here with the general. Make him ready to move.' He glared at the Hammer Bearer. 'You'll show us the way to the cart.'

# SIXTEEN
## Shallya Receive You

REINER AND THE Blackhearts raced with the Hammer
Bearer down the winding, always descending passage,
torches in hand. Every second counted, for the longer
they left the tunnel open the more ratmen would descend
on the unsuspecting fort. As they ran, the Hammer Bearer
told Reiner what Shaeder had intended.

'The commander never meant to betray the Empire. He
only wanted to discredit Gutzmann and prove himself to
Altdorf by winning a great victory over a terrible enemy.'

'So he did all this out of jealousy?' asked Reiner, incred-
ulous.

'Not jealousy,' said the greatsword stiffly. 'Duty. Gutzmann meant to desert. Shaeder had to stop him, but
unless the general was made to look a traitor to his
troops, they would have revolted, and the border would
have been undefended. Shaeder didn't know how to pro-
ceed until the engineers discovered the rats.'

Reiner frowned. 'So he set up that charade with the
dead ratmen and the dinner table to make it look like
Gutzmann was conspiring with them?'

'Aye,' said the Hammer.

Reiner nodded. 'And he planned to bring down the tunnel after only half the rat army had come out, so the men would see the threat, and yet would have an easy victory?'

The greatsword nodded. 'Aye. You have it. Brilliant, was it not?'

'Except it didn't work,' growled Hals.

'The ratmen betrayed us,' said the Hammer Bearer, angry.

Reiner rolled his eyes. 'You shock me!'

The Hammer held up his hand and they slowed to a stop. 'Around the next bend,' he said, catching his breath.

Reiner nodded. 'Right. Giano?'

Giano handed his torch to Gert and crept forward into the darkness. After a short wait, he returned, eyes bright and eager.

'They making to be moving it. Six, seven soldier-rat, and ten maybe slave-rat,' he said. 'They putting rope on back to let down slow.' He grinned. 'We take 'em easy, hey?'

'Have they started?'

Giano shook his head.

'Good,' said Reiner. 'And the cart. It's still full of powder kegs?'

'Aye.'

Reiner grunted, satisfied. 'Right. Then we leave our torches here, and go in swift and silent. Gert, Giano, Dag and Franka, bolts and arrows on the string. The rest, stay low. The moment they see us coming, you four let fly, and we run in swinging. We want to take 'em all in the first charge, aye?'

The others nodded.

'Good, then off we go.'

The men laid their torches in a line on the floor and drew their weapons. Gert and Giano set bolts in grooves as Franka and Dag nocked arrows.

Hals glanced at Franka. 'Shouldn't the lass stay back here?'

Reiner's jaw tensed. 'We need all the cover we can muster.'

'But…'

'This isn't the time, pikeman.'

Hals grunted and looked at his boots.

'Don't worry, Hals,' said Franka. 'I'll do my best not to shoot you in the back.'

'She can put a rabbit's eye out at fifty paces,' said Pavel.

Hals glared at him.

The men started down the passage, hunched low, with Dag, Giano, Gert and Franka at the rear. Reiner, Pavel and Hals shared the front with Jergen and the greatsword. As they rounded the bend the darkness was absolute for a moment, and then a faint purple glow lit the walls ahead. A few more steps and the cart and the rats were revealed. It was as Giano had said. Seven rat soldiers stood around the cart, directing a crowd of starved and stunted rat-slaves who were tying ropes to the back of the cart, which was almost as wide as the tunnel itself. There was another rope, stouter, that was lashed to a ring set in the tunnel floor. This held the cart in place at the top of the rails that disappeared down the steep slope into darkness.

Reiner quickened his pace, but stayed on his toes, holding his sword behind him so the blade wouldn't reflect the purple light. The others sped up as well. Twenty paces to go. Fifteen.

A ratman lifted his nose, then twitched his head toward them. He squealed a warning.

'Now!' cried Reiner, and pounded forward with the others, silence forgotten.

Bolts and arrows sprouted from two ratmen's chests as they drew their swords. Then Reiner and the Hammer Bearer and the Blackhearts were among the rest. Slashing and chopping. Two more went down immediately, but the slave-rats were running every which way in a panic and got in the way. Reiner and the others kicked and shoved through a swamp of furry, filthy bodies as the last three rat soldiers retreated around the cart.

Franka, Giano, Dag and Gert leapt up onto the back of the cart. Franka and Dag fired over it at the retreating rats as Giano and Gert reloaded their crossbows. Franka hit a slave-rat.

Jergen and Reiner forced their way down the left side of the cart as the Hammer Bearer went down the right, chopping through the slave-rats like dense undergrowth. Hals and Pavel followed the Hammer, gutting the fallen, and spearing the slave-rats who tried to swarm the greatsword.

Giano and Gert fired again as Franka and Dag got off their third shots. One of the rat warriors fell with an arrow and a bolt in his back, but before the archers could load again, slave-rats crowded onto the cart, trying to escape the three swordsmen, and got in their way.

Reiner and Jergen stumbled out on the far side of the cart and lunged at the last two rat soldiers. The greatsword staggered out as well, throwing and kicking slave-rats in every direction, but one swung by his jaws from the man's neck like a pit-dog hanging from a bull. With a cry, the greatsword thrust it away and it fell to the ground, but it had a bloody chunk of his neck in its teeth. The Hammer dropped to his knees, his gloves shiny red as he tried to stop the fountain of blood that pumped from his jugular.

One of the rat soldiers hurled a dagger at Reiner. He flinched, and it spun by his ear. A slave-rat screamed behind him. Jergen ran the knife-rat through as Reiner angled for the other. It threw a glass globe at the ground and the tunnel filled with smoke. Reiner slashed where he thought the rat was, covering his nose and mouth with the crook of his arm. He hit nothing.

'Fire!' he cried. 'Fire!'

He heard bolts and arrows thrum past him into the smoke, and a rattish squeal, but couldn't tell if it had been a fatal shot.

Jergen charged into the smoke, his sword spinning in a figure eight, but Reiner heard no cries or impacts. He ran in after him, heart thudding – fighting blind was for fools. After a few steps he was beyond the smoke, but the clouds blocked the light and the tunnel was pitch black. He heard Jergen returning.

'Get him?'

'No.'

Reiner sighed and turned, stumbling over the rails. 'Then they will be coming.'

'Yes.'

The others were finishing off the last of the slave-rats as he and Jergen stepped out of the dissipating cloud.

'Clear the rails,' said Reiner. 'We must light the fuses and cut the anchor. One got away. They'll be coming back.'

The Blackhearts kicked and rolled slave-rat bodies off the rails. On the cart, Gert began checking the powder kegs. After a second, he groaned.

'Captain,' he said. 'They've pulled the match cord.'

'The what?'

'The fuses. They've taken them from the powder. And I don't see 'em.'

Reiner cursed. 'Check the bodies.'

The Blackhearts frisked all the rat-corpses, both slave and soldier, but none had the match cord.

'Captain,' said Pavel. 'They're coming.'

Reiner looked up. Far down the slanting passage a purple light was moving along the walls. 'Ranald's loaded dice!'

'Can y'just stuff bits of rag in and light them?' asked Pavel.

Reiner shook his head. 'The engineers would have timed it to a nicety. Too short and the cart blows before it reaches the tunnel. Too long and the rats snuff 'em when the cart hits the bottom.'

'Somebody would have to ride down with it, torch in hand,' said Franka. 'But that would be suicide.'

Reiner nodded. Someone would have to light the powder by hand just as the cart reached the ratmen's tunnel, but whoever did it... Reiner looked around, trying to decide who he could most afford to lose. His eyes fell upon Dag. The boy had been trouble from the beginning – a loose cannon who had done more harm than good, and whom no one in the company could trust. And he was fiercely – foolishly – loyal to Reiner. He would do it if Reiner asked. On the other hand, the boy was so scatterbrained and unreliable that it was better than even odds he would muck it up. He cursed. There was no time to think. He had to make a choice now. He...

'I do,' said Giano.

Everyone looked up.

'What?' said Reiner.

The Tilean was white faced. He swallowed. 'I do. This I want whole my life. I vow revenging on ratmans ever they kill my family. How I can kill more ratmans than here? With sword and bow, I kill ten, twenty, fifty? This I do, I kill hundred, thousand.'

'But, lad, you'll die,' said Hals.

Franka looked horrified. 'You can't.'

'We need you,' said Reiner. He could pick out the faces of the advancing ratmen now. There were thirty or more, all warriors.

'You need me do this,' said Giano. 'I get torch.' He turned and ran back up the corridor out of sight.

The others looked at each other blankly.

'Will you let him do this?' asked Franka.

'Someone has to,' said Reiner.

'Aye,' said Pavel, his eyes sliding toward Dag like Reiner's had done. 'But...'

'Someone who can do it,' said Reiner. He turned. 'Gert, chop open the kegs. As many as you can.'

Gert nodded and climbed on the cart, drawing his hand axe. He began staving in the tops of the kegs.

Giano reappeared carrying two torches. He hopped onto the back of the cart and swung his legs in. Jergen stepped to the anchor rope and raised his sword.

Giano faced Reiner. He swallowed again. 'Captain, you good man. I happy to fight for you. Grazie.'

'You are a good man too, Ostini. Giano.' There was a lump in Reiner's throat. He forced it down. 'Shallya receive you.'

The ratmen were a hundred paces away. They were sprinting.

Gert jumped down off the cart. 'Ready.'

Giano raised a torch in salute. 'Cut rope.'

Reiner tried to think of something noble to say, but Jergen didn't hesitate. He chopped through the heavy hawser with a single stroke and the cart began rolling down the sloping rails. Giano threw his arms wide and opened his mouth. At first Reiner thought he was screaming, but his cry became a word, and Reiner realized he was singing some wild Tilean song.

'Damned fool,' said Hals thickly.

Franka turned away, hand over her eyes. Reiner heard her sob.

The cart rapidly picked up speed. The approaching ratmen saw it coming and threw themselves to the left and right, but there were too many of them. They couldn't get out of the way. As the cart blasted through them, they were thrown up like a bow wave, pin-wheeling and smashing against the walls. Some were cut in half under the iron wheels. A few got caught on the sides and were dragged, heads bouncing and cracking as they hit each successive tie.

And then the cart was gone, vanishing into the black of the passage beyond the ratmen's purple light. Reiner stared after it for a moment, but the surviving ratmen were picking themselves up and finding their weapons.

'Right then,' he said hollowly. 'Let's be off.'

He started up the passage with the others following, their faces grim.

'But how do we know it worked?' asked Hals, as they ran. 'How do we know the poor lad didn't kill his fool self for naught?'

'We don't' said Reiner. They reached their line of torches, now two fewer. He picked one up. 'We'll just have to pray.' He looked back down the tunnel. 'Come on now, hurry. We don't want those rats catching us up. And all that powder might shake things up down–'

Before he could finish there was a huge boom, and a blast of hot air hit them like a ram. Reiner clapped his hands to his ears, which felt like they might explode from the pressure. The shock came a second later. It knocked them all off their feet. Before they hit the floor another thunderclap deafened them, and then another, each bigger than the one before. The concussions pushed them up the passage like a giant hand shoving at them. Then twin shocks shook the passage so hard that Reiner was lifted off the ground and slammed into the wall. He landed on top of Pavel, who was screaming and holding his ears. Reiner couldn't hear him.

The walls, ceiling and floor cracked, pebbles and dust sifting down on them like snow. A chunk of stone the size of Reiner's head landed next to his foot. Then all was still. Reiner stayed where he was, waiting for more explosions and working his jaw to try and pop his ears. When no blasts came, he sat up. The tunnel spun around him.

'Come on, lads,' he said, staggering to his feet. 'The place might come down any minute.'

'Hey?' said Hals, putting a hand to his ear.

'Say again?' said Gert.

'What?' said Franka.

Reiner could barely hear them. He pointed up the tunnel. 'Run!' he shouted. 'We must run!'

The others nodded and tried to stand, weaving and staggering like drunks. Reiner clung to the wall, dizzier than if he had spun in circles. They started up the hall at a zigzagging trot, stumbling over their own feet. Before they had gone twenty paces a rushing wall of smoke caught them, billowing up out of the passage. At first it had the sharp battlefield tang of blackpowder, but behind that came an eye watering alchemical stink that had them all retching and gagging. Through his tearing eyes Reiner swore that the smoke that buffeted them glowed a faint green.

'Hurry!' he choked.

They ran as hard as they could, covering their faces with their shirts and jerkins as they went.

'Must have hit one of their weird weapons,' rasped Franka beside him.

'Or a whole wagon full,' said Reiner.

THEY RAN OUT of the fireplace into the parlour of the stone house to find Gutzmann lying still and alone on the floor, surrounded by mounds of dead ratmen. The room was filled with a smoky haze.

Reiner stepped to him uneasily. 'General, do you live? Where is Karel?'

Gutzmann raised his head weakly. He smiled. 'Success, then? We... felt it.'

'Aye, but...'

Karel ran in from the foyer. He saluted. 'Captain, I am glad to see you. The ratmen have stopped. After the explosion some turned back, but no more come from the tunnel.'

'Praise Sigmar,' grunted Pavel. 'Maybe Ostini didn't die for nothing.'

Karel turned to him. 'The Tilean is dead?'

'And the Hammer Bearer,' said Reiner.

Karel made the sign of the Hammer and bowed his head.

'I hope it weren't for nothing,' said Hals bitterly. 'So many got out before he blew it. Might not make a difference.'

'They were only beginning to bring their siege engines out,' said Karel. 'So we are saved that.'

'We must return to the fort... immediately,' said Gutzmann. 'But first, cut off a ratman's head and... and give it to me.'

Reiner made a face. 'Whatever for?'

'I shall show it… to the men.' Gutzmann raised an eyebrow. 'As you should have done, when… when you came to me.'

RETURNING TO THE fort was easier said than done, for though no more ratmen poured out of the tunnel, many still milled about in the entry chamber, though whether they meant to dig out their brethren or were just unwilling to continue toward the fort without the full might of their army, Reiner couldn't decide. Either way, it made exit that way an impossibility.

'The hill track,' said Gutzmann from the stretcher Pavel and Hals had made of their two spears and a red brocade drapery. A bundle of blankets shielded him against the cold. He cradled the severed head of a rat in his arms like a baby. 'The chief engineer told me once. They cut a… a hidden staircase behind an upstairs closet. It leads… to the mountainside above the… the mine, and from there to the fort.' He chuckled. 'In case of cave-in, he said. But I begin to think it had… another purpose.'

'We'll look for it,' Reiner said, wincing. Gutzmann's words bubbled in his throat and he had to take two breaths for each sentence. He was not long for the world.

After a mad search through the upstairs rooms – a series of beautiful, stonework suites that the engineers had turned into a fetid dormitory hung with grimy clothes and littered with papers, books, and the strange tools of their trade – they found the stairs at last behind a door in the back of a closet in what had once been a grand boudoir. The secret panel was opened by pressing in the eyes of a bas-relief griffin that stood rampant above the closet door. Behind it, a crude, narrow spiral staircase had been cut into the rock. It was too tight, and the angle too steep, to manoeuvre Gutzmann's stretcher, so Jergen, the sturdiest of the men, carried him on his back.

After a hundred steps, the stairway ended at a stone door. When they pressed a lever, the door swung in smoothly, revealing a small cave.

Reiner stepped into it cautiously. Some animal made the cave its home, but it was not here now. He crept to the jagged mouth and peeked out. The cave opened onto a narrow goat path high up on a sharply sloping mountainside. Below were the outbuildings and the fortifications of the mine, almost invisible in the cloud cloaked night.

Reiner beckoned the others forward and he stepped onto the path. The wind that had blown them into the mines was still whipping around the crags. He shivered as the others filed out, Hals and Pavel once again carrying Gutzmann on his stretcher.

The general pointed south. 'Follow the path. It leads to the... the hills above the fort. You will find a branch that... brings you beyond. To the Aulschweig side. As long as we still hold... the south wall...'

Reiner motioned the Blackhearts forward, then walked beside the general. 'This path allows one to circumvent the fort?'

Gutzmann grinned. 'This and others. The bandits... They go where they please. But not... not worth defending. No army could navigate... this.'

Reiner caught his balance as the wind nearly blew him off the mountain. He swallowed. 'No. I suppose not.'

They hurried on as quickly as they could, but it was difficult going, particularly for Pavel and Hals, carrying Gutzmann. There were places where the path went straight up a rock face and the general had to be passed up it from hand to hand. In other places it was barely a lip of stone on the edge of a cliff and his weight threatened to pull them into space. At one point the path went under a jutting rock and everyone had to crawl. Pavel and Hals pushed and pulled Gutzmann along on their hands and knees.

But though they bumped and jarred him, and twisted him into undignified and uncomfortable positions, not once did the general complain, only urged them to go faster.

'If those vermin have hurt my men,' he said more than once, 'I shall slaughter all of them, above and... and below ground. They shall be... wiped from the earth.'

It took the company twice as long to reach the latitude of the fort as it would have if they had walked the pass, but at last they came over the spine of a pine covered hill and saw it below them. The battle had not yet begun. The rats were still forming up in the darkness of the pass, keeping out of sight of the tent camp. They needn't have bothered. No one manned the north walls. No one was in the camp. The entire force of the fort was on the great south wall, crossbows loaded, handguns primed, cannon ready, all waiting for the Army of Aulschweig to march up the southern pass. Shaeder's ruse was a complete success.

Reiner wished he could reach out an unimaginably long arm and tap the defenders on their collective shoulder, make them turn about and take notice of the menace to their rear. But a warning was impossible. Even if he shouted at the top of his lungs no one would hear him.

'Skirmishers!' said Franka, pointing.

Reiner looked. Furtive figures were snaking through the empty camp. The first of them were already at the north wall, peeking through the undefended gate.

He turned to Gutzmann in his stretcher. 'It begins, general. We must hurry. Tell us where the path to the far side is.'

The general didn't respond.

Reiner stepped closer. 'Sir?'

Gutzmann was staring up at the stars.

Reiner knelt beside him. His hand was halfway to his mouth, which gaped open. It looked like he had paused in the middle of a cough.

'General.'

Reiner shook him. He was stiff and cold. Hals and Pavel moaned and lowered the stretcher to the ground. The others gathered around.

Reiner grunted and hung his head. 'What a bastard Sigmar is,' he said under his breath.

'Hey?' said Hals. 'Blasphemy?'

'Sigmar says he wants his champions to die fighting, and here's one of his best, and what does he do?' Reiner swallowed. 'He pinches out his flame right before the fight of his life.' Reiner looked up at the sky. 'You can kiss my arse, you great hairy ape.'

Pavel, Hals and Karel shied away from him, as if afraid they might get caught by the thunderbolt that would shortly stab out of the sky and burn Reiner to a crisp. The others shifted uncomfortably.

'We must still warn them,' said Karel at last.

'To what purpose?' said Reiner, standing. 'They'll know soon enough. Look.'

The others followed his gaze. The ratmen were on the move, a living carpet that filled the pass from wall to wall. Dotted among them were a few weird artillery pieces, but not, at least, any siege towers. Those hadn't made it out. As the rat army exited the pass it spread out like molasses spilling from a jar, and flowed through the neat ranks of tents. No alarm had yet sounded. If there had been any guards on the wall, the skirmishers had silenced them.

'But we could warn the men Shaeder sent south,' said Franka. 'If we reached them quickly enough they might make the difference.'

'Aye,' said Reiner. 'They might, but they're led by Nuemark, who is undoubtedly in on Shaeder's scheme. He'll kill us before he listens to us.'

Karel frowned. 'I think we must still try.'

Reiner nodded unhappily. 'Aye, lad. I'm afraid we must.'

'There is some cavalry there,' said Franka. 'I heard Nuemark calling the captains. They can't be in on it, can they?'

'No,' said Reiner. 'I doubt it.' He frowned, thinking. 'Matthais will be there, under Halmer. Maybe we can convince them to stage a mutiny.'

Hals cursed and looked down at Gutzmann. 'Why'd y'have to die, y'mad jagger. If it was ye coming to 'em, the whole lot'd follow you to the Chaos Wastes themselves.'

Pavel nodded. 'That they would. And I'd join 'em.'

'We'd best bring him with us,' said Reiner. 'Him and his rat head are the best evidence we have of Shaeder's treachery.'

Pavel and Hals lifted Gutzmann on their spear stretcher again, and the party started south.

# SEVENTEEN
## To Betray a Traitor!

THE BLACKHEARTS CONTINUED along the ridge, doing their best to find the path among the black shadows of the thick pine forest. A half league beyond the fort, they found Gutzmann's split and followed it down to the floor of the pass. Hals and Pavel continued to carry Gutzmann, but they were no longer so gentle.

Just as Reiner and the others stepped onto the road, an eerie echo of a thousand voices rose behind them. Everyone stopped and looked back towards the fort. The roar continued, punctuated with faint crashes and explosions.

Gert cursed. 'It's begun.'

Reiner nodded, a shiver running up his spine.

Hals made the sign of the hammer. 'Sigmar protect ye, lads.'

They turned and jogged quickly south, but less than a league later they slowed again. There were torches ahead. They drew their weapons. Reiner pulled Gutzmann's blankets over his face.

Four silhouettes stood before them. One held up his hand. Reiner could see he was a sergeant of pike. 'Halt! Who comes?' he said. 'Stand where you are.'

Reiner saluted and stepped into the light. 'Sergeant, we come from the fort with desperate news. The invasion from Aulschweig was a trick. We are attacked from the north instead. The detachment must return immediately.'

But the man didn't appear to be listening. He peered behind Reiner. 'Who's that behind you? How many are you?'

The others came up around Reiner.

'We are eight,' he said, continuing to walk forward. 'Now let us pass. We must deliver our message.'

'Er.' The sergeant stepped back. He shot a glance towards the trees. 'Can't allow that. We've orders to… to stop anyone who might be…' He looked at the trees again. 'Er, be an Aulschweig spy.'

Without warning Reiner leapt ahead and put his sword to the sergeant's throat. The man's companions stepped forward, crying out, but then stopped, not daring to move. The Blackhearts spread out to encircle them.

'Call 'em out,' Reiner said. 'Call 'em out or you're dead.'

The sergeant swallowed, his adam's apple pressing against the tip of Reiner's blade as he did. 'I… I don't know what you mean.'

Reiner extended his arm a little, pricking the man's skin. 'Don't you? Shall I tell you, since you've forgotten?'

The sergeant was too frightened to respond.

'You are here to stop anyone from the fort from warning Nuemark's force,' said Reiner, then stopped, holding up a hand. 'No. I am wrong. You are to let one man through. A messenger from Shaeder, who will make sure that Nuemark arrives just in the nick, and not a moment before.' He raised the sergeant's chin with his blade. 'Do I have the right of it?'

The man sighed, and waved a defeated hand towards the woods. 'Come out, Grint. Lannich. He has us.'

After a moment, there was a snapping of twigs on either side of the road and two sullen handgunners stepped out of the brush.

'We should kill you for this,' said Reiner. 'But there will be enough Empire blood spilled this day.'

'We was only following Shaeder's orders,' said the sergeant.

'To betray your general. Very nice.'

'To betray a traitor!' the sergeant said.

Reiner laughed unpleasantly. 'Well, ease your mind. Gutzmann is betrayed and Shaeder commands. But he needs your help in the fort's defence. Leave your weapons here and return. With luck, the men on the walls won't mistake you for Aulschweigers.'

'But how are we to help in the defence if you take our weapons?' the sergeant pleaded.

Reiner sneered. 'You will find plenty of weapons in the hands of the comrades who are dead by your treachery.'

The sergeant reluctantly began unbuckling his sword belt. His men followed his example.

AFTER SUPPLEMENTING THEIR kit with the guns, swords and spears of the sergeant's men, and sending them scurrying for the fort, Reiner and the Blackhearts continued south through the pass. After a quarter of an hour, the mountains began to draw in and grow steeper.

'There they are,' said Pavel, pointing forward.

The road twisted behind a screen of trees as it entered Lessner's Narrows, and the armour and helmets of soldiers glinted yellow and orange through the branches in the light of an orderly row of small campfires.

'And there.' Dag pointed towards the highest, narrowest part of the trail. Against the cloudy grey of the night sky, Reiner and the others could see the outlines of mounted scouts watching for the army that wasn't coming.

Reiner called a halt and squatted down in the road, thinking. 'There will be a picket, and it will be Nuemark's greatswords. He doesn't want any messenger to come except the one he expects. We'll need to draw 'em off.' He raised his head suddenly. 'Dag. How would you like to make a little trouble?'

Dag grinned. 'Ye want me to kill 'em for ye?'

'No, no,' said Reiner hastily. 'Only start a fight. I want you to run down the road like a madman, screaming about ratmen attacking the fort, aye?'

Dag chuckled. 'Aye.'

'Be loud. Act drunk. And when the picket comes, punch as many of them in the nose as you can, aye?'

Dag smacked his fist into his palm eagerly. 'Oh, aye. Oh, aye. Thank'ee, sir.'

Reiner looked around to be sure the rest were ready to move, then nodded at Dag. 'Right then, off you go.'

Dag giggled as he stood, and began trotting off down the road that curved around the stand of trees.

The others looked at Reiner, eyes wide.

Hals voiced what they all were thinking. 'They'll kill the boy.'

Reiner nodded. 'Oh, aye.' He stood. 'When the shouting starts, we cut through the woods. Got it?' He hoped none of them could see the flush that rose on his cheeks. As much as the lad deserved it, Reiner still felt ashamed. It was like kicking a dog who'd done wrong. The dog wouldn't understand why you hurt it.

Franka looked up at him, eyes unreadable, as the company moved towards the woods.

Reiner swallowed a growl. 'Don't tell me you're disappointed in me?'

Franka shook her head. 'No. On this I am with you.' She shuddered and squeezed his hand.

From a way off came a cry. 'Ratmen! Save us! Save us, brothers! Ratmen attack the fort! Get up ye sluggards! Ride! Ride!'

Reiner could see movement in the camp, soldiers turning their heads and standing. There were more furtive movements as well. Men in the trees closed in on the road, quietly drawing weapons.

'That's our cue,' said Reiner.

The Blackhearts started through the woods, angling away from Dag's shouting. Other voices soon joined him, shouting challenges and questions.

'Take me to Nuemark,' shouted Dag. 'I wan' tell him about the ratmen!'

The Blackhearts reached the far edge of the trees. The makeshift camp spread out before them. The infantry sat in formation on the road, looking towards Dag's shouts. The lancers waited in a slanting meadow off to the left, their horses tethered in neat lines. A small command tent had been set up between the two forces. Nuemark's Carrolsburg greatswords stood on guard before it.

Dag's shouts ended in a yelp of pain as Reiner peered through the trees beside the meadow, searching for Matthais among the lancers who stood or squatted by little fires, rubbing their hands and stamping their feet in the cold wind that swooped down from the mountain. At last Reiner saw him, sitting on a flat rock, talking to Captain Halmer.

Reiner groaned. Halmer had disliked him from the moment he rode out onto the parade ground that first day. Reiner didn't want to have to tell his story in front of him. He'd call for his arrest before he got out two words. But there wasn't time to wait for him to leave. The battle at the fort was raging. Every second meant more Empire men dead.

Matthais and Halmer were three ranks in. Reiner was trying to think of a way to reach them without being taken for an interloper, when the answer nearly stumbled on him. A lancer strode into the woods and began relieving himself against a tree not ten paces from the Blackhearts. They held their breath, but he didn't look their way.

When he had gone, Reiner turned and took the wrapped rat-head from Gutzmann's dead hands. He tucked it under his arm. 'Wish me luck,' he said.

The Blackhearts murmured their replies, and he started for the edge of the woods, undoing his flies. As he stepped into the meadow he began doing them up again, as if returning from a piss. No one remarked his passage. He walking as nonchalantly as he could manage to Matthais and Halmer and squatted down beside them.

'Evening, Matthais,' he said.

'Evening, lancer,' said Matthais, turning. 'What can I…' He stopped dead, his jaw hanging open. 'Rein…'

'Don't shout, lad. I beg you.'

'But you're meant to be in the brig!'

Halmer turned at that. 'Who? Isn't this…? You're Meyerling. Gutzmann put you in stir.'

Reiner nodded. 'Yes, captain. I escaped. But I have…'

'Sigmar, sir!' choked Halmer. 'You've some nerve. Where are Nuemark's guard. I'll have you…'

'Please, captain, I beg you to hear me out.'

'Hear you out? I'll be damned if…'

'Sir, please. I won't fight. You can take me to Nuemark and be done with me. But I beg you to listen first.' He looked at Matthais. 'Matthais. Won't you speak for me?'

Matthais sneered. 'Why should I? You came here to assassinate the general. You lied to me.'

Halmer stood, drawing his sword. 'Enough of this. Give me your sword, villain.'

'This is not a lie,' said Reiner, angrily, and flipped open his bloody parcel. The rat-head's death filmed eyes stared blindly up at them. Matthais and Halmer gasped. Reiner closed it again.

'Now will you listen?' he asked.

Halmer sat down on the rock with a thump. He stared at the bundle. 'What… what was that.'

'A ratman,' said Matthais, wonderingly. 'So all that was true? The ratmen in the mine? Attacking the fort?'

'Ratmen don't exist,' said Halmer, angrily. 'It must be something else.'

'Would you like another look?' asked Reiner. He opened the bundle again. Halmer and Matthais stared.

Halmer shook his head, amazed. 'It seems incredible, but I must believe my own eyes.'

'Thank you, captain,' said Reiner. 'Now, believing that, will you also believe what I told Gutzmann about Shaeder? That he is in league with these horrors?'

Matthais made a face. 'But Gutzmann proved you wrong about that. Shaeder would never betray the Empire, and certainly not for gold.'

Reiner nodded. 'I was wrong about him betraying the Empire. He was betraying Gutzmann because Gutzmann was betraying the Empire. He is jealous of the general, as you may know, and so meant to ruin his name and take his position in one sly move.'

Halmer and Matthais stared at him, agog.

'Shaeder meant to allow the ratmen to attack the fort, and make it seem that Gutzmann was in league with them. Then by defeating the vermin, he would prove to Altdorf that he was the man to replace the traitor.'

Halmer closed his mouth. His lips pressed into a thin line. 'That sounds like Shaeder.'

'Unfortunately,' continued Reiner, 'he has been too clever for his own good. He planned to blow up the ratmen's tunnel before their full strength emerged, but they discovered his black powder and stopped him.'

'What!' barked Halmer.

'They...?' Matthais jumped up. 'You mean this happens now? The rats attack the fort now?'

Reiner hauled him down. 'Be quiet you fool!' He lowered his voice as nearby lancers looked around. 'Yes. The rats are attacking as we speak. Shaeder intended to call you back to make a last minute rescue, and so increase his glory, but he has many more ratmen to deal with than he expected.'

'I don't understand,' said Halmer. 'Where is the general? Is he not in command of the fort?'

'No,' said Matthais, his face falling. 'Shaeder drew him away to the mines. I remember now. He invited him to see the tunnel. The devious...'

'Gutzmann is dead,' said Reiner.

The two lancers gasped, staring.

Reiner nodded. 'He died fighting Shaeder's Hammers in the mine.' He looked toward the woods. 'My men carry him.'

Halmer and Matthais made the sign of the hammer and bowed their heads. Then Halmer stood. 'We must return at once. We must tell Nuemark.'

'But he is Shaeder's creature,' said Reiner. 'He already knows.'

'Not all. Surely when he learns that Shaeder's trick has failed…'

'If he believes it.'

There was a sudden clatter of hooves on the road. Reiner, Matthais and Halmer turned. A rider was pulling up before Nuemark's tent.

The obercaptain stepped out as if on cue. 'What news?' he asked in a loud voice. 'Is something amiss at the fort?'

Reiner rolled his eyes at this display. The man would never make an actor.

Nuemark frowned, confused, as the rider got off his horse and whispered in his ear instead of crying his news to the heavens. Reiner didn't need to read the rider's lips to know what the message was, for even in the uncertain flicker of the torches, he could see the obercaptain pale as he took it in. He looked around, then motioned to his infantry captains, and dragged the rider into his tent.

'What does he do?' asked Matthais. 'Why isn't he calling us to order? Why aren't we getting under way?'

They waited a moment, thinking the obercaptain would come out again and make his announcement, but he did not.

'He's bunking it,' said Reiner. 'He's going to cut and run.'

'Impossible,' said Halmer. 'Leaving the fort in enemy hands would be treason.'

Reiner shook his head. 'You saw the fear in him. He's in there now, looking for an excuse. I'll lay odds on it.'

'But we must go back!' Matthais insisted. He turned to Halmer. 'We can't leave when there's a chance!'

'Unfortunately I am not the obercaptain,' Halmer growled. 'I cannot give the order.' He glared at the company of greatswords standing before Nuemark's tent. 'And I wouldn't care to fight through his Carrolburgers to usurp him.'

Reiner's head lifted slowly and he turned to look at the captain, eyes wide.

Halmer drew back, uneasy. 'What?'

Reiner grinned at him. 'Captain, you have given me an idea. Will you allow me?'

Halmer nodded. 'Speak.'

Reiner leaned in. 'We will need a horse, armour, a lance, and as much rope as we can gather.'

# EIGHTEEN
## Shoulder Your Weapons

A SHORT WHILE later, Infantry Obercaptain Nuemark stepped from his tent with his four infantry captains behind him. He was sweating despite the cold night. The messenger he had brought in with him was conspicuously absent.

He spoke to the cavalry captains, then mounted his horse and waited while they sent their corporals to bring the lancers and knights down to stand alongside the foot soldiers who were rising and turning to face him at their sergeants' urging.

When all were assembled, Nuemark saluted the troops and cleared his throat. 'Friends.' He tried again, raising his voice. 'Friends. Comrades. We have been betrayed by one whom we held dear. Our removal here was a trick perpetrated by General Gutzmann. There is no army coming from Aulschweig. The general has turned against us and sided with an army of monsters. The fort is overrun.'

A low, questioning murmur came from the troops, and quickly became a roar of disbelief and anger.

'Yer off yer head, Nuemark,' cried a handgunner.

The obercaptain waved his hands for silence. 'It is true! I have just received word from the fort. General Gutzmann attacked the fort at the head of an inhuman army. Lord Shaeder defended it as best he could, but at half strength he could not hold it. It is lost.'

The roar became a howl, and the troops, both infantry and cavalry surged forward. Only the curses and punches of their sergeants and corporals held them back.

'Believe me,' cried Nuemark, his hands shaking. 'I am as grieved and outraged as you are. But we cannot prevail. We must retire to Aulschweig and help Baron Caspar defend the border until word can be sent to Altdorf and reinforcements can be brought.'

'If General Gutzmann has taken the fort,' shouted a knight, 'then we are with General Gutzmann, whoever he sides with.'

'Fools! You don't understand! General Gutzmann is dead!' bellowed Nuemark. 'Killed by his vile compatriots!'

The howl dropped to a murmur as the troops took this in. They were stunned. They asked each other if such an impossible thing could be true.

Into this lull came a new voice, calling, 'General Gutzmann is not dead! The fort is not lost!'

The troops turned. Nuemark and his captains looked up.

Down the road that curved around the stand of trees came a knight on horseback, holding aloft a lance tied with pennons of blue and white. He was led by two men, and followed by a ragged company. As they walked into the light, the troops erupted in cheers, for the knight was General Gutzmann.

Reiner, holding the general's bridle, raised his voice again. 'Your general is here, lads! To lead you against the vermin who storm the fort! And against the coward Shaeder, who betrayed us all.'

The cheers echoed off the mountains. Reiner saw Captain Halmer and Matthais and their company at the front of the troops, doing as he had bidden them and crying loudly for Shaeder's head. Good men.

Nuemark was staring, his jaw unhinged. The infantry captains were the same. Reiner beamed. Was ever an entrance so perfectly timed? Had even the great Sierck ever written so stirring a scene? It was perfect. A masterpiece, worth every moment of sweat and furious, grisly effort. For it hadn't been easy. Gutzmann had been frozen with rigor mortis and they had had to break his limbs to get him into Matthais's armour. They had had to clean his face and cut off his eyelids so his eyes would stay open. Matthais had wept. Karel had vomited.

Tying the general to Halmer's second horse had been more difficult than expected as well. He weighed a ton, and tended to hang to one side. Fortunately, Matthais's cloak was made for winter weather, long and heavy, and hid a multitude of ropes, straps and stays. Unfortunately, the youth's head was smaller than Gutzmann's and they had had to force his helmet down over the general's brow most cruelly. It had been essential however. The ruse wouldn't work in full light. Not even in the flickering light of a torch. They needed the shadows of a helmet to hide the stillness of Gutzmann's face.

'Command us, general!' cried a lancer. 'Lead us to the fort.'

Reiner swallowed. Now came the hard part. He raised his voice. 'The general was terribly wounded defending the fort and cannot speak nor fight, but he can yet ride. He will lead you! He will command you! Mount up, knights and lancers. Mount up, pistoliers! Shoulder your weapons, ye pike and sword and gun! We've a battle to win!'

The troops cheered.

'Wait!' cried Nucmark, desperately trying to shout them down. He seemed totally undone by the situation. 'We dare not... we... This is madness! The fort is taken, I tell you! Even with the general at our head we cannot hope to prevail. We must retire!'

'Don't listen to him,' shouted Matthais. 'He is Shaeder's creature! He betrays us as well.'

'A lie!' yelped Nuemark. 'I only urge caution!'

'And look what he betrays us to,' said Reiner. He nodded to Franka, who stood in the shadows behind Gutzmann's horse. She stepped back, pulling surreptitiously on a rope that ran up under the general's cloak. Gutzmann's arm raised – somewhat mechanically – but at least it raised, thought Reiner, exhaling with relief. Hanging from the general's hand was the bloody head of the ratman.

'Look what foul monsters kill our brothers as we speak!'

The troops stared, repulsed, at the long-nosed, long-toothed head, with its mangy brown fur. Its black eyes glittered evilly in the torchlight, looking strangely more alive than Gutzmann's.

'The ratmen!' Reiner cried. 'The ratmen are real! They are slaying our comrades!'

The troops bellowed their fear and rage. Captain Halmer and Matthais mounted their horses and clattered to Gutzmann's side as Reiner turned Gutzmann's horse and Franka lowered his arm.

'Form up!' Halmer yelled. 'Form up behind your general, lads! We march for the fort, and victory!' He winked down at Reiner as the men cheered and began lining up in their ranks. 'Nice work, pistol. You've a talent for mummery. I'll handle him now.'

Reiner bowed, hiding a smile. The captain wasn't about to allow Reiner to be Gutzmann's voice for a second longer than necessary. He turned away as Halmer began barking at one of Matthais's lances. 'Skelditz, ride to Aulschweig and remind Baron Caspar of his sworn duty to help the Empire defend this border. Ask him to bring as many men as he can, as swiftly as he can.'

Wandering through the column in search of the Blackhearts, Reiner saw Nuemark before his tent, sitting slack on his horse. He stared at the ground while one by one his captains deserted him to take up command of their companies.

The Blackhearts were forming up in the last rank of the first company of pike. Reiner joined them.

'Not riding with the pistols, captain?' asked Hals.

'No fear,' said Reiner. 'I've no wish to be first in. If I thought we could get away with it, I'd wait here until it was all over. We've done our part.'

'No thank'ee,' said Pavel, grinning as he touched his missing ear. 'I owe them ratties a few lopped ears. I want at 'em.'

'Aye,' said Karel. 'Me as well.'

'And me,' said Gert.

Jergen nodded.

'Hoy, captain!' came a voice.

The company looked around. Dag was stumbling towards them, waving and grinning. He had a black eye and a missing tooth.

'I did good, hey?' he said, falling in with them.

Reiner flushed. 'Aye, it worked. Er, sorry you were ill used.'

Dag shrugged. 'Had worse.' He pointed to his purple eye. 'And I broke three of this one's fingers, so I got mine in.'

'Well, that's a comfort at least.' Reiner turned away, exchanging uncomfortable glances with the others. The boy seemed to have no inkling that Reiner had hung him out to dry.

At the head of the column, Matthais raised his bugle and blew 'forward,' and the column got under way. Reiner groaned as the foot soldiers fell into a brisk trot behind the cavalry. He couldn't remember the last time he had rested. It felt a decade since they had escaped the cell under the keep, and not a single break from running, fighting and sneaking since. Oh, for the quiet life of a gambler.

The pikemen on the other hand were well rested and eager for action, inspired by the presence of General

Gutzmann at their head. They made the trip back to the fort in half the time the Blackhearts had taken, and Reiner and Gert and some of the others were gasping when Halmer slowed a half a league from the fort.

Reiner looked ahead. A trio of men, wounded and ragged, had waved down the column and were now jogging beside the captain and talking to him in urgent tones. Halmer nodded and saluted, and the men stepped to the side and watched the column pass.

Reiner called out to them. 'What news, lads?

'Bad, sir,' said one, a lanky fellow with a wounded arm. 'Very bad. The rat-things have all the fort but the keep and the main gatehouse. Even the great south wall is theirs. And there are many dead.'

Reiner saluted the man. 'Thank'ee for the warning.'

'Sigmar!' moaned Karel. 'Are we too late then?'

'They won't have an easy time breaching the keep,' said Reiner. 'There may still be hope.'

As the black battlements of the great south wall rose in the distance, Halmer stood and turned in his saddle, calling back to his captains. Reiner could only just hear him. 'Pass back General Gutzmann's commands! Cavalry will enter the fort at the charge! Infantry will follow and hold our position! Do not allow the enemy behind you!'

Halmer's captains repeated the orders to the men behind them and the command echoed down the column.

Two hundred yards out, Matthais raised his bugle again and began blowing 'rally,' a three note tantara, as loud and as often as he could.

Reiner and the others craned their necks, trying to see around the horses before them. Reiner found his teeth were grinding with tension. If the ratmen had since taken the gatehouse, then this attack was over before it began. They would be locked out of their own fort, a besieging army with no ladders, siege engines or cannon.

At last Pavel breathed. 'It opens.'

Reiner leaned to one side and saw it through pumping horse legs – the iron portcullis rising, the massive oak doors behind it swinging in. He sighed with relief.

Matthais's bugle blew 'charge' and the horsemen before the Blackhearts' adopted company of pikemen began to pull away. Reiner fought down a surge of regret as he watched the lancers and pistoliers move through the familiar rising rhythms of trot, canter, and gallop. What a thrill to be sprinting in, pistols at his shoulders, closing with the enemy. But then he saw a lancer fall, and another, and heard the reports of the ratmen's jezzails firing from the walls. He shivered. Better not to be a gunner's first target.

Led by Gutzmann, who held aloft the borrowed lance in his dead hand, Halmer, Matthais and the lancers plunged into the black hole of the gate four abreast, howling fierce battle-cries. The knights and pistoliers charged in behind them without pause.

Pikemen fell, screaming, to Reiner's left and right in a rain of bullets as the company ran after the horsemen. The bullets seemed to explode on impact, ripping through breastplates as if they were muslin. At last they reached the gate and ran out of the deadly hail. The thunder of hundreds of boot heels ricocheted off the walls of the arched tunnel, almost drowning out the roar of battle that came from within. Reiner drew his pistols. Franka, Dag and Gert readied their bows and crossbows. The others drew their swords.

And then they were in.

Directly ahead, the lancers and knights hit the back of a solid mass of ratmen with an impact Reiner could feel through his feet. Rat soldiers flew through the air, blood spraying, as the first rank of knights raised them on their lances. More were crushed under the charge. Reiner saw an iron shod hoof pop a ratman's skull like an egg. The ratmen recoiled from the unexpected attack, screeching and terrified.

In the centre of the line, Gutzmann's horse reared and kicked while the general sat bolt upright, the pennons of his lance waving bravely. And it seemed that nature – or perhaps Sigmar – conspired with Reiner to help him with his grand illusion, for just as the charge hit, the clouds above the fort broke and the light of Mannslieb shot through, haloing Gutzmann in an unearthly blue-white glow. His armour gleamed, the rat head he held shone silver and black.

Rat gunners, drawing a bead on the beacon of the general's breastplate, raised their jezzails and fired. Bullets punched hole after hole in his armour, but Gutzmann remained ram-rod straight, not even flinching. The ratmen before him fell back, awed, at this miracle.

Inspired by their general's superhuman fortitude, the lancers and knights pressed forward, their ardour for battle redoubled. They left their lances in the backs of the first rank of rats, then drew their swords and hammers and laid about them in a fury. The pistoliers swung left and right, emptying their pieces into the ratmen, then wheeling in to meet them sabre to sword. The infantry captains screamed at their troops to block the sides, and the four companies of pike spread out in a long curving line as the force's lone company of handgunners fired into the ratmen's right wing. Reiner and the Blackhearts ran in the last rank of their adopted pikes to close with the rats on the left.

They had to chase them, however, for already the ratmen were retreating. Panicked by the sudden shock to their rear, and as unnerved by Gutzmann's invulnerability as his troops were inspired by it, they fell back in confusion, leaving a putrid animal musk in their wake.

'By Sigmar,' said Hals. 'We've done it. They've broken.'

'To the keep! cried Halmer.

The knights and lancers surged forward, but were not able to overtake the ratmen's scampering retreat. The rest of the troops followed at a run, and found themselves stumbling over the bodies of fallen men and horses, lying on the blood slicked flagstones. They had been hacked to pieces.

Karel choked as he tripped over a gilded helm. 'Captain, look! Cavalry Obercaptain Oppenhauer! Was he caught unawares?'

Reiner looked back. Oppenhauer's round, rosy-cheeked face was gazing at the sky, an expression of horror frozen upon it. It was missing an eye, and his beard was matted with clotting blood. His breastplate was pierced with the heads of three halberds. The jolly old fellow didn't look right without a grin on his face. Reiner swallowed as he ran on. 'They're in full kit. They tried a sortie.'

'A sortie? But that is madness! A single company?'

Reiner looked darkly at the keep. 'Maybe they were ordered to.'

Karel goggled at him. 'But... but why?'

Reiner shrugged. 'Shaeder continues to remove all who might challenge him.'

Ahead of them, the sea of ratmen surrounded the keep, and lapped halfway up it like drifts of dirty brown snow. Some mounted ladders, but just as many were climbing the great piles of their dead that hugged the walls. The defenders fired down into them from the battlements, killing many, but never enough. The keep's gate burned with a weird green fire.

To the right, the stables and some of the other outbuildings were aflame as well, painting the scene a garish orange. From above, cannons roared, and stones and masonry exploded from the walls of the keep. Reiner could see ratkin crews silhouetted on the main battlements as they worked the fort's great guns.

'Our own cannon, turned against us,' said Gert, bitterly.

As they ran through their fellows, the fleeing ratkin alerted their besieging brethren to the threat at their back, and they turned, rat commanders laying about them with whips and staves and squealing orders. In seconds what had been the ratmen's unprotected flank now bristled with spears and swords.

The cavalry slammed into the ratmen first, but armed only with swords now, and facing a prepared enemy, the charge was not as successful. Reiner saw men and horses go down, impaled on the ratmen's polearms.

Next came the pikes and swords. As the Blackhearts raced toward the ratmen with their pike company, Reiner fired into the seething mass with both pistols, then holstered them and drew his sword. Gert shot his crossbow before tossing it aside to pull his axe. There would be no time to reload. Pavel and Hals began pushing up with their spears to the first rank.

Reiner cursed. 'Stay back, fools! Let the pikes make the charge!'

They ignored him.

The company hit the rat-wall as one, pikes punching their first line back into their second, but there were more behind them, and more behind those. The vermin swarmed forward, trying to overwhelm the men's line with sheer numbers.

'Don't let 'em through!' cried Reiner.

Reiner and the Blackhearts slashed and thrust from the third rank, stabbing at the vermin who attempted to get behind the front line. It mattered not where they struck, there was a furred body there to receive their blades. The ratmen went down like wheat before the reaper, but there were always more – an endless tide of monsters: yellow teeth snapping, curved swords slashing, gashing arms, biting fingers, clawing eyes. Reiner was almost instantly bleeding from a dozen wounds, and pikemen fell all around him. Hals and Pavel were stabbing and thrusting like machines. Jergen spun his sword around him with deadly grace. Gert cleft rat skulls with his axe. Dag flailed like a drunk with a fire iron. Franka lost her dagger in a ratman's ribs and was punching rats with her off hand as she blocked attacks with her short sword.

All along the line, the men of the Empire slowly brought the ratmen to a standstill, and then started to press them back. The gate of the keep was coming into reach. But just as Reiner thought they might break through, men and rats began dropping all around him, screaming and writhing, as exploding bullets ripped through them. The jezzail-rats who held the great south wall had found them. Worse, they had turned the fort's artillery away from the keep. A cannon boomed and a horse reared, its head missing. Another collapsed, legs gone. Another cannon fired and ploughed a trench through the front lines, dismembering man and ratman alike.

'Do they not care about their own troops?' asked Franka, horrified.

Reiner shrugged. 'Would even a ratman like another ratman?'

The knights and lancers redoubled their efforts to reach the keep's gate, in a frenzy now to get out of range of the gunners on the great south wall. They hacked a bloody path through the carpet of ratmen as more and more men fell under the deadly barrage. And the ratmen were flowing around the ends of the men's lines now, trying to surround them. To protect their flanks, the pike companies folded back like two wings, at last meeting behind the cavalry to form a rough square, pressed on all sides by ratmen.

Matthais's bugle blew the rally again and again as Halmer bellowed up at the keep. 'Open up! Open the gates!'

Reiner wondered if that was even possible, for behind the portcullis, the huge wooden doors were a roaring green inferno. Teams of ratmen stood before them, aiming weapons that Reiner recognized from his adventure in their tunnels. A brass tank carried by one rat, connected by a leather hose to a gun aimed by the other that painted the door with flames that stuck like syrup. The great oak beams were being eaten away, and Reiner realized with horror that the ratmen might be thin enough to fit through the iron bars of the portcullis.

'Pistoliers! Handgunners!' came Halmer's cry, and the gunners fired into the flame-crews. Four of the rats jerked and twitched as the bullets smashed into them. A flame gunner dropped his gun as he fell, and it sprayed fire all around, catching his tank-carrying comrade on fire. The burning rat danced and screeched, trying desperately to unbuckle the straps of his unwieldy canister.

The flames spread to his back, and with a blinding explosion, he was no longer there. A boiling ball of flame erupted where he had stood, and knocked the other rat-men in the vicinity flat, catching them on fire.

The first rank of knights were pushed back into the second by the blast, shrieking in pain, bits of red hot brass sticking out of their breastplates and faces. Their horses screamed as well, similarly wounded.

The way to the gate was clear, though it was still aflame. Matthais blew the rally blast again, as Halmer's force pushed forward. Halmer and the other cavalry men screamed up at the keep. 'Open the gate! Open the gate!'

The portcullis didn't move.

Matthais blew his bugle again, then shook his fist at the keep's walls. 'Let us in, curse you!' he cried. His forehead exploded in gore, and he sagged back in his saddle.

Halmer cried out. Reiner looked up. The shot had come from the keep. Someone in the murder room above the gate was shooting at the knights. Another shot fired, and another. Two hit Gutzmann, one in the head, one in the chest. The general never wavered. Matthais, however, toppled slowly off his horse and crashed to the ground, face first, his bugle rattling across the flagstones. Reiner swallowed. The poor lad. A shame for one so faithful to be so faithlessly cut down.

Another shot took Halmer in the shoulder. He gripped his arm and spurred his horse into the lee of the gate. 'What are playing at, y'madmen?' he cried. 'We come to your aid!'

Reiner groaned. He had a fair idea of who was firing on them.

More shots came, but the target was still Gutzmann. The worse problem was that if the portcullis stayed closed Halmer's force would remain completely exposed to the guns on the great south wall, which were picking them off in twos and threes. Halmer rose in his saddle and bellowed at the square of troops. 'Around the keep! Put it between you and the walls!'

The square began to shift around obediently, pressing against the wall so the pikemen only had three sides to defend. Reiner swallowed as he saw one of the giant rat-monsters wading toward them through the rat army.

'Hetsau!'

Reiner turned. Halmer was waving at him.

Reiner hurried to the captain, hunching low, though what protection that was from bullets from above he didn't know.

Halmer was in a heated discussion with the other captains as Reiner stepped up to his horse. 'It's the only way!' he barked, then turned to Reiner. 'Hetsau, you broke out of our keep. How would you like to try breaking in?'

'Er, if it's all the same to you, captain…'

'It wasn't a request, Sigmar take you! Someone must enter the keep to stop those guns and open the cursed gates, someone who ain't afraid to disobey Shaeder.'

'Yes, sir,' said Reiner. 'But how am I…?'

'There's an underground passage from the gatehouse in the great south wall to the keep dungeon.'

Reiner looked back to the gatehouse in the southern wall – the distance they had just come. There was a roiling mass of ratmen in the way. 'Sir…'

'Yes, I know,' snapped Halmer. 'We are discussing that. Someone must get you to the gatehouse, then try to retake the south wall's battlements.'

'Captain,' said a voice behind Reiner. Everyone turned. It was Nuemark. He was almost as pale as his hair. His greatswords were behind him. He swallowed and squared his shoulders. 'Captain. I… I have much to make up for. Let me and my Carrolsburgers do this thing.'

Halmer looked taken aback. 'Er, you… you outrank me, Obercaptain. I will not command you. But if it is your wish….'

'It is my duty.'

'Very well.' Halmer turned to Reiner. 'Gather your men. The obercaptain will escort you.'

Reiner saluted, and returned to the Blackhearts, still fighting in the last rank of their adopted pike company. His stomach sank as if it had been loaded with rocks. Charging across the battlefield under heavy fire from the walls was certain death. On the other hand, staying here outside the fort was certain death as well. Better perhaps to be moving.

'Blackhearts!' he called. 'To me. General's orders.'

The Blackhearts backed out of their rank, allowing their pikeman comrades to fill their gaps, then joined him. The square had now tucked in behind the keep, out of the great south wall's line of fire, and the shooting from the keep had stopped as soon as they had moved away from the gatehouse. In fact, here, handgun and crossbow fire from the keep was supporting them, dropping rats all around Halmer's force.

'What's the job?' asked Hals.

'There's a passage into the keep dungeon from under the main gatehouse. We're to go in and open the gates.' He looked up at the walls. 'And discover who's shooting at the general.'

'A passage into…' Pavel cursed. 'Would've been nice to know that when we was trying to break out, hey?'

Reiner led them to where Nuemark was forming up his twenty greatswords. He looked even more scared than before, his face grey and slick.

Reiner saluted. 'Ready, obercaptain.'

Nuemark nodded. 'Very good.' He turned to his men. 'Swords of Carrolsburg, I have dishonoured your name with my cowardice today, and you should not die that I may make amends. Do not make this sacrifice for me, but to save the lives of your comrades, the men I helped betray to these foul vermin.'

The greatswords drew their weapons, their faces grim. Their sergeant saluted. 'We are ready, obercaptain.' They fell into two rows, one on either side of the Blackhearts, shields on their outer arms. One of them growled in Reiner's ear.

'Y'better be worth it, boy.'

Nuemark turned. 'Gunner captain! When you are ready.'

The captain of the handgunners nodded and signalled his men to advance to the southernmost edge of the square. Nuemark's greatswords and the Blackhearts fell in behind them. The handgunners stopped directly behind a triple rank of pikemen. Every other man knelt. 'Pikemen!' called the gunner captain. 'Make a hole!'

The pikemen looked behind them, then parted ranks. Ratmen tried to flood the hole, but they were not quick enough.

'Fire!' called the gunner captain, and his men unloaded their shot directly into the narrow gap, slaughtering four ranks of ratmen in one volley.

'In!' cried Nuemark. 'Carrolsburgmen charge!'

The greatswords ran into the opening made by the dying ratmen, swords high, roaring the name of their city. Reiner and the Blackhearts ran with them, hunched down to hide behind their massive, armoured bodies and their round shields. The greatswords hit the massed ratmen like a boulder smashing into a mud lake. The sound of steel chopping rat-flesh and rat-bone was music to Reiner's ears.

The party rounded the corner of the keep, a tiny raft of humanity in a swamp of vermin. The greatsword who had growled at Reiner went down beside him, a rat-spear thrust through his groin. He held his killer's severed head in his shield hand. Another Carrolsburger went down on the other side. The others closed ranks.

A third dropped, shrieking, as a bullet ripped through his breastplate. The metal of the breastplate seemed to melt away from the bullet, and the flesh beneath it boiled. The rats on the walls had found them. The Carrolsburgers raised their shields over their heads. Reiner wondered if that would help.

A rat spear darted through between two greatswords and stabbed Reiner through the thigh. He stumbled as his leg gave out, but Gert caught him and hauled him up again.

'Steady, captain.'

Reiner looked down. The wound was deep. Blood was crimsoning his leggings. 'Bollocks!' He couldn't feel it, at least. And then he could, and he grunted. It hurt like fire. He almost fell from the pain. Gert caught him again.

'Can you walk, captain?'

'I'll manage.'

Reiner limped on, his leg jolting agony with every step. Fortunately, the ratmen thinned out the closer they got to the gatehouse, for their attentions were on the keep. But in a way this was also unfortunate, for it made the men clearer targets for the gunners on the wall. Two more greatswords fell, and Dag screamed and shook his left hand. It was missing two fingers. Blood poured from the stumps.

At last they ran under the shadow of the main gate, a thick crowd of rats still harassing them. Nuemark beat on the thick gatehouse door with the pommel of his sword. 'Let us in! Let us in!'

A voice came through the studded wood. 'Commander Shaeder's orders. No one to come though this door.'

'We are on General Gutzmann's orders, curse you!' cried Nuemark. 'Let us in.'

There was a short pause, then Reiner and the others heard bolts being drawn and crossbars raised. Reiner's leg was making him feel nauseous. The gatehouse door swam before him. He gripped the wall and steadied himself.

'All right, captain?' asked Franka.

'Not in the least,' he said. 'But there's nothing for it now.'

The door opened to reveal a few terrified guardsmen. Nuemark shoved Reiner through. 'Skirmishers. In. Hurry.'

The Blackhearts pushed in behind Reiner and turned. It was a tiny room, already crowded with guardsmen, who had to press into the corners to make room for the new arrivals. There was a table and chairs in the centre, racks of weapons on the walls, and a spiral staircase in one corner that led to the battlements. The left wall was filled with the machinery that raised and lowered the portcullises.

The greatswords made to follow the Blackhearts in, but the rats, seeing an opportunity to take the room, attacked furiously. Another greatsword went down. The rest faced out, chopping into the mass of rats.

'In, curse you!' roared Nuemark. His knees were shaking. He nearly lost his grip on his sword.

One by one the greatswords backed into the door as Pavel and Hals stabbed at the rats over their shoulders with their spears. But with each one through the door, those left outside were pressed all the harder. Another went down, and another. At last there was only Nuemark and one other, and the rats were beginning to slip around them.

Nuemark pushed his last man through the door. 'Close it! Close it, you fools,' he cried. He was weeping with fear, but he never stopped slashing with his sword.

The greatsword sergeant slammed the door shut and the gatehouse guards dropped the heavy bar.

Through the thick oak, Nuemark's voice rose to a wail. 'Sigmar forgive me! Sigmar forgive…' His words were cut short as the sound of halberds cutting through armour and into human flesh made every man in the cramped room shudder.

Nuemark's sergeant made the sign of the hammer as he finished his captain's plea. 'Sigmar forgive him.'

'We could have had him in,' said Hals.

'He didn't wish it,' said the greatsword sergeant.

Reiner collapsed on the stone stairs and cut at his leggings, exposing his wound. A ragged trench had been dug in his left thigh by the spear. The very sight of it made the pain worse. Franka hissed when she saw it.

With more than twenty men in it, the room was terribly cramped. A few of the greatswords were seeing to wounds of their own. Dag was giggling hysterically as he tied his kerchief over the stumps of his missing third and fourth fingers.

'All right, archer?' asked Reiner as he stripped out of his jacket and tore the sleeve from his shirt.

Dag grinned glassily and held up his ruined hand, waggling his first and middle finger. 'Fine, captain. Still have my shooting fingers.'

Reiner ripped his sleeve into strips. He glanced up at the guardsmen. 'Have any of you some water? Or better yet, kirschwasser?'

A guard pulled a flask from a cupboard and handed it to him. Reiner uncapped it, and had it halfway to his lips before he remembered his vow. He cursed. Damn Ranald anyway, another nine hundred and ninety-six men at least before he could drink again. What had he been thinking? He poured the liquor on the wound. It stung like wet ice. Reiner hissed. Franka tied the strips of cloth tight around the wound. Reiner's vision eclipsed at the pain, and he turned quickly away to avoid vomiting on her. He vomited on Pavel instead.

'Thank you very much,' said the pikeman, recoiling.

'Sorry lad. Surprised me, too.' He pushed himself up and faced the guard room sergeant. His leg screamed but held. 'Where is this trap?' he asked through clenched teeth.

The sergeant pointed to a rack of spears built into the wall. 'Lundt. Corbin. Open the bolt hole.'

Two guardsmen tugged four heavy pegs from the frame of the rack then lifted it away from the wall, revealing a narrow staircase that descended into darkness.

'So Gutzmann's alive?' asked the guard sergeant.

'Aye,' said Reiner as he helped Gert to his feet. 'And he commands you hold this door at all costs. Let no rat in.'

'Aye, sir. No fear of that.'

The Blackhearts and Nuemark's greatswords stood and made themselves ready. Reiner saluted their sergeant. 'Thank you for the escort,' he said. 'Sigmar watch you.'

'And you as well,' said the greatsword. He turned and led his men up the stairs.

Jergen stood and faced Reiner. 'Captain.'

Reiner nearly jumped out of his skin. He wasn't sure the swordsman had ever addressed him voluntarily before. 'Aye, Rohmner?'

Jergen nodded at the greatswords. 'I will be best used with them.'

Reiner looked at the greatsword sergeant. 'Will you have him?'

'Can he fight?'

'Like several tigers.'

The greatsword chuckled. 'Then fall in, bravo.'

Jergen joined the men climbing the stairs.

Reiner turned to the Blackhearts. 'Ready lads?'

They nodded. Reiner took a torch from the gatehouse wall, then ducked through the secret door and they all went down into the dark.

The passage was narrow and direct. At the end, there was a second staircase and a door in the ceiling. Reiner found the catch and shot it back, then pressed his back against the door. It didn't budge.

'Steingesser. Kiir,' he called, limping down. Gert and Hals squeezed around the others and stepped up to the trap. They pushed with hands and shoulders.

A muffled 'Hoy!' came from above, and they heard a confusion of steps.

The trap slammed open, and a ring of handgunners aimed down at them, fingers on their triggers. Gert and Hals threw up their hands.

Reiner did too. 'Hold, brothers. We are men.'

The handgunners eased back, but continued to look at them warily. 'What men are ye?' asked a sergeant.

'I bring a message for Commander Shaeder,' said Reiner as he and his companions stepped slowly up the stairs.

They were coming up in the guardroom just outside the cell Gutzmann had imprisoned them in the night before. The room was packed with a company of handgunners, sitting in rows with their guns across their laps. Gert and Hals had apparently lifted a few of them along with the trap. Their sergeants were their only commanders.

'Is the battle over?' asked a redheaded sergeant.

'What?' said Reiner. 'Hardly. What are you doing down here? Where is your captain?'

'We was told to bide here 'til the order came to retake the walls, sir,' said the sergeant, saluting. 'But it never come. Captain Baer went to ask, but he ain't come back.' He coughed, nervous. 'Er, is it true the general's returned, sir?'

'Aye, sergeant,' said Reiner, smiling as big as he could manage. 'Returned to lead us, and he commands you to take the great south wall. There's a company of greatswords clearing the way for you now. Away with you. And Sigmar guide your aim!'

'But our captains…'

'There's no time. I'll send 'em after you. Go. Go!'

'Aye, sir!' said the sergeant, grinning. 'This way, lads! Action at last!'

The handgunners jumped up, relieved to be doing something, and began clattering into the trap after him.

Reiner and the others hurried for stairs.

Franka shook her head. 'I don't understand. I know Shaeder wished to kill Gutzmann. But at the cost of killing himself as well?'

Reiner shrugged. He had no answer for her.

The gate at the top of the stairs was open and there was no guard. The boom of guns and a buzz of voices echoed from outside, but the hallway was empty. Reiner held up his hand, then crept forward. The door into the dining hall was open. They looked in. The room was packed with pikemen, all staring glumly towards the main entrance.

The fort shuddered as a cannon ball struck it.

'The ratmen still control the guns, then,' said Karel.

'Jergen'll see to them,' said Hals, then spat to be sure he hadn't cursed the swordsman by speaking too quickly.

The Blackhearts passed on to the courtyard door and looked out. A crowd of lancers and pistoliers filled it, waiting on their horses in full kit, but like the hand-gunners in the dungeon, they had no captains. They were rigid with tension, every fibre ready to charge out, but instead only their eyes moved, darting from a knot of men banging on the north door of the murder room, to the burning doors of the gate, which looked about to collapse, to the clamour of desperate battle coming from over the north wall, where Halmer's force fought the rat army. Reiner could see that the thud and clash of weapons, the screams of men and horses, the high chittering of rats, were driving the cavalry men insane. Their fellows were dying not twenty yards away, and they could do nothing but sit and listen.

Reiner's pistolier company was near the door, arguing amongst themselves as they watched the walls.

'Hist!' Reiner called, stepping out. 'Grau!'

The corporal turned. Reiner beckoned him over. He dismounted and hurried to the door. Two of his men came with him.

'Where have you been, Meyerling?' asked Grau. 'Vortmunder's been calling for your head.'

'Never mind that. What's all this? Gutzmann's getting chopped to bits outside. Why do you not ride out?'

'We want to,' said Grau, angrily. 'But Shaeder's lads have barricaded themselves in the murder room and that is where the winches are. He's locked us in, the traitor.'

'Shaeder ain't a traitor,' said Yoeder. 'It's a trap, like he said. Aulschweig men, dressed up as Reiksmen to lure us out to our doom.'

'Yer mad,' said the third, a stout fair-haired man Reiner didn't know. 'That's Gutzmann out there. I saw his face.'

'It ain't!' said Yeoder. 'Gutzmann couldn't ride so poor if he tried. Damned imposter sits a horse like he's made of sticks.'

'It is Gutzmann,' said Reiner. 'I've just come from him. He's grievously wounded, but he wouldn't stay away while you were trapped here.'

Yeoder stared at him. 'It's Gutzmann? Truly?'

'Truly.'

Grau cursed. 'Some of the captains are up trying to break down the door. The rest are in arguing with Shaeder in Gutzmann's quarters.'

Reiner pushed a hand through his hair. 'This is madness. You must ride out.'

'Too bad old Urquart ain't still with us,' said Pavel. 'He'd knock them doors down with one swing.'

'If only we had one of them glass balls the ratties got,' said Hals. 'We could smoke 'em out.'

Reiner looked at him, eyebrows raising, 'Amazing. A pikeman with a brain.' He turned, looking around the courtyard intently. 'Franka, a feedbag from the stables. And fill it with hay. Oh, and a good length of rope. Karel, a keg of powder from the armoury if you please. Pavel and Hals, lamp oil and bacon fat from the kitchen. As much as you can carry. And a big pot. Hurry. Meet us on the wall at the south door. Aye?'

As they ran off, the gate's wooden doors finally collapsed with a great roaring and eruption of sparks. Through the smoking rubble Reiner saw the forms of ratmen trying to eel through the bars of the portcullis.

'And pray we are not too late.'

# NINETEEN
## All Must Die!

REINER, DAG AND Gert ran up the stairs to the murder room as sergeants called squads of handgunners and swordsmen to defend the gate below it. The gunners fired through the inner portcullis at the ratmen that squirmed through the outer one. The murder room had two heavy, banded doors that opened onto the battlements to its left and right. Narrow arrow slot windows pierced the inner and outer walls. There were no other openings. Reiner listened at the south door when they reached it. He could hear the captains pounding uselessly on the north door and demanding that the men inside let them in. There was an iron ladder bolted to the wall. He looked up it then turned to the others.

'Dag, I'll have you here. Gert, can you make it onto the roof?'

Gert scowled. 'Ain't that fat, captain.' He started up the ladder.

Franka was first to return to them, a coil of rope slung over her shoulder and a leather feedbag stuffed with hay dangling from one hand.

'Good, lad. Er, lass,' said Reiner. 'Now get that rope around your waist.'

'What?' Franka looked alarmed.

'Not afraid of heights, are you?'

'No, but…'

'Once knew a topside monkey with a second storey mob. Made his living this way. Here, let me tie you off.'

Karel came back next, holding a keg of powder like a baby.

'Now pour as much of that as you can down into the hay,' said Reiner. 'But don't pack it.'

Pavel and Hals ran up just as Karel was finishing. Hals had two jugs of lamp oil. Pavel carried a big iron pot with a jar of drippings in it.

Reiner grinned. 'Excellent. Pavel, smear some fat on the bag. Hals, pour the lamp oil in the pot.'

Pavel made a face, but dug some of the fat out with his dagger and scraped it off onto the bag as Hals filled the big pot. When he was done, Reiner took the bag and lowered it into the pot of oil, pushing it down with the butt end of Pavel's spear until the hay and the leather were well saturated with the volatile oil.

As Reiner was lifting the bag out, Pavel raised his head. 'The cannon have stopped.'

Reiner cocked his head. It was true. The guns on the great south wall had gone silent.

Hals grinned. 'That's our Jergen. Lets his sword do his talking.'

Reiner hung the dripping bag from the point of the spear. The fumes made his eyes water. He stood. 'Hals, Pavel, Karel, stay here with Dag, ready to run in when the villains run out. Franka, up the ladder. I'll hand your weapon to you.'

Franka looked at him askance as she climbed the ladder. 'I begin to like this less and less.'

Reiner handed the spear up to her, then climbed up himself, carrying his torch. He stepped to the courtyard edge and looked over. Franka joined him. She swallowed. It was a long way down.

'Sorry, beloved,' he said. 'You are the lightest.'

He handed the end of her rope to Gert. 'Keep it taut, and pay it out slowly when I tell you.'

Gert gathered up the slack. 'Aye, captain.'

Reiner turned to Franka. 'Ready?'

Franka made Myrmidia's sign, then stepped up onto the wall, her back to the courtyard, and held the spear out to her side. 'Ready.'

Reiner crossed his fingers to Ranald and held the torch under the feed bag. The oil caught with a *whump* and a ball of fire boiled up from the bag, followed by oily black smoke.

'Lower away.'

Franka stepped backward off the wall as Gert let out the rope, and as Reiner watched, walked slowly down the wall, the bag roaring and smoking at the end of the spear like a filthy comet. The entire courtyard was watching as well, the pale, upturned faces of the lancers and pistoliers frowning in confusion.

A few more steps and Franka was at the level of the window slots.

'Now lass! Now!'

Franka jammed the spear point into the window on the left. For a moment Reiner thought all was lost, for the flaming bag became caught between the bars, but Franka pulled the spear back and stuffed the burning mess through like a handgunner jamming wadding into his barrel.

The violence of her action caused Franka to lose her footing, and she banged against the wall, dropping the spear.

'Up!' Reiner called over his shoulder. 'Pull her up!'

Gert hauled away. Reiner held down his hand and caught Franka's wrist as she bumped up the rough wall.

'Did it work?' asked Gert, when Franka had tumbled over onto the roof.

Reiner looked over. Black smoke was beginning to curl out of the murder room windows, and he could hear shouts and choking from below. He grinned. 'I believe it did. Ware the doors!' He cried.

He helped Franka up, and they stepped with Gert to the ladder and looked down. With a frantic turning of bolts and scraping of bars, the door flew open and three Hammer Bearers flew out, gasping and retching, accompanied by a great cloud of greasy black smoke. They were in no mood to fight, and Karel, Pavel and Hals just shoved them past as they coughed and wept sooty tears.

Reiner heard the south door crashing open as well, and a cheer going up from the men outside it. He clambered down the ladder and snatched Hals's spear, then dashed into the room, ducking low and covering his mouth and nose. The burning bag was under the courtyard-side windows. He stuck it with the spear and hurried back to the door, his eyes streaming, and flipped it out over the battlements.

'In lads!' he coughed, beckoning them. 'Man the winches!'

The Blackhearts ran in, stepping to the great spoked wheels that raised the two portcullises. They fell to with a will, pulling on the spokes with all their might, and a great cheer came from the troops in the courtyard below.

More men ran into the room from the south door – the captains. Vortmunder was at their head.

'Meyerling!' he cried. 'You surface at last! Good work! I'll take a day off your stable duty for this.'

Reiner saluted. 'Thank you, captain! May I suggest you return to your company. Your way will be clear momentarily.'

'Very good! Carry on.'

Just then the cheers in the courtyard turned to shouts of alarm. Reiner, Vortmunder and the other captains ran out and looked down. Squirming under the slowly raising portcullis was a spreading tide of ratmen. The handgunners were falling back as a company of swordsmen ran in to meet the invasion. Steel clashed on steel.

Vortmunder turned to Reiner. 'Raise it as fast as you can, corporal, so that we may charge.' He ran off with the other captains.

Reiner ran into the murder room. 'Put your backs into it, lads. We…'

'What is this!' cried a voice. 'Who disobeys my orders?'

Reiner looked up. Standing in the south door was a crazed figure. It took a moment for Reiner to realize it was Shaeder. His grey hair was disordered, his eyes wild. He looked like he had aged ten years in a night. He stepped into the room, drawing his sword. The Hammer Bearers who had held the murder room came in behind him, as did their glowering, white-bearded captain.

'Lower those portcullis, curse you!' shouted Shaeder, and lunged at Dag, who was hauling one-handed on the left-hand wheel with Gert and Franka.

'Sod off, y'berk!' said Dag, and punched him in the nose with his ruined hand as the others turned, drawing their weapons. The wheels stopped.

Shaeder stepped back, cursing, blood running over his lips. 'You… you dare? You peasant.' He ran Dag through the chest. A bright spike of steel sprouted from the archer's back. He convulsed, vomiting blood, then raised his head and sneered through bloody teeth. 'Get stuffed.' He poked Shaeder in the eyes with his two remaining fingers.

Shaeder howled and jerked back, clutching his face. Dag dropped off Shaeder's sword and flopped bonelessly to the floor, dead. An unexpected pang of sadness struck Reiner at the sight. He had spent all the time that he had known Dag trying to be rid of him. The boy had been a dangerous madman, but dead, Reiner felt a strange fondness for him. He chuckled sadly to himself. That was the best way, really. Better for Dag to be dead and miss him, than have him running around wreaking havoc.

Shaeder and his Hammer Bearers attacked the Blackhearts on the wheels. Shaeder flailed wildly, half-blind. The Blackhearts defended themselves. A cry of dismay came from the courtyard as the wheels started to spin backwards.

'Damn you, Shaeder!' Reiner ran forward, swinging his sword. He caught Shaeder's blade before it came down on Pavel's head. 'Gert! Hals! Franka! Stay on the wheels. The rest, defend them!' The Blackhearts turned to their tasks as Reiner thrust savagely at Shaeder, 'What ails you? We must attack!'

Shaeder riposted, forcing Reiner back. The whites of his eyes were blood red. 'No! We must die! All must die!'

'You're mad. We might still win.' Reiner parried desperately. Mad or not, Shaeder was still the better swordsman, and his frenzy gave him strength.

'And have Altdorf learn of this?' Spittle flew from Shaeder's lips with each word. 'No one must survive to get word back. They won't understand. They won't see that it was Gutzmann who was the traitor, and I the patriot! We will stay here until the rats overwhelm us!'

The Hammer Bearers shot uneasy glances at him. Their swords faltered. 'Do we not wait for Gutzmann to be defeated?' asked the white-bearded captain. 'You said Aulschweig came to reinforce us.'

'I said what was necessary.'

Reiner sneered. 'So you kill an entire garrison to hide your foolish manipulations? You are worse than a traitor. You are a bad general.'

Shaeder's eyes went wide. 'Villain! Take back that slander!' He rushed forward, swinging wildly. Reiner caught Shaeder's blade on his hilt, and his shoulder on his chest. The commander clawed for his dagger.

Reiner got his boot up between them and kicked with all his might. Shaeder flew back, flailing for balance. He stopped in the door – or rather, something stopped him. The doorway was filled with dark, hunched figures.

Shaeder looked around as clawed hands gripped his arms and legs. 'Who…?'

Reiner and the Blackhearts and the Hammer Bearers stared as a jagged bronze blade reached from behind the commander and sawed his neck open from ear to ear. Ratmen poured into the room over his body before his blood began to flow.

There was a cry from the courtyard. 'They're over the walls!'

The Hammer Bearers stood shoulder to shoulder with the Blackhearts to meet the ratmen's charge. Hals, Franka and Gert left the wheels to help.

'No!' Reiner ran forward. 'Keep turning! We'll hold 'em back!'

Hals cursed. 'But, captain…'

'You've the strongest back, laddie.' Reiner cleft a ratman's skull to its curved front teeth as he joined the line. 'Push 'em out! Franka! Close the other door!'

Franka ran to the north door. She slammed and locked it as Hals and Gert hauled on their wheels. With only one man turning each, they raised by inches instead of feet at a pull.

Reiner found himself fighting beside the captain of the Hammer Bearers.

'I swear to you,' the captain said, 'I swear we didn't know.'

The ratmen swarmed around them, trying to reach the wheels and cut at the ropes. Reiner cut one down and kicked a second back. Karel blocked a bronze halberd and gutted its owner. Pavel wielded his spear like a quarterstaff, knocking heads left and right. The Hammer Bearers stabbed and sliced around them like men possessed. One went down, impaled on a hooked spear. Reiner feared it was all in vain. More and more ratmen were squeezing through the door.

An arrow sprouted from the eye of a rat swinging a cutlass at Reiner. It fell, shrieking.

'Franz,' Reiner called over his shoulder. 'Get back to your wheel!'

'No, captain,' said Franka.

Another arrow appeared in a rat's throat.

Reiner grunted. Even with her arrows they were certain to be overwhelmed. But just as he thought it, the ratmen who still filled the door began turning and squealing. Battle cries echoed into the room from the battlements.

'For Gutzmann!'

'For the Empire!'

Reiner's heart leapt. The keep's sword company! He raised his voice in answer. 'For the Empire! For Gutzmann!'

The others joined him. 'For Gutzmann! For the Empire!'

Outside, the swordsmen cheered.

Reiner could see a wave of panic ripple through the ratmen as they realized they were caught between two forces. They began slashing about themselves in a frenzy, striking at their comrades as often as their foes. Reiner caught a wild slash in the forearm. He dodged back.

'Press forward as one!' cried the leader of the Hammer Bearers. They and the Blackhearts walked forward, jabbing at the ratmen in unison until the vermin fought each other to get out of the door and collided with those who were fighting to get in. Through the doorway, Reiner saw the swordsmen on the battlements, holding off a wave of ratmen that were pouring over the wall.

'Franz! The door!'

'Aye, captain.'

As Reiner and the others backed the ratmen into the doorway, Franka edged around and squeezed behind the door. She began pushing it closed. Reiner stood at its edge, defending her and adding his shoulder to her weight, but there were too many ratmen in the way.

Reiner waved at the Blackhearts and the Hammers. 'Jump back! All at once!'

Pavel scowled at him. 'Hey?'

'Trust me, curse you! Jump back! Now!'

The Blackhearts jumped back. Shaeder's Hammers were only a step slower. The ratmen in the door, suddenly without resistance before them, stumbled forward into the room, off balance.

'Now!'

Reiner and Franka pushed at the door as one and got it nearly closed before it hit the crowd of ratmen beyond it. It started opening again. The Hammers waded into the ratmen in the centre of the room. Pavel and Hals dodged around them and charged into the door, slamming it closed. Outside, a ratman shrieked. Reiner looked down. A naked pink tail lay on the floor, severed from its owner.

Reiner turned the lock. Franka dropped the bar. They ran back with Pavel and Hals to the wheels as the Hammer Bearers finished off the remaining ratmen. The Blackhearts threw down their weapons and pulled on the spokes for all they were worth. After a moment the Hammers joined them.

A roar of triumph rose from the courtyard as the wheels jarred to a stop. The portcullises were open at last. A horn blew 'charge,' and hooves thundered below them.

Reiner locked his wheel and breathed a sigh of relief. Gert did the same at the other wheel. The Blackhearts ran to the arrow slots, but could see nothing. Franka darted to the south door and threw it open. The Blackhearts and the Hammer Bearers ran out and looked over the parapet, craning their necks to see the scene below. The lancers were already through the gate, wheeling left toward the thick ring of ratmen that surrounded the ragged remains of Halmer's square. The pistoliers were right behind them, arcing wide to broadside the ratmen as they raced past. Next came a stream of pikemen, ten wide, running at full charge. The Blackhearts and the Hammer Bearers joined the swordsmen cheering them from the walls.

The companies hit the rats' flank with a devastating triple impact, all their enforced inaction and pent up rage exploding in bloodthirsty fury. The rats fell before them like trampled grass, crushed under the hooves of the lancers, riddled with bullets from the pistoliers, and impaled by rank after rank of pike.

It was too much. The ratmen had expected the battle to be over almost as soon as it had begun. Instead they had fought Halmer's troops to a standstill for more than a quarter of an hour, all the while taking heavy crossbow fire from the walls of the keep, and now fresh troops were crashing into their rear. The ratmen turned and fled before the charge. Seeing them flee, their brethren fled too, and soon the entire rat army was scrambling away, some on all fours, in full rout, with the lancers and pistoliers chasing them down.

Reiner would have wagered that Halmer's men would have called it a day and let their comrades finish the job, but to his surprise, they joined the pikemen and trotted north after the cavalry. At least those still standing did. At Reiner's guess, more than half the men who had ridden into the fort with Halmer lay dead or wounded below the wall of the keep. Others were too tired to move and sat down unheeding among the broken bodies and spilled viscera of their enemies and friends.

Hals let out a huge sigh. 'So we did it, then.'

Reiner nodded and closed his eyes. He leaned against the battlement. 'Aye. Well done, lads. Well done.'

'Manfred damned well better thank us for this one,' said Pavel.

'Aye,' agreed Franka.

'It weren't the job he sent us on, that's certain,' said Gert.

'Oh, Sigmar,' said Karel. Reiner thought he was about to kneel in prayer, but the boy sobbed and retched. 'Oh, Sigmar, they're eating them.'

'What's the matter?' Reiner opened his eyes. 'Who's eating who?'

Karel was looking over the wall. 'The rats. They're eating the dead.'

'The rats?' asked Reiner, turning with the others to look. 'The ratmen?'

'No. Rats. Big rats.'

Franka choked. 'They're eating Matthais!'

# TWENTY
## Heroic Deeds

THE BLACKHEARTS RAN down to the courtyard and out of the keep. The grounds of the fort were strewn with the dead and dying. Men and ratmen lay in long heaps of bodies that defined where the lines of battle had been, highest where the fighting had been the fiercest. To the left of the gate was the place Halmer had called to the keep to open the portcullis.

Reiner peered at the bodies there. Things were moving among them, but he didn't wish to believe they were rats. They were the size of pit dogs, and as muscular. They scurried over the bodies, gnawing and clawing at them. And they didn't just prey on the dead. Reiner saw a wounded man try to push away a rat with feeble strength. The rat sat on his chest and chewed through his throat.

'It's horrible,' muttered Franka. 'Horrible.'

'Begone, beasts!' cried Karcl, stamping his feet and waving his sword.

The rats looked up, but failed to run at his advance. Their eyes glowed red in the light from the keep's gate.

Reiner grunted and waved the others ahead. 'We get Matthais, but no more. There are too many. We'll tell someone once we're back inside.'

As they started moving through the bodies, Reiner saw Jergen crossing towards them. He saluted as he approached.

'Rohmner,' Reiner said, nodding. 'How went the battle for the walls?'

'Well.'

Reiner snorted. 'A veritable fountain of words, aren't you, Rohmner?'

Jergen nodded, then fell in with the others. Reiner sighed. The man was unreachable.

After a moment, Reiner saw the body of Matthais's horse. They picked their way to it, keeping wary eyes and weapons on the huge rats. Matthais lay behind it, almost lost in shadow but for the bright, straight line of his sword. Two huge rats hunched over him, one chewing on a leg, the other on an arm.

'Shoo!' called Karel. 'Go away, you horrible things!'

'Ware, laddie,' said Reiner.

He hurried after him, stepping on bodies as he went. One squealed and squirmed. Reiner stopped and turned. The squeal had not been human. A plump ratman in long robes knelt among the bodies, a scalpel in its hands, a handgunner neatly laid open before it. It blinked up at Reiner through thick spectacles. Reiner frowned. He knew this creature.

'The surgeon!' cried Franka. She started forward, her teeth bared. 'I want his spleen!'

The ratman snarled in anger, and started to crab backwards.

Franka lunged at it, slashing with dagger and short sword. The rat scrambled away with surprising speed, chittering in his own tongue and pointing at the Blackhearts. The giant rats looked up like dogs hearing their master's voice, then leapt to the attack.

Reiner sprang back, slashing at three rats that snapped at his legs. The others were similarly infested.

'Ahoy the keep!' Reiner cried. 'Help us!' No one responded. He cursed. 'Back to the fort!'

But it was difficult to disengage. Hals pinned a rat to the ground but another had him by the boot. Pavel flung one over his shoulder on the point of his spear. A second jumped on his back. Franka kicked one back and stabbed another as she tried to reach the surgeon. Gert hacked one with his axe and stomped another flat. Two more leapt at his chest. Jergen decapitated one and cut another in two. He stepped toward Pavel to help him with his. Karel cut at two, backing away from their claws and teeth. A huge shadow loomed out of the darkness behind him. He didn't see it.

'Lad!' called Reiner. 'Behind you!'

Karel turned, and ducked a great, chisel-shaped claw. The monster slashed at him again. The thing was the size of an ogre, rippling with fur-covered muscles. Karel dodged back, then lunged at it, slashing it across the arm. It roared and attacked.

Reiner rushed in with Franka and Jergen, but before they could reach the beast, the surgeon skittered ahead of them. 'Such brave,' it cried. 'Such courage! Take! Take!' It gibbered an order at the rat-ogre, and the thing curled its fist and clubbed Karel to the ground instead of gutting him. The boy's sword clattered to the flagstones.

Reiner tripped on a pile of bodies trying to reach the monster. He fell. Jergen leapt the pile and swung at the beast, gashing its shoulder. It backhanded him, knocking him into Pavel and Franka.

Before they could regain their feet, the rat-ogre caught up Karel's limp form with one claw while the surgeon clambered up on its shoulders. The ratman rapped his monstrous mount on the head with his bony knuckles and pointed to the north wall, squeaking all the while. The beast vaulted over a dead horse and disappeared into the shadows, Karel tucked under one arm. The giant rats ran behind it in a bounding carpet.

Reiner clenched his fists. 'Curse the boy! The battle's won! The day is saved! Why does he have to go and get himself taken now?' He looked around at the Blackhearts. They were waiting, expectant. He sighed. 'All right. Come on.'

They ran for the north gate, Reiner's wounded leg, screaming with each step, as stiff as a tree branch.

THE PASS WAS strewn with dead ratmen. Their panic had apparently not abated, for they had all been cut down from behind. Reiner and the Blackhearts jogged through it, peering ahead anxiously into the darkness. Only occasionally did the clouds part to allow them to see their quarry bounding before them. They were gaining on the rat-monster, but slowly. Reiner's breath was like knives in his throat. He couldn't remember when he had run more in one night.

They veered into the branching ravine that led to the mine. The dead rats were thicker here where the narrowing walls had slowed their retreat, and the Blackhearts stumbled over bodies and were forced to weave around abandoned flame guns and other strange equipment.

Soon they saw the outer walls of the mine before them, and a moment later the weird silhouette of the ogremounted surgeon lurching through the gate, followed by its boiling shadow of rats. Reiner expected to hear echoes of battle from within the compound and see the light of torches, but it was silent and empty.

As they ran in they saw at last evidence that the ratmen and the soldiers had come this way. A crowd of armoured horses milled about in front of the mine entrance, waiting for their riders to return. The soldiers have chased the rats to their hole, thought Reiner. He prayed the vermin the explosion had trapped hadn't dug themselves out.

'There,' said Hals, pointing.

In the centre of the compound, the rat-ogre was shambling wearily on, its burdens at last slowing it down. Franka stopped and nocked an arrow, then pulled her bowstring back to her ear. She let fly. The rat-surgeon squeaked and toppled off his mount's shoulders, arms flailing. The rat-ogre stopped and turned.

The Blackhearts sprinted forward while Gert and Franka stayed back and fired at the beast. Jergen shot out ahead, holding his sword out to his side. The rat-ogre saw them coming and dropped Karel to step over the surgeon, roaring defiance. The giant rats surrounded it, hissing and snarling.

Jergen leapt over them, sword high. The rat-ogre raised an arm instinctively. A clawed hand spun away, severed cleanly by Jergen's flashing blade. The beast bellowed its pain and knocked Jergen sideways. The swordmaster landed shoulder-first among the rats and rolled. They snapped and clawed at him.

Reiner kicked left and right at the rats and aimed a thrust at the monster. His blade slid off its ribs, opening a crimson gash in its dark fur. It clubbed him aside with its bloody stump. Reiner staggered, his vision blurring from the impact, his bad leg buckling.

Pavel and Hals tried to reach the rat-ogre as well, but found themselves fending off the rats instead. The monster surged forward, swinging at Pavel. Franka and Gert peppered it with arrows and bolts, but it kept coming.

Reiner limped forward again, but as he waded into the rats, chopping in all directions, Karel stood up behind the rat-ogre, weaving and drawing his dagger.

'Get away, laddie!' Reiner shouted.

But the boy leapt on the beast's back, stabbing it in the neck. It howled and clawed behind it in agony, catching Karel by the arm. Reiner lunged in at its exposed side and plunged his sword into its guts. It roared and smashed Karel down on top of him, flattening him to the cobbles. The boy's elbow cracked him in the cheekbone. Reiner gasped, trying to suck air into his collapsed lungs. Karel's weight lifted off again and he rolled away, slashing blindly to keep the rats away.

He looked up. The rat-ogre towered above him, its hideous face contorted in a snarl. It had Karel by the leg now and was swinging him around like a club. Pavel and Hals were flying back, knocked off their feet. Franka and Gert were holding fire, afraid to hit Karel.

Reiner tried to rise, tried to get his sword in front of him. The rat-ogre glared down at him and raised Karel over its head. Reiner threw himself aside. The beast brought the boy down like an axe. Karel smashed onto the cobbles with a sick smack Reiner felt through his hands.

Pavel and Hals staggered up, shaking off rats and wading towards the beast. Franka and Gert fired.

Reiner rolled to dislodge a rat and saw the rat-ogre raising its human weapon again. Reiner flailed, but he couldn't get out of the way. He was covered in rats. One bit his arm, another his side, another his foot. He felt none of it. His whole world was the rat-ogre.

Motion flickered in the corner of his eye. Jergen. The swordsman ran up the monster's back, blade high. He chopped down like an executioner. The ugly head split in two, gushing blood, Jergen's steel lodging between its two front teeth. The beast fell like a tree, face first, right beside Reiner. Karel flopped flat to his right.

Jergen sprang off the monster and laid into the rats around Reiner.

Reiner killed the one on his chest and flung it at two more. He rolled to his knees, slashing in a circle, then staggered to his feet and joined Pavel and Hals, who stabbed and kicked and chopped at the vermin in a frenzy. Franka and Gert shot arrows and bolts into them as fast as they could. After a red blind moment, Reiner stopped and looked around, breathing heavily. The others were doing the same. They had run out of targets.

'All dead?' Reiner asked.

'Aye,' said Hals.

'There's one moving,' said Gert.

The Blackhearts turned. The rat-surgeon was writhing about in agony, Franka's arrow still lodged in his back. He had lost his spectacles.

Franka approached him, sword out, her face blank and hard. The surgeon squinted up at her, trying to back away. 'Mercy... Mercy please!'

Franka sneered. 'This is mercy, torturer!' She chopped at his neck. The first cut failed to decapitate him, and he shrieked as she hacked at him a second time and cut his head off. The headless corpse flopped and spasmed.

Franka collapsed to her knees.

Hals nodded. 'Well struck, lass.'

There was a moan behind them. They spun around, swords at the ready.

It was Karel. The boy's hands were moving weakly, but he was not long for the world. Reiner knelt stiffly at his side. The others gathered round. Franka retched and sobbed. Karel's chest was an odd shape. A red rib jutted up though his jerkin. He had a gash in his scalp Reiner could see his skull through. It was cracked. The boy lay in a lake of his own blood.

'Lad. Are you...' Reiner swallowed. 'Are you still with us?'

'Row...' Karel was trying to beckon to Reiner, but he hadn't much control of his hands. His breath whistled through his teeth in short gasps.

Reiner leaned close. 'What is it, lad?'

'Rowena.' Karel clutched Reiner's arm. His grip was painfully strong. 'Tell her I died... thinking of her.'

Reiner nodded. 'Certainly I will.' The poor fool, he thought. The girl had likely forgotten him as soon he had left her sight.

'But,' Karel pulled him closer. 'But... invent a better death.' He grinned up at Reiner, though his eyes gazed past him. 'You're good at that, aye?'

Reiner smiled sadly. 'Aye, laddie. That I am.'

Karel relaxed his grip and sank back. 'Thank you. You aren't... what Manfred said.' His eyes closed.

'Poor foolish boy,' said Hals.

Pavel made the sign of the hammer. Franka murmured a prayer to Myrmidia.

'He'd no business being mixed up in all this,' said Gert.

Reiner snorted. 'None of us did.'

A noise brought their heads up. They looked around. The sound came from outside the compound – the slow hoof steps of a single horse, echoing hollowly off the walls of the ravine. As they watched, it wandered through the gate, unguided by its rider, who was revealed slowly as it moved out of the shadow of the wall. The knight hung sideways from the saddle at an unnatural angle. A broken lance drooped from his mailed hand, blue and white pennons smeared with blood and dirt. His eyes stared vacantly beyond them.

'Sigmar!' hissed Pavel. 'It's Gutzmann!'

They all stood and turned to face the dead general, but no one seemed eager to approach him. They were transfixed. A chill ran up Reiner's spine as Mannslieb cut through the clouds and haloed the dead rider. Where had he come from? Had he got lost in the army's pursuit of the ratmen? Had he followed the Blackhearts?

The horse stopped in the centre of the compound, its head low, as noises began to come from the mine – the thud of boots, the creak and jingle of armour and sword, and above it all, loud laughter and exuberant banter – the voices of a victorious army returning from battle. Reiner stole a look behind him. Lancers, swordsmen and pikemen were swaggering out of the mine, boasting to each other of their exploits. Others came limping, or carrying fallen comrades, but even these seemed to be in an ebullient mood. The enemy was vanquished. The Empire – or their little corner of it – was saved.

Their merry chatter faltered and fell silent however, as one by one they noticed the lone knight sagging gracelessly from his saddle in the moon glow. They came forward in small groups to stand with the Blackhearts, until at last the entire garrison – or what was left of it – stood in a half circle, looking at their leader, who in life had nearly led them to folly, but in death had led them to victory.

They watched thus for many minutes, no one wanting to end the unearthly eeriencss of the moment. But then, with a loud snap, one of Gutzmann's ropes broke and he crashed to the ground.

The garrison gasped and cried out. Then Captain Halmer, who had been standing with his men, stepped forward. 'Make a bier. Carry him back to the fort.' He raised his hands. 'May Sigmar bless our fallen general!'

The garrison raised their voices in unison. 'Hail Gutzmann! Praise Sigmar! Long live the Empire!'

The crowd of soldiers began to break up as some of Halmer's lancers went forward and started making a makeshift stretcher of their lances. Riders found their horses, pikemen and swordsmen formed up in their shattered companies.

Halmer saw the Blackhearts and saluted. He crossed to Reiner and clasped his hand, then leaned in. 'The garrison and the whole of the Empire owe you. I owe you. Unfortunately, for the morale of the men, I think it might be best if they were allowed to continue to believe that Gutzmann died here, now, after the battle was won, rather than before it began.'

Reiner exchanged wry looks with his comrades. 'That's all right, captain,' he said. 'We're used to it. Heroic deeds play best when it's heroes that perform them. Nobody wants to hear a ballad about the blackhearts that propped a would-be deserter on his horse and sent him off to save the day.'

Halmer scowled at that. 'Good. Then you would do well to keep it to yourself.' He turned on his heel and began calling the troops to order.

Franka rolled her eyes. 'The soul of diplomacy as always.'

Reiner shrugged, grinning. 'The truth is never diplomatic.'

* * *

THE SUN ROSE on a cold, bright morning as General Gutzmann led his army for the last time. Four knights carried him back to the fort on crossed lances as their comrades marched silently behind them, heads uncovered, and swords, lances and pikes held at the shoulder. The ceremonial mood was marred however, when it was discovered that another army occupied the fort. A thousand fresh Aulschweig knights, spearmen, swordsmen, and crossbowmen held the great south wall and the keep. An Aulschweig captain at the head of a company of swordsmen held up a hand as the column entered.

'Baron Caspar Tzetchka-Koloman's regards,' he said, 'and would you be so kind as to ask your captains to meet him in the great hall?'

Halmer stiffened. 'A foreigner gives orders in an Empire fort?'

'It is a request only,' said the Aulschweiger, bowing.

'Very well,' Halmer said. He dispatched a corporal to summon the other captains.

Reiner didn't like the look of things. He motioned his comrades off to one side. 'I think, lads, that it is time for us to go. Collect your things and meet me back here as soon as you can. We'll want to be away before…'

'Hetsau!' came Halmer's voice.

Reiner cringed. He turned and saluted. 'Captain?'

Halmer dismounted and stepped close to him. 'I may have need of your guile just now. You will attend me as my assistant. Come.'

Reiner sighed. 'Right ho.' He looked back at the Blackhearts as Halmer led him towards the keep. 'Get ready,' he mouthed.

BARON CASPAR WAITED for the garrison's captains on the steps of the great hall. He looked every inch the dashing hero, dressed in armour of silvered plate, with a cloak and surcoat of blazing white over it.

'Welcome, gentlemen,' he said. 'Pray come in.'

He turned and led them into the great hall, which was still in great disarray after being used to house pike and sword companies the night before. Caspar pushed through the clutter of benches and tables and stepped up onto the raised dais, extending a gracious hand. 'Take your seats, gentlemen.' He circled the table and dropped into Gutzmann's chair.

The captains froze where they were.

'My lord,' said Halmer. 'That is the general's chair.'

Caspar shrugged. 'I am a general, yes?'

'Yes, but not...'

The hall's great double doors boomed closed behind them. Reiner looked around with the others. Armed men filed through the side door and surrounded them.

'What is the meaning of this?' asked Captain Vortmunder.

Caspar smiled. 'It means I now have the right to sit in this chair.'

Vortmunder stepped forward. 'But you were the general's friend. He was helping you...'

'And the general is dead,' Caspar cut him off. He sighed. 'I was becoming tired, anyway, of all the delays. All the shilly-shallying. Of having to beg for Gutzmann's gold and make extravagant promises to get it.' He sat forward. 'Now I no longer have need of such compromises. Now I no longer have to buy the golden eggs, since as of this moment, I own the goose that lays them.' He laughed. 'This is the best of all worlds! With the mine and the fort in my possession, my brother will not long stand against me. I will rule Aulschweig, and soon all the principalities!'

'You swine!' cried a knight captain. 'You break treaty!'

'The Empire will destroy you!' said Vortmunder.

'You won't get away with this!' said Halmer.

'The Empire will never know,' said Caspar. 'For no one will leave here. Besides, as long as I continue to send Altdorf a few meagre shipments of gold they won't bother to ask who sends it to them.' He smiled. 'And if they do someday learn who holds the pass, it will be too late, for I will have built my own empire by then.'

'You madman,' cried Vortmunder. 'You are a mere tick on the backside of the Empire. You…'

Caspar shot to his feet. 'I will not be insulted in my own keep!' He shouted. 'Speak to me that way again and you will be shot.' He sat back down, composed again. 'Now. You will be held hostage against the good behaviour of your men until I decide how to dispose of them.'

Reiner watched the captains seething with impotent rage as Caspar outlined his commands and conditions. Their hands clenched. Their eyes bulged with fury. They were too angry to think, too outraged by this grievous insult to the Empire to examine the situation. At any moment one of them might explode and say something that would get them all killed. Reiner didn't wish to die. Something had to be done. He leaned in and whispered in Halmer's ear. After a moment, the lance captain nodded.

'My lord,' he said, stepping forward. 'I regret to inform you that you are too late. Altdorf will be sending a force to reinforce this garrison within a month.'

'What do you say?' asked Caspar, sitting up. 'What's that?'

'A messenger was dispatched before we left the mine, my lord,' replied Halmer. 'Informing Karl-Franz of our battle with the ratmen and requesting reinforcements. There will be a full garrison on its way as soon as he reaches Altdorf. And though you may well hold the fort against that force, you won't hold it against the force that will come after the first. The Empire is relentless against its enemies, as you know. It will not stop until you have been wiped from the face of the earth.'

Caspar turned red. He turned to one of his captains. 'Send a squad to hunt down this messenger. I will kill him before he leaves the mountains.'

'You might, my lord,' said Halmer levelly. 'And you might not. He has quite a lead.' He coughed. 'I have another suggestion that you might find palatable.'

Caspar glared at him. 'You think to make terms with me? You are my prisoners!'

'It is only a suggestion my lord. You may do with it as you will.'

'Speak,' snapped Caspar.

'You might, my lord, allow a second messenger to be sent after the first, informing Altdorf that you hold the fort for them. That after Commander Shaeder's betrayal of General Gutzmann to the ratmen and the subsequent loss of the fort, you rode in and saved us.'

Vortmunder turned on Halmer, eyes wild. 'What horrible lie is this! We needed no help! We defeated the ratmen! We held the fort!'

'But we don't now, captain,' said Halmer. 'Would you rather lose the fort to assuage your pride, or serve the Empire with your humility?' He turned back to Caspar. 'My apologies, my lord. As I was saying, you could send a message to Altdorf that you have saved us, and that you hold the fort for Karl-Franz until reinforcements can be brought up, thereby keeping the Empire's southern border safe.'

Caspar sneered. 'And why should I do that? Why should I kiss Karl-Franz's spotty behind?'

The captains bridled at that, but Halmer only smiled. 'Because, my lord, just as the Empire's vengeance is relentless, so is its benevolence limitless. In return for your help in this matter, the gracious Empire would support you against your brother and very likely back you in your ambitions against the other princes of the region. Altdorf has for centuries longed for more stability on its southern border.'

Caspar sat back in his seat, brow furrowed. Reiner could see his suspicious nature fighting with his greed and ambition. He smiled. He knew which of those combatants always won out with a man like Caspar. He exchanged a look with Halmer and nodded. The captain had done a masterful job. He hadn't made any demands, any threats. He had laid it out as Reiner whispered it to him. A reasonable plan presented by a reasonable man.

After a long moment Caspar nodded. 'Very well, send your messenger. But you will be held as hostages in Aulschweig. If Altdorf betrays me, you will all die. You understand me?'

Halmer and the others nodded, their heads held high. They knew that, in reality, the Empire would come for Caspar's head, and Caspar would kill them for betraying him, but they were knights of the Empire. They were ready to make this sacrifice.

Reiner, on the other hand, was not. 'Er, captain,' he said to Halmer. 'I would be honoured to be allowed to convey this message to Altdorf.'

# TWENTY-ONE
## Freedom

REINER CHIVVIED HIS comrades out of the fort as quickly as he could. His shoulders remained tense as they waited while horses were found and they were outfitted and provisioned. At any moment Caspar might change his mind and lock down the fort, or Halmer might decide he had too much need of Reiner's guile to let him go. But at last they were all kitted out and mounted up, with a little pony cart following them to carry their supplies. Reiner had insisted on the cart.

Hals spat over his left shoulder as they got under way, riding into the pass out of the shattered remains of the tent encampment outside the fort's north wall. 'Ain't sorry to be showing that place my backside.'

'Didn't think I'd get out with mine intact,' said Gert.

Pavel laughed. 'Ye've enough. Y'could've left some of it behind.'

Franka shivered. 'The sooner we're out of these accursed mountains the better.'

Jergen nodded.

Reiner spurred his horse. 'I agree. But we have a stop to make first.'

THE MINE'S THIRD tunnel was choked with the bodies of ratmen, piles of them, their limbs and torsos broken and cut to ribbons. At the end of the tunnel where the explosion had closed it off the bodies were packed to the ceiling, and it appeared that these had torn each other apart in their frenzy to return to their underground world. The wounds that had killed them weren't the straight cuts of swords, but the ragged shredding of claws and teeth.

But though the stench of blood, bile and filth was unbearable, Reiner had searched every foot of it, for he couldn't find Gutzmann's gold. Reiner had led the Blackhearts to the spot where he had discovered the crates, but they were no longer there. At least he was almost sure they weren't. He couldn't be certain he hadn't missed them somehow.

He cursed. 'We'll search again as we go up,' he said.

Hals made a face. 'But what do we look for?'

'Is it really worth all this stink?' asked Pavel.

Reiner shot a look at Gert and Jergen. They were all that was left of Manfred's new men. Either one could be his spy. And at the same time, neither could be. The spy might have been... Dag? It hardly seemed possible. More likely Abel. But if that was the case, he had decided early on to switch from observer to leader. And what had become of him anyway? Reiner hadn't seen the quartermaster since he had betrayed him to Gutzmann.

'Aye, it's worth it,' Reiner said at last. 'It's evidence. For Manfred. Something that'll impress him. That we might be able to use to convince him to free us. Now come. Pavel and Hals, look on the left. Gert and Jergen on the right. Franka, stay with me in the centre. Don't miss an inch.'

The Blackhearts groaned and began trudging back up the tunnel.

* * *

HALF AN HOUR later Reiner had to admit defeat. The crates were nowhere in the tunnel. The Blackhearts returned to their horses and the cart, and at last got on the road for Averheim and Altdorf.

Reiner was glum, his shoulders slumped. The gold had been their chance at freedom, and now it was gone. They were back were they were before Manfred had sent them on this fool mission – firmly in his clutches with no way that Reiner could see to get out. It was maddening.

As they passed out of Brunn and started up the next rise Franka patted his arm.

'Don't feel so bad,' she said. 'Didn't we survive?'

'Aye, but for what? More servitude?'

Franka looked at him. 'Don't you feel any pride in what you've done? If you hadn't put Gutzmann on his horse and tricked all his men into following him, the day would have been lost. The ratmen would hold the fort, and everyone would be dead. You...'

'A thousand men!' said Reiner suddenly.

'What?' Franka frowned. 'Where?

Reiner laughed, loud and long. 'Pavel,' he cried. 'Open a bottle of wine.'

'Hey,' said the pikeman. 'Now?'

'Yes now. I need a drink. We all do. A celebration.'

Pavel shrugged and dug through the supplies on the cart.

Franka scowled at him quizzically. 'What are you on about?'

Reiner wiped his eyes and shook his head. 'When I was in the ratmen's tunnels trying to free you, and it looked like we wouldn't make it, I made a pledge to Ranald that if he saved me, I would not touch drink again until I had tricked a thousand men.' He grinned. 'Well, he saved me.'

Franka smiled. 'And you tricked a thousand men.'

'And now I need a drink.'

Pavel handed Reiner a bottle and he raised it. 'Here's to luck and the brains to use it.' He took a long drink and passed it to Franka.

'Here's to those that didn't make it, and to us that did. Sigmar bless us all,' she said, and tilted the bottle up for a few swallows. 'And Myrmidia.' She passed it to Pavel.

'Here's to home and hearth,' he said. 'May we see them again at last.' He drank and passed the bottle to Hals.

'Here's to Gutzmann,' he said. 'May he sup with Sigmar tonight.' He drank deep and handed the bottle to Gert.

'Here's to new friends,' he said. 'May we drink again in better circumstances.' He gulped down two big swallows, then passed it to Jergen.

The swordsman raised the bottle, but not his eyes. 'Freedom.' He drank and returned it to Reiner.

The others nodded, and echoed him. 'Freedom.'

Reiner finished the bottle, then tossed it at the rocky wall of the pass. It smashed into a hundred pieces. Red drops spattered the rocks.

A FEW MILES later, the companions came around a bend in the path and saw a cart up ahead. It was in a ditch, and the horses and driver nowhere in sight. As they got closer, Reiner noticed crates on the back of the cart, and his heart jumped. He recognized them. He spurred his horse forward. He was shaking. Could it be?

The crates had been opened, the tops pried off. Reiner stepped off his horse onto the cart, and looked inside them. They were empty. His fists clenched. Empty!

He kicked one to the ground. There was a single gold ingot beneath it, missed by whoever had looted them. He snatched it up. Hardly enough to buy an hour of a sorcerer's time, let alone pay him to remove whatever poisonous curse Manfred had put on them. He hurled it into the brush.

'Reiner,' said Franka, as the others caught up to him. 'Look.'

Reiner turned to where she was pointing. On the far side of the cart was a body. He jumped down and turned it over, then recoiled. The Blackhearts gathered around him, staring and gagging.

It was Abel. He was dead, but not from any weapon of steel. Reiner was almost certain he had been dead before those who had robbed the cart had struck. His face was stretched in a hideous rictus grin, as if something inhumanly strong had grabbed the flesh at the back of his head and pulled it tight. His tongue was thick and black and protruded from his mouth like a sausage. His hands were so flexed that the bones of his fingers had snapped, and his arms and legs were as rigid and hard as iron.

'Tis the poison,' breathed Pavel. 'Manfred knew he betrayed us and he set it loose.'

Reiner swallowed. 'So it isn't a ruse after all.'

'He can see us all,' moaned Hals. 'He knows what we're thinking.'

'But how can that be?' asked Franka, shivering. 'It's impossible.'

It was impossible, thought Reiner. But that left an even more unpalatable option – that Manfred's spy still lived. That he was one of them. Reiner looked around. Gert or Jergen – which was it? Then an even more horrible possibility struck him. What if Manfred had reached one of the original group? The spy could be any of them. Any of them.

Reiner and the others mounted up again and continued north, but the mood of camaraderie that had united them mere moments ago was lost, replaced by an uneasy silence.

A cold wind began to blow. Franka urged her horse up beside Reiner's and rubbed her leg against his. He instinctively returned the sweet pressure, but then stopped. What if it was she who…?

He edged away from her, hating himself. Suspicion was a poison that would kill them all. She looked up at him, confused.

He pulled his cloak tighter around him and rode alone

*Nathan Long* has worked as a screenwriter for fifteen years, during which time he has had three movies made and a handful of live-action and animated TV episodes produced. He has also written several award winning short stories. When these lofty pursuits have failed to make him a living, he has also been a taxi driver, limo driver, graphic designer, dishwasher and lead singer for a rockabilly band. He lives in Hollywood.

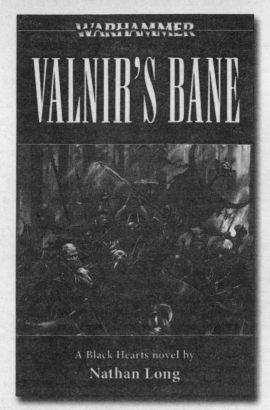

WARHAMMER

VALNIR'S BANE

A Black Hearts novel by
Nathan Long

## Valnir's Bane
Nathan Long

**They're not fighting for their Emperor.
They're not fighting for their country.
They're definitely not fighting fair!**

**www.blacklibrary.com**

# READ TILL YOU BLEED

## DO YOU HAVE THEM ALL?